Muddy Bayou

A Raleigh Cheramie Mystery

By

Jessica Tastet

This is a work of fiction. All the characters and events portrayed in this novel are fiction.

Muddy Bayou

Copyright 2011 by Jessica Tastet

Cover photo by Paula A. Clement

Cover Design by Ashley Comeaux-Foret

ISBN: 0615574688
ISBN-13:978-0615574684

DEDICATION

Andrew and Cara

My Inspiration in life

ACKNOWLEDGMENTS

Many thanks to Donna McBroom-Theriot for her invaluable critiques. Thanks to Paula Arcement Clement for the cover photo. Thanks to all those who shared their knowledge of the bayou with me.

Also By Jessica Tastet

THE RALEIGH CHERAMIE SERIES

Muddy Bayou

Muddy Grave

Muddy Hearts

Chapter One

Raleigh Cheramie bolted up in bed, head snapping forward, heart throbbing in her chest. Perspiration beaded over her body and her throat burned as if she'd gulped a shot of tequila from the bottle.

She swallowed, flinched with the pain, and caught her reflection in the ornate framed mirror leaning against the wall. Blue lips stared back at her and thick red blood trickled down her forehead.

Her fingers sprung forward, touching the smoothness of her face. She felt around, kneading her fingers into her temple. Nothing wet or sticky made contact with her scouring fingertips.

She shut her eyes to the paleness of her reflection and willed her heart to slow with each measured breath she drew. When her heart had returned to a somewhat normal pace, she forced her eyes to open again. Her normal, if not disappointing, reflection greeted her.

She'd dreamed it. She hadn't been about to drown in a car, under the muddy water of the bayou, in a miniskirt. A miniskirt? Where had that come from? She hadn't worn a miniskirt since she was twelve and wanted to be like Madonna.

A laugh swelled in her chest as relief flooded her clinched muscles. Why couldn't she dream of drowning in the blue Caribbean? Always dirty, dark, bayou water. Always. She didn't even live near the bayou she'd almost drowned in as a teenager. Two hours away and she still went back to that place. Maybe she needed to look into some dream therapy. Would there even be a listing for that in Baton Rouge?

A nagging voice that sounded too much like Me'Maw, her grandmother, chided her from inside her head. Raleigh hadn't nearly drowned inside a car. She'd had to kick and fight her way to the surface, unable to tell if she was going to break through the surface or dig into the muddy bottom.

She didn't own a car that would have a child's booster seat in the back seat or a manila envelope in the passenger seat. She hadn't had a busted head.

Raleigh groaned as her head throbbed once again. Had it been a dream after all?

Panic tingled around her middle. It couldn't be anything else. That was impossible. She shouldn't even consider it really. She didn't connect to the dying anymore. She'd pushed that skill so far that it had broken. She'd felt the break inside her mind as if something had clicked and the static in that part of her brain had all gone silent. It had to be the complete lack of direction her life had nosedived into that she was thinking about the bayou she'd grown up on, where her family still lived.

Family. Her Me'Maw's nagging voice sounded louder in her head. Me'Maw was the traiteur, the community healer. Raleigh was just a freak of nature, healer to the dead as Me'Maw affectionately nicknamed it.

Raleigh groaned as her head gave a dull throb in response to her dismissal. She was going to just tell herself it was a dream. Besides, someone would need to know her to connect to her as she died. It's not as if she advertised. She could imagine the billboards. Have a message for a loved one before you go? Connect to Raleigh Cheramie and give your loved ones peace of mind.

No, that particular skill had broken long ago. It must have been a dream. She tried to push the dream away as she pushed the pale yellow comforter to the edge of her full-size bed.

Cardboard boxes filled the room and encroached on her space. Six months of living at Cassie's and she hadn't unpacked a single box labeled clothing, books, or miscellaneous. She guessed it was better than the literal meaning of living out of a cardboard box.

Her stomach rumbled from beneath the sheet.

Oh well, what was one more day of digging for underclothes and a descent top in a box?

Her head throbbed again, the pain duller than before. The dream tried to press back into her cranium. Raleigh stretched, pushing her arms toward the ceiling, trying to shake it away.

Her alarm clock blinked red from the nightstand. Strange how the electricity blinked so often these days. Sunlight didn't spill through the gauzy linen curtains, though. It was probably some ungodly hour not meant to be seen by the living.

What she needed was chocolate: the cure to all that ails.

Raleigh stood and stretched her legs. Her body ached strangely, as if she'd been clenching her muscles all night. Had she? Had there been another dream she didn't remember?

She stumbled toward the mirror, checking out her slightly ruffled brunette hair. She'd recently chopped several inches off its long length and she couldn't get it to stay put. It didn't look much different when she tried to fix it, so she moved on to the dark circles under her amber eyes. The green flecks were dull this morning. Okay, so she wasn't going to impress anyone today. It's not as if she had tried much lately, anyway. Cassie had seen her worse than this. A morning after an all-night party in college came to mind.

She strolled to the door, dodging the boxes with her toes that she'd more than once stubbed against the cardboard stacked two high. She peeked into the hallway, wondering if Cassie had brought home company after her date. It was her house after all, and a house she was used to living in alone. A fact that Cassie tried tactfully not to remind her of, but a fact that always seemed to hang between them.

The door to Cassie's room and the home office were closed and the only sound that Raleigh heard was the soft swooshing sound of the grandfather clock in the living room. She tiptoed toward the end of the hall before she saw Cassie perched on her tan leather barstool, leaning over the Baton Rouge *Advocate* with a spoon of oatmeal resting in her hand. Her gray pantsuit was unwrinkled, and her hair was pulled back without a strand daring to protest.

This waking up before the living was the reason Cassie owned a house and Raleigh was only a squatter. Cassie was a real estate agent, who could hold her own in a testosterone-filled room. Secretly, Raleigh sometimes thought she had her own influx of testosterone, but that was another one of those bits of information that would never be said aloud.

Cassie also had a mean right hook, and her favorite form of exercise was boxing.

Raleigh paced toward the pantry. Her head was still throbbing in that 'I'm not about to let you forget about it just yet' way. "Any good news in the paper today?"

Cassie frowned without glancing up from the paper. "Only murder, deceit, and Louisiana politicians. Good news doesn't sell."

As she rummaged through the candy basket, Raleigh couldn't help but smile, though she knew that Cassie didn't find it funny in the least. Finally, her fingers embraced a Twix. She tore the paper and bit eagerly into it, feeling her headache dissolve into millions of particles as the chocolate lifted the dark mood pressing into her.

Chocolate should be advertised as the miracle cure.

"I can't believe you still eat candy for breakfast. We're not in college anymore."

Cassie's voice pierced her reverie. Cassie's mocha eyes now bore down on her from behind her black wire frames.

"We can't all be health nuts. Besides, people eat sugary cereal and breakfast bars. I eat Twix. There's not much difference."

Cassie grunted and folded the paper up. "Let's not go with that argument again this morning. What has you awake so early, anyway?"

Raleigh leaned against the black granite countertop. "Just the usual. Drowning in bayou water."

Cassie shook her head, her eyebrows raised above the square rims of her glasses. "You need to see someone. That can't be normal."

Raleigh smirked at her as she bit into the Twix, again feeling a surge of chocolate-covered happiness.

Cassie clamped down on her lower lip, studying Raleigh's face. Raleigh stared back, unblinking. "Well, I guess you're not really normal, huh?"

A towering mass of chest strutted from the hallway toward Cassie. Raleigh drank in the broad chest and tight abs that disappeared into drawstring pants. He lifted his arm and ran his hand through his curly dark hair, and Raleigh choked on the bite she'd just taken as his biceps rippled.

Cassie turned toward him and allowed him to embrace her in a bear hug with those gorgeous arms. Raleigh blushed, feeling as though she were eavesdropping. Cassie wasn't usually one for displays of affection, but Raleigh thought anyone, including hard-nose Cassie, would make an exception for underwear model material. Raleigh forced her eyes down toward the terra cotta floor, a pang in her chest again at the disturbance she was creating in Cassie's life. Maybe she should seriously look for her own place.

"I thought I'd take a shower and then drive in to work with you."

Cassie smiled, the creases around her lips relaxing. "Sounds good. This is my roommate I told you about. Raleigh, this is Greg."

Raleigh smiled, her throat still burning and eyes tearing from the Twix that had slid down the wrong way. "It's nice to see, I mean meet you."

He nodded, but his almond eyes crinkled into a smile. "Likewise."

He brushed Cassie's forehead with a kiss and then strutted back toward the hall. The back view was just as nice, even in drawstring pants.

Raleigh waited until she heard the soft closing of the door before she pounced. "Please tell us lesser mortals where'd you find Greg?"

A faint tinge flushed Cassie's cheeks. "He's a new agent, but he used to own a few restaurants. He's still invested in one or two."

"So he looks like that and he's smart. How do you get so lucky?"

Cassie sipped her cappuccino. "It has nothing to do with luck. I asked him out."

Raleigh laughed. "Have you ever let a guy ask you out?"

Cassie's forehead wrinkled. "I never wanted to date the guys who asked."

Raleigh stifled her laugh with another bite. Cassie had been her dorm-assigned roommate freshmen year. She'd lucked out in the roommate department with Cassie, who hadn't changed much since college. Always sensible, persistent, and in-control. All traits Raleigh would never possess, no matter how hard Cassie tried to teach, or more like preach, to her.

The familiar chords of Raleigh's cell phone filtered through the room. Raleigh glanced at the red numbers on the stove. 6:45. Who would call so early? Who would actually think she was awake this early?

She threw her jacket and a few t-shirts to the side to uncover her cell phone resting on the table. The screen lit up with her dad's number.

He should be at work. The throbbing in her head increased again as if to remind her that it was still there making a home for itself today.

Cassie called to her as she walked to the sink with her bowl. "I want that mess cleaned up."

Raleigh rolled her eyes before flipping it open and clearing her throat. "Dad?"

"Raleigh, is that you?"

As usual, her father spoke too loudly and harshly. She called it his telephone voice.

"Yes, Dad, it's me."

A pause followed, as though he were waiting for her to tell him what he'd called for. She fiddled with the shirts, items they'd been giving out at a radio-sponsored fundraiser last night. She'd attended with co-workers, and it had made for a dull evening. Yet another sign that her new job was going nowhere.

Finally, after seconds passed in silence, he decided he knew why he'd called. "Did Madison or Claudia call you last night?"

Raleigh turned over the words in her head, which had decided to ease its rhythmic pulsing for a moment. It was so random. She hadn't spoken to Claudia, her first cousin, in years, and her sister never called. She only returned calls if she were in the mood.

"No."

"Are you sure?"

Was she supposed to have called Madison this week? Had she forgotten something important? She didn't think so, although she should probably remind him about her birthday since he'd forgotten last year. "I think I would remember, Dad."

"When did you talk to your sister last?"

"I called Madison last week. What's this about?"

"Did she say anything about going somewhere? Maybe a trip?"

Raleigh's headache pushed back into her skull with a bursting throb. Damn. She'd left her Twix on the counter. "No, she didn't mention anything."

Again, there was silence on the other end of the phone. That feeling that something was wrong constricted her airway. The chocolate seemed to rise in her throat, bringing a harsh burning with it.

"Claudia and Madison are missing. They didn't report to work last night, and Madison didn't pick up Mason from the babysitter."

A familiar numbness scratched at her chest. Her head prickled, and her lungs felt as though they would burst. She shook it off. "Did you call all their friends?"

"Uncle Jude and I drove to their houses and all the usual places."

Her forehead grew warm as she pushed her hand into her chest, attempting to rub away the pain. It was a strange feeling, but familiar. She couldn't be having a heart attack. She was too young, right? When had she felt this way before?

An acid taste rose into her throat and her closed eyes flashed to her dream. A girl drowning in a car. A girl in a miniskirt which Raleigh would never wear.

Raleigh hadn't almost drowned in a car. She'd swallowed the water and felt it crawling inside her, but most of all she remembered how it felt not to be able to breathe. She remembered what it felt like to drown.

It hadn't been a dream at all.

She was going to be sick. She felt it rising in her throat.

"Dad, I'm going to call you back."

Raleigh dropped the phone and bolted toward her bathroom.

Cassie called after her. "See, I told you not to eat candy for breakfast."

Raleigh shut the door behind her and lay down on the cold, murky blue tile floor, the coldness seeping through her cheek, the shock of it easing her nausea. Even the hardness didn't bother her as her fingers ran over the ecru bath rug.

She felt the tightness in her chest ease, and her lungs relaxed with the inflow of oxygen. The throbbing numbness in her head even dwindled to a dull ache, and the vanilla potpourri in the bowl on the counter didn't make her want to vomit anymore.

She was going to be okay.

But she knew someone else who'd dared to wear a miniskirt; someone like Madison or Claudia perhaps, had drowned.

It hadn't been a dream. Just her nightmare she called Traiteur to the dead.

Chapter Two

Raleigh tapped on the steering wheel with her fingers. Her insides jittered as her rent-a-car propelled her forward. She'd turned the radio off a few miles back when she kept losing focus on the road. Even her usual sing-along didn't distract her thoughts from what lay before her. She slowed her hurtling pace as she approached the town, but no matter the sixty or forty-five mile per hour speed, the car would eventually reach the girl in that miniskirt.

She sighed. Her body had calmed its violent reaction, but the tiny seed had planted itself in her mind and it was acting like a honing device straight to the bayou.

Up ahead, there it was. The weathered cypress wooden sign burned black with Welcome to Barbeaux Bayou. Home of about ten thousand at last count. Ten years ago when she'd left with that sign at her back, a couple thousand less had lived here. Some things had stood still, but others had changed as quickly as a Mardi Gras parade during the rain.

That two-story brick probably still belonged to Drake Defelice's family. The trees still grew thick along this part, blocking the view of the bayou, and the *Cynthia* was still docked in its battered state along the bayou. She noticed new larger homes spaced on their acres of land, and she'd been told that the new spacious Wal-Mart was behind these upscale homes on the back highway. The bayou meandered fifty feet to her left. She was aware of the prickling on her left side, but she pushed it down into the pit of her stomach. The bayou could wait.

She braked at the red light, studying Nick's gas station at the intersection. It was falling apart, and it had been turned into a seafood market. In junior high, she'd had such a crush on Nick's son, Frank. She'd ridden with her Paw to the gas station just to see his reaction as she stepped out of the truck in her short shorts. She'd cornered him out back where they stored the old tires and given him her first kiss. He'd been four years older and still unsure what to do with her.

It had all been so easy in junior high. Where had that confidence gone? She must have left it out back with the tires. Maybe if she stuck around these parts long enough, she could go see if it was still back there.

14

It would sure be nice to feel that again. Raleigh laughed out loud. The sound echoed around the hollow car, and she realized she hadn't made a sound in the last thirty minutes.

It was like a funeral procession. She kept dreading that moment of stepping out of the car to confront the dead.

A loud honking from behind caused her to jump, and she noticed the light had turned green. She accelerated and pushed further into town. She remembered several homes she passed, but new structures dotted the highway. Large homes with perfectly landscaped Crepe Myrtles and some homes even surrounded with palm trees, as if the muddy bayou water had suddenly turned into the beach from the sugar cane and the cows once there. As she traveled further in, the houses became closer and closer until the narrow streets seemed to be less than one hundred feet apart.

She unconsciously slowed as she reached the yellow double shotgun house at the front of Cheramie Lane, but accelerated when she realized that instinct.

It wasn't that she was avoiding her family, she assured herself unconvincingly. She'd driven these two hours for a reason, and it wasn't down that street. At least not yet.

At the bridge, she signaled and turned left. Upset with herself that she held her breath as she crossed, she muttered "coward" under her breath, but knew from experience that it wouldn't help. She would still feel the fear no matter what insults to her confidence she flung. She'd just feel guilty, too. At least she didn't raise her feet up off the floorboard as she'd once done.

At a shell road between a crumbling tin shed and rows of full grown sugar cane, Raleigh signaled and turned. One hundred feet before her stretched the canal. Raleigh shifted into park and sat staring at the water. Her breathing was irregular and her body prickled with a growing numbness, but she knew she would need to step out of the car. Oh, how she hated bayou water. She couldn't even begin to say how she hated the bayou.

With a painful gulp and a slight dizziness, she heaved the car door open and stumbled out.

Raleigh took measured breaths, inhaling the stench of lily pads, stagnant water, and sugar cane. Her stomach lurched and she held onto the car for balance.

Slowly as vapor, it seeped into her. She felt it traveling from her toes, wrapping her in a cocoon.

This was the place.

The car was beneath the bottom of the canal. The dead girl waited, recognizing her nearness.

Raleigh avoided the water, her feet inching further from it. In high school, this had been the hangout. Cars would line the shell road. Someone would blare their music from a truck, and several boys with access to alcohol would break out ice chests of beer. Predictably, at around midnight an officer would come break it up, send everyone home, and make sure everyone had a safe ride. It was Barbeaux, after all. The officer was probably the dad, the brother, the uncle or a cousin of someone at the party.

From the looks of the untouched grass, the level ground, and the quietness, high school students didn't hang here anymore.

The familiar chords of her cell phone vibrated through the quietness. A squawking bird flew from the canopy of the nearby oak behind the tin shed.

Raleigh reached in and grabbed the phone, her eyes still avoiding direct contact with the bayou.

The screen flashed Me'Maw. Raleigh sighed. Me'Maw would have sensed her here as Raleigh had sensed the girl below.

"I'm here, Me'Maw."

Me'Maw cleared her throat. "I knew you'd come, but child, you had your dad worried when you didn't call him back."

"I just needed to be here first."

Me'Maw's weak, wispy voice made Raleigh's chest tighten and her outside was having a difficult time keeping it casual as well. "What's going on, Raleigh?"

Raleigh closed her eyes to the picturesque setting. The great oaks with moss draping down, touching the grass in places, and blades of grass waving in the breeze framed the dark waters. Beautiful hiding place for

16

the ugliness. It made her knowledge of what lay beneath more horrific. "You need to call Cousin Joey and ask him to get a diver down by the old canal."

The deep gasp registered in the quiet of the clear connection. "Is it Madison and Claudia?"

Raleigh's insides clinched. "There's only one. You know I haven't been real accurate, so there's a chance it may not be either."

Even as she spoke the words aloud, Raleigh felt a tug from below the surface of the murky water. As she'd died, the girl had reached out to Raleigh, knowing Raleigh could feel her.

"If it's only one, it can't be them. They left together. A nice detective is here right now, so I'll send him to meet you. I know how you don't like that water."

The relief in Me'Maw's voice made Raleigh's throat swell. She didn't want to break Me'Maw's heart, but the girl below knew her. She'd known that Raleigh could find her. "Okay."

"Don't leave without seeing us."

Raleigh swallowed as she closed her phone. About as much chance in that as there being a parade to welcome her home.

Chapter Three

Raleigh yanked the grass out by its roots and flung it into the field. Her frustration eased for about as long as it took the grass to plop down and get lost in the long weeds.

She'd tried sitting in her rent-a-car, but she was too conscious of the girl below in a car, swimming in fear and anxiety. So now she sat in the field, trying to feel the life of the grass, the insects, and the critters that weaved their way below.

It didn't work that way. She only connected with the dying. As Me'Maw would put it, her special talent was feeling the dead's final moments. It didn't hurt to try to connect to the living, though. Her Me'Maw could do it. She was the one with a connection to the living. As a traiteur in these parts, Me'Maw was a healer, but she had the extra, added kick of what Raleigh liked to call physic ability. Of course, she didn't say it in earshot of Me'Maw, or she might have a slipper thrown at her. Me'Maw didn't own up to that part of her ability since she wasn't quite sure of the Catholic church's opinion on the matter. If there were any fairness to genetics, Raleigh would have had her talent. But no, Raleigh had to pull from even further in the gene pool. She didn't feel it was a talent, though, more of a genetic deformity.

Raleigh ripped another blade of grass out, feeling its essence fade before flinging it into the air.

How long could it take to get here? It was Barbeaux, for Heaven's sake! She could throw a rock and hit Bois, the next town over.

Just as she ripped another blade of grass from the earth, tires crunched on the gravel behind her.

It was about time.

Raleigh stood as the navy Caprice rolled to a stop next to her Ford. She squinted in the sunlight, guessing it was about ten A.M. now. She'd forgotten her watch in her haste this morning, but she knew it would be a long day, whether she knew the time or not.

The car door slammed, shattering the stillness. Birds fluttered from their branches, squawking at the interruption, and then settled again among the branches. Quietness settled eerily again over the field. Raleigh heard the static clatter from below the surface of the gumbo water.

The detective strolled toward her in an even gait and an unwavering gaze. His light blue polo tugged at his broad shoulders, with just enough room to not be too tight. His perfectly groomed black hair contrasted nicely with his pressed khaki slacks. As he approached, the sunlight hit his eyes in the right direction for them to flash gray, and his olive skin deepened.

Her face flushed. She needed to get out more. Apparently, men were starting to look better after her self-inflicted abstinence. Maybe that was the abstinence talking.

He squinted at her. She felt him appraising her, and she straightened her posture. She wondered if it were her ponytail and jeans he was evaluating or something else. Paul Siminoux, a detective she'd worked for in Texas, could list a page of description after a five minute interview with a person. He always said health, wealth, and body tics said pretty much all you needed to know about a person. "Raleigh?"

"Yes."

"I'm Detective Max Pyles. I believe it's your Me'Maw that told me you'd be waiting down here for me?"

"Yes, did Me'Maw call Cousin Joey?"

He scanned the area. His eyes seemed to suck up every detail from the rustle in the nearby oak to the stillness of the water. Raleigh wondered what he was looking for and even scanned the area to see if something was there. Of course, she was quick in her check over the Bayou. There was no sign of anything disturbed here. The car lay beneath the surface, not above in this tranquil backdrop. "She did, but I don't quite understand what we're doing down here."

She fidgeted. "A young woman is in a car at the bottom of the canal. We're here to get her out."

He studied her with a concentrated look on his face. Her face flushed again although it wasn't a particularly warm day in October. Raleigh could imagine all the thoughts behind those gorgeous eyes, and none put her in a good light. She knew what it sounded like to an officer. She'd been there before way too many times.

"Did you see the young woman go in?"

Raleigh shook her head, but then stopped. "Not in the way you're asking."

She didn't look at him, though she could feel him looking at her. Paul, her former boss, had warned her not to do this, but she couldn't help it. She was growing warm under his gaze.

He didn't lift his gaze. "What way did you see her go in then?"

Raleigh flushed. "I'm not making it up if that's what you're asking."

She didn't explain her "talent" as Me'Maw called it very well. She'd never been able to put it into words. How did you tell someone that you could live the dying's last moments? Any sane person would think she was loony, right? Me'Maw had connections, why had she sent a stranger?

"Did someone tell you about it?"

"No, I didn't need any help," Raleigh cringed, knowing that it hadn't come out very well. She'd be lucky if she didn't end up in handcuffs today. "Did you call the diver?"

"Joey did."

He studied his surroundings, glancing at her periodically. Raleigh fought the urge to laugh. Nothing was funny about the situation, but she had the feeling nonetheless when she was uncomfortable and nervous. The idea of Detective Max's reaction to a sudden outburst of laughter increased the urge until she was biting down on her lip. He would think she was nuts.

Who knew? Maybe she was, but there was still a girl at the bottom of the canal. She didn't even allow herself to give the girl a face. That idea was enough to sober her up.

"Are you sure about this situation?"

Raleigh didn't want to tell him that she could feel the dead girl. That she floated below, bayou water surrounding her as well as filling her. She was waiting and would keep waiting until she was found. Raleigh would continue feeling her until it was over.

No use he waste their time calling for a doctor, or depending on his skepticism, arresting her. He would definitely think she'd gone around the bend if she explained it to him now. Raleigh might be inclined to agree with him, given the edginess and deep panic pressing against her chest

20

from her insides. She hated the bayou and as long as that girl was in it, Raleigh would feel as though the water was inside of her.

Raleigh brought her eyes to his and was surprised by the force his green eyes packed. "She's there."

His eyes softened at the edges. He believed her. A sense of relief rushed through her. "Do you know who she is?"

Raleigh looked away from him, some of the seasickness settling. "I'm not sure."

He stepped forward into the area that Raleigh wouldn't approach. "Why don't you show me where you think she is?"

Panic churned in her stomach. "I can't go any closer to that water than I am."

"Can't?"

Raleigh glanced away, looking back at the stretch of empty highway. Very few cars had passed in this direction this morning. "Phobia."

His voice was thick with skepticism. "Aren't you from this area?"

Raleigh felt her chin rise slightly and her expression freeze. "I moved away, didn't I?"

The crunch of gravel under tires disturbed the quiet once again. Raleigh looked back to see two new vehicles pulling up: a squad car and an old Ford truck. Raleigh recognized Buddy in the truck. He must have followed in his father's footsteps and gone into diving. Sure enough, his father hobbled out the passenger side as she watched. Cousin Joey stepped out of the squad car.

Joey walked toward her, his brown eyes zoning in on her. He resembled Uncle Jude down to the thinning brown hair sticking up in the front. "Raleigh, are you okay?"

She frowned. If the seasickness didn't end soon, she'd lose the Twix she'd eaten this morning. Certainly not a pretty thought. "I've had better mornings."

"Why don't you go wait at Me'Maw's house until we're done?"

Raleigh shook her head, feeling the girl reach and tug on her. She didn't want to be left alone. "I need to be here until she's found."

His face was grim, but he nodded in understanding. Her family knew her better than anyone. Just this assurance spread a tiny burst of comfort through her edginess.

Joey walked down to the launch, pointing out tire marks, indicating the path of the current to Buddy, who was handling his gear. Detective Max joined them. Raleigh studied his perplexed forehead. Raleigh figured by this time he thought her whole family was nuts. He'd already met Me'Maw. If Me'Maw hadn't sealed the deal, Cousin Joey and she had. He didn't comment much, but he listened. He observed the tire marks. He even followed the marks into the grass. He picked something up and bagged it in a brown paper bag. Though Raleigh leaned dangerously in, she couldn't make out what it was.

More tires crunched on the shells. Raleigh turned around and noticed a tow truck and another squad car crawl to a stop. A wave of nausea washed over her as she realized she'd have to watch them pull the girl up. She'd really have to see a dead body, again. She was really regretting that Twix this morning, and not just for what it was doing to her thighs.

The clinginess was so familiar. Someone hanging onto her for the comfort only family could give. She knew it was Claudia or Madison. She pushed the thought away, staring up into the sun until everything evaporated into spots.

She wished she could fast-forward through this day. Why couldn't that be a "talent" that was part of their gene pool? Now, that would be a useful talent. Junior Prom would be one of those moments she'd love to fast-forward. Not to mention that awkward date last week Cassie had arranged. That would be a talent she wouldn't want to send back to her ancestors with a "thanks but no thanks" card.

The officer in the squad car began to roll out the yellow tape to secure the perimeter. He didn't even glance at her as he passed in front of her. It was okay by her. She didn't want to be on the other side. She'd like to be on the banks of a different kind of water.

Again, tires crunched on the gravel. The birds squawked loudly and then flew off further down to another set of trees. A white Jeep Wrangler pulled up next to her. Raleigh smiled. This certainly was a flashback to high school.

A lanky blond bounded from the driver door. Mike, best friend and reporter. She knew which one he'd come as.

He wrapped his tan arm around her, and she breathed in amber and spice. "I heard a rumor you were here."

"So the tongues are flapping already?"

Mike relaxed his arm. "C'mon Ree, You really should wait at Me'Maw's. This isn't something you want to see."

Raleigh swallowed as the water splashed around Buddy as he disturbed the calm of the murky water. "She wants me here."

They watched as Buddy waded his way further in. "Who is she?"

"I don't know, but she knows me."

They waited in silence as Buddy went under. A strong comfort seeped through Mike's arm that still hung around her shoulder. Mike had once told her that they could eat the mud pies they had made on the playground. After, of course, she'd told him he had to taste it first. They had been three, and they had been friends ever since. He was her only bridge to this town these days besides Me'Maw. He felt like a warm electric blanket on a cold day.

Ten minutes later, Buddy surfaced twenty-five feet into the canal and slightly downstream. He raised his thumb to indicate he'd found the car. Raleigh could feel an anxiety building in her chest. It wasn't just coming from her, though. It seeped through her toes and surrounded her as the girl below anticipated being brought above.

Thirty minutes later, after what seemed like forever, the tow truck was finally latched on properly. Buddy returned to the surface with another thumbs up, and the grinding motor on the tow truck added to the orchestra of sound surrounding the area that now included a local camera crew.

Raleigh's stomach flip-flopped with each lap of the cable. Her body tensed and she gritted her teeth in determination not to bolt.

As the back end of the car emerged from the water, Raleigh shuddered. The black Ford Escort was Madison's car. She'd driven it to Baton Rouge just a few months ago for a strange visit. She'd come to check on Raleigh as she'd said. Madison had never once asked about anything in Raleigh's life, hence the strange part.

Raleigh edged to her left, staying behind the yellow tape. She needed a view of the driver-side door. The need to know who was in the car struggled against her panic at seeing the girl.

Mike kept close, one arm gently touching her waist.

Water poured from under the doors as well as a broken passenger window. The grinding of the cable stopped. Raleigh's heartbeat seemed to continue in sync.

Cousin Joey stepped forward and with a gloved hand, opened the driver side door. Water gushed out, spreading the grayness through the white shells.

She no longer felt the girl. Her fear and anxiety had gushed out with the water. The connection had broken.

Raleigh first absorbed the plaid mini-skirt and once-white shirt. Her conscience then wrapped around the white skin and oval face with matted dirty blonde hair that stared blankly in her direction.

Raleigh leaned back against Mike's chest, the feeling of waking up from a dream prickling through her.

"Claudia."

Chapter Four

Raleigh again released a deep breath through her mouth and her fingers trembled a little less against the steering wheel. She signaled and turned down Cheramie Lane. She wasn't sure if she was feeling the remnants of nervousness at seeing Claudia's water-logged body, or the dread of telling her family about Claudia. A dull throb was beginning behind her eyes. The all-too-familiar sign of a stress headache.

What she wouldn't do for even half a Twix right now.

Cheramie Lane was home to thirteen Creole or shotgun-style homes all belonging at some point in time to a Cheramie. Of course people got old, died, and their family didn't want to own these small, old-fashioned homes. As a consequence, not many Cheramies still resided on Cheramie Lane. It was a source of unending anger for Paw. He thought of the land as Cheramie land, not land for sale.

She noticed the four-foot weeds growing up around Aunt Clarice's old Acadian. This had been her favorite house as a teenager. She loved its sweeping front porch, pitched roof, and three wooden French doors opening out to the porch. She vaguely remembered some gossip about this house. Nothing prior to this morning's events wanted to settle within her reach. Everything seemed to buzz around her head like a kid on a playground.

Lingering over the trivial gossip was a nice attempt at a stall, though. Unfortunately, the car was still going to propel her to the back of the street, no matter how much she slowed down to catch up on small town life.

Cars speckled the front yard of Me'Maw's home and even overflowed onto her parents' lawn next door. These were the last two houses on Cheramie Lane, blocking any access the street could have had to the highway that ran a thousand feet behind them. Paw had actually been mighty glad of this.

Raleigh pulled up next to a green Ford SUV and shut off the engine. Why did so many people have to be here? This was going to be hard enough without having to retell it to half the town. It was Barbeaux

Bayou, though. Half the town turned out for a tragedy. The other half would be waiting by their phones for the news.

She steadied her hands with one last deep breath and got out the car before thinking it through any further and probably fleeing back to Baton Rouge. She muttered "coward" beneath her breath again for the second time today. She was just all about that positive self-confidence building. Right.

She approached the white Creole slowly. The men on the front porch registered, but she didn't allow herself to drink them in yet. Instead she focused on the house; the house she'd dreamed about often and had sometimes been more homesick for than her family. The paint had faded to a dingy gray and someone had attempted to paint the shutters a deep blue, but the house still stood tall and clean. Even the stained glass dormer window from the second story was spotless, and Raleigh knew Me'Maw could not be climbing those stairs these days; Me'Maw's carnation bushes anchored each side of the house. Paw sure kept his yard neat, although Raleigh thought it was probably harder than it used to be for him now at eighty-eight.

At last, she breathed in the gentlemen on the porch. Uncle Jude sat on the cement porch steps. His jeans were smeared with grease and an old khaki hat covered his thinning brown hair. Her father sat in the rocking chair to her right. A much too blue pair of jeans and a black t-shirt with several holes swallowed his once heavy frame. His few strands of brown hair on top hadn't been brushed down this morning. Uncle Camille sat in the rocking chair to her left. His blue Dickie's were four sizes too big on his skeletal frame. He had none of his brown hair left on top, and his face was the yellowish-brown color of his alcohol. Paw, her grandfather, leaned against the porch to her right. He was stooped over in his blue Dickie's, the only outfit she'd ever seen him wear besides a white striped dress shirt. All three of his sons had his long nose, almond-shaped brown eyes, and long face. Supposedly, Uncle Davy was the only son who'd resembled Me'Maw, and he'd died in the war long before Raleigh was born.

Her dad and Uncle Camille stood as she approached, and she couldn't settle her gaze on either of them. Although she knew she must be the one to tell, she wished for someone to hide behind. She wasn't feeling very grown-up at the moment. Especially with these four pairs of eyes on her, the same eyes that would watch them run around the back yard as children. She looked from one to the other, opening her mouth, but she couldn't find any words there.

The screen door screeched in the silence, and Me'Maw hobbled half-way out.

Me'Maw peered into her with her soft blue eyes, the wrinkles only softening the force after she'd looked into Raleigh. It was as if Raleigh were made of transparent glass, and Me'Maw's eyes were the light by which to see the whole of her. Then Me'Maw gasped and her blue-tinged hand clasped over her mouth.

Tears burned the brim of Raleigh's eyes.

Me'Maw's pain was visible in her trembling body and her drooping eyes. She'd broken Me'Maw's heart. Me'Maw had always been able to see through her like a snow globe.

She looked to Uncle Camille, the alcohol swimming in his yellowish eyes. He waited with breath caught, leaning forward.

"I'm so sorry."

He stared at her blankly, unable to grasp the words. She felt the moment it clutched his body in an unflinching grasp. He fell back into his rocking chair, unmoving.

The screen door flung open, smacking the siding on the house, the sound shattering the growing stillness in the neighborhood. Raleigh's mother stopped at Me'Maw's side, a terror clearly visible in her darting pupils.

"Madison?"

Raleigh shook her head, unable to look at the men. "She wasn't in the car. It was just Claudia."

Me'Maw collapsed. Raleigh bounded up the stairs, past the unaware Uncle Jude. Her mother just stared blankly at her, unflinching. Her father reached Me'Maw's side at the same time Raleigh did.

Raleigh gently shifted Me'Maw's weight to her shoulder. The five-foot woman was heavier than her thin frame appeared. Uncle Jude swooped in from behind, and her father and he lifted her weight from the ground. Me'Maw's complexion was as white as the old flour jar she used to stuff money in for a rainy day. Raleigh shuddered as Me'Maw's lips twitched and her eyelids fluttered.

They pushed into the darkness of the house. Spots appeared, blurring her vision, as Raleigh turned her back to the sun.

Her father grunted as he banged the side of the solid oak doorframe with his shoulder. "Raleigh, get a wet towel and a glass of water from the kitchen."

Raleigh pushed forward as they ventured to the left. Although it had been ten years since she'd spent any real time in this house, she knew the towels would be in the drawer under the sink and the glasses would be in the cabinet to the left of the "ice box" as Me'Maw insisted on calling it. She also preferred gallon water to tap, saying they put too much chemicals in the tap.

Raleigh ignored the turned heads as she passed through the living room to the kitchen in the back. She could imagine what was being said as word spread that she had come back here to find a body. She was sure they would eventually hint around and then someone would come out and ask, unable to live with that burning curiosity.

Me'Maw's carnations were drooped over in the small glass vase that always sat on her gold speckled laminate table. She'd tried to spruce up her white cabinets with hardware that wasn't rusted, but everything else was exactly the same down to the broom that leaned against the back door. Raleigh could remember running through the kitchen out the back door after Sunday dinner, making sure to snatch a candy in the special drawer near the door before running through Paw's garden.

She hadn't felt any uneasiness in her stomach then. The neighbors hadn't known about her special talent because Me'Maw had wanted it that way.

Raleigh was rummaging around in the refrigerator for Me'Maw's gallon of water when she was startled by someone clearing her throat behind her.

Raleigh turned and she felt her heart stop as Ms. Bethany English stared at her.

Her pink lips curved into a hesitant smile and her hands clasped together in front of her. Raleigh's heart roared back with a thunder in her ears.

"We heard what you did to help the police find Claudia."

Raleigh stared at her. Her vocal chords seemed to have dried up when her heart stopped.

Ms. Bethany's pink lips trembled as her hands wrung together. "I know you had a little block after that incident in the bayou, but I thought that it might be over now since you were able to find Claudia."

Was there some cap on the amount of emotions you could experience in one day? What about a six-hour period? Raleigh sure had to have reached her max by this time. She felt the twangs of exhaustion in the muscles of her legs.

Raleigh cleared her throat; a searing pain tore at her vocal chords. "Ms. English, I don't know where, um... I don't know where Katherine is."

Ms. Bethany glanced away, but not before Raleigh saw the tears brimming in her brown pencil-lined eyes. "I just thought... If you could try now..."

Paw limped in. "Girl, what's taking so long?"

Raleigh just stared at him, unable to focus clearly on his darkened scowl. For an instant he glanced from one to the other, and then nodded at Raleigh. "Get going now. The past isn't going anywhere today."

Raleigh grabbed the towel and a bottle of water from the refrigerator door and scooted out the room.

Paw had perfect timing.

Raleigh weaved her way through the crowd standing in Me'Maw's living room, careful not to look at anyone's face. She could see Me'Maw slumped over on the covered loveseat, a seat she'd never seen her sit on growing up. Finally, Raleigh squeezed between her mother and Uncle Jude to rest the wet towel on Me'Maw's forehead.

Her egg-white skin had darkened a shade, but her hands still trembled and her weight still sagged heavily against the loveseat. Raleigh sank down next to her and leaned gently against her. Raleigh breathed in her Avon perfume and the lingering aroma of a bacon breakfast.

Gradually, Me'Maw's fingers brushed against her own, and Raleigh felt the deep sigh heave against her side. She passed the bottle of water over to her shaking hand, the lines creasing on her hand like the lines of a road map. Strange, how age went unnoticed until time separated you. Me'Maw hadn't seemed so old when she'd left.

For the first time, Raleigh noticed the soft humming from the room. A crowd of people in a small room were all mumbling, creating the humming of a small outboard engine. Raleigh relaxed further into Me'Maw, feeling her steady heart against her shoulder. It wasn't difficult to figure out what the topic of talk was today.

Uncle Jude moved to the side and lanky Mike appeared before her. Raleigh smiled, but then frowned as he jerked his head in the direction of the porch.

Raleigh leaned over and kissed Me'Maw's cheek, her skin like crushed silk. Me'Maw squeezed her hand and Raleigh lifted herself from the loveseat, her shoulder instantly feeling the loss of Me'Maw's heat.

Raleigh followed Mike through the crowd as he led her to the front porch. She could feel the eyes scolding her as she followed him out the front door. They were probably thinking that the two of them were back at getting into a wasp nest of trouble.

Raleigh breathed in the air and blinked against the glaring sun.

Mike walked to the edge, away from Uncle Camille's chair and Raleigh's father sitting at his feet.

Raleigh moved in closer as they huddled near the porch post. Mike glanced toward them and then lowered his voice to a whisper. "The police didn't say much, but she had a wound to her head. They wouldn't say if she drowned or she was gone before she went in."

Raleigh glanced back. Uncle Camille sat in his chair unmoving while her father stared at him, waiting. "She drowned. She woke up before... she was conscious when the water filled the car. The window wasn't broken yet."

Mike nodded his head. "I'll have to wait until the autopsy, of course. I saw them trying for fingerprints. Dealing with water, we'll have to wait and see. There was nothing in the car. At least, that is what they are releasing."

"I saw an envelope. The kind for a large picture or a paper."

Mike swore under his breath. "The new detective doesn't release information at the crime scene."

Raleigh frowned. "It could be nothing."

Mike ran his fingers through his hair. "Or it could be important. It could lead us to Madison."

Raleigh bit down on her lip. "She's alive; I know that, but..."

Mike reached out and embraced her in a hug. Raleigh relaxed into his chest, feeling the muscles beneath his t-shirt. Mike wasn't a scraggly teenager anymore. In fact, he was quite well-built and attractive. Hmm. "We're going to find her. I'm going to go back and make Detective Max tell me what was in that envelope."

Raleigh's lips curved into a semi-smile. "Don't get arrested."

"Nah, I only get in trouble when you're with me."

Raleigh laughed. It was a bad joke, a joke that would be an insult from anyone else but Mike. The fact that it seemed to be absolutely true made it hilarious.

The rocking chair scraped against the porch board. "Why didn't you save my baby?"

Raleigh pulled herself from Mike's grip to see Uncle Camille facing her. His eyes were at once accusing and forlorn. Raleigh's lip trembled and she couldn't breathe. Finally, Uncle Camille stumbled down the porch steps and hobbled in the direction of his white shotgun house. Her father stood, stared off the front porch and then walked off the front steps toward his own house in the opposite direction.

"I don't guess they've welcomed you home yet."

Raleigh looked at him, his green eyes cloudy. "I'm sure the welcome parade is just late." Raleigh shrugged, "But it feels good, anyway. Not the Claudia and Madison part, but the being home part. It's a different smell here."

Mike nodded. "Me'Maw will be glad."

It had felt good to be near her, to feel as if she belonged to her. Raleigh smiled. "You go give that detective a hard time. I'm not going anywhere."

Mike squeezed her shoulder one more time and then jumped off the front porch and trotted to his Jeep.

Raleigh breathed in deeply the aroma of sugarcane at its peak. It did feel good to be back here. More familiar than Baton Rouge, and not the painful heartbreak of Texas.

Another car pulled into the front yard. Another carload of people dropping in to see if everyone was okay and to carry away any gossip floating around.

Raleigh sighed. The downside to a small town was how quickly word traveled.

Chapter Five

The screen door snapped behind Raleigh as she stepped out onto the back porch. She could see Paw's old beat-up Ford parked inside the old cypress barn's dirt floor. A black bicycle leaned against the front shadows of the barn. Paw's rows and rows of garden stretched out behind, disappearing into the tree line.

Raleigh breathed in deeply. Sugarcane, Me'Maw's carnations, and a hint of tobacco filled her body, pushing out a heaviness that had settled in. These were the smells of her childhood.

The porch boards shook beneath her as a ding resounded in the open air. Mason sat to her left, leaning against a four by four post, a metal baseball bat gripped in his small hands. He again kicked it with his foot and it swung back, banging it into the porch boards.

"Do you mind if I sit out here with you?"

Mason turned his head slightly toward her, and Madison's face stared at her. His round, brown eyes, protected by those dark eyelashes, wore the same expression as when Madison begged to follow her.

Where was Madison?

Mason shrugged, scowled, and returned his focus back onto the bat.

Raleigh sat down on the steps, relishing the stillness. The voices inside the house had risen in volume until her head vibrated to a steady hum. More and more people had come by to console the family and check on Me'Maw. Me'Maw had many friends, and many who had sought out her traiteur skills.

The metal bat vibrated through the quiet once again. Raleigh closed her eyes to the sunset. How old was Mason? Madison was twenty-three now, so Mason must be about five. Why must children make so much noise?

Again, the ding vibrated through the quiet.

Raleigh gritted her teeth and resisted the urge to grab the bat and fling it into the field. "Why are you out here by yourself?"

Mason shrugged and kicked the bat again. Raleigh wanted to laugh at how much he was like his mother. Madison would behave the same way when she was angry. Raleigh could remember a time when Madison had torn her notebook apart and sat sullenly refusing to explain she was upset because Raleigh had gone to sleep at Katherine's house instead of watch her dance team perform.

"Have you been out here all day?"

Mason flung the bat into the yard. It landed a few feet in front of him. "Do you want me to go away, too?"

"I was wondering if you wanted me to go away."

"Nanan, I'm five years old. I'm not stupid. Momma makes me go away when something's wrong. I'm in kindergarten now. They can tell me."

Raleigh didn't know if she wanted to laugh or cry, but after the day she'd had, she could probably do both at the same time. How was that for multitasking? "Well, Sweetie, Aunt Claudia had an accident today."

"Did she go to live with the angels? Alex in my class had an accident, and Momma said he went live with the angels."

Raleigh nodded, thankful that Madison had explained death in her own way already. How was she supposed to know how to handle a five-year-old? No sane person would trust their child to her. At ten, she'd killed her goldfish after forgetting to feed it. Not to mention the countless plants that had shriveled and died under her care. A kid? She might forget a child in the grocery store. "She's gone to live with the angels, so everyone is real sad."

He was quiet as he kicked his feet under the porch boards. "Where's Momma?"

Raleigh looked up into the salmon sky. "I wish I knew, sweetie, but we'll find her, I promise."

"Nanan?"

"Yes, sweetie?"

"I'm glad you came down to see me. You're not as bad as Mamma says."

Raleigh smiled. Maybe children weren't all bad, even if they obviously didn't keep secrets. It was okay. Raleigh knew Madison blamed her for many things that had gone wrong. Some she'd been responsible for, and some that would have added more hot sauce to her ordinary life.

The grass rustled to her right, and Raleigh looked over into the sunset to see Detective Max coming around the corner of the house. Apparently, she needed to go further than the back porch to find sanctuary.

He nodded, "Good evening."

Raleigh frowned and appraised him. This close, she could see the tightness of his blue polo shirt on his biceps, how it tugged across his broad chest. The chick of hair that now stood straight up was natural, and after his long day, it had escaped his methods of keeping it down. His olive skin was a shade or two lighter than this morning. Still, even in his rugged condition, he was still appealing.

"Do you have news or questions?"

Max's gaze settled on Mason. "Buddy, why don't you go find your mom?"

Mason's eyes narrowed, and he scrunched up his nose as he jumped off the porch. It was so unfunny, but Raleigh had to bite down on her lip to stop a second laugh from escaping.

"If I knew where she was, I'd find her."

"Mason!"

Mason turned his angry face on her, and the need to laugh evaporated. A five-year-old Madison stared at her, angry at the world, yelling in her famous words that it was all unfair.

"I always have to go away. I'm not stupid."

Raleigh straightened her shoulders. She could do this. She could be a grown-up, though she'd like to stomp around the ground and yell that Max needed to find Madison right now. "Mason, go next door and find a picture of Momma. This man is going to need a picture to help find her, and I know you want to help."

His nose relaxed as the dark clouds in his eyes lightened. "What kind of picture?"

Raleigh smiled. "Find a good one. You know Momma doesn't like people to see just any old picture of her."

Mason sprinted toward the house. "Okay!"

Max stepped closer. "I apologize. This morning he wasn't here, so I thought he belonged to someone else."

Raleigh gazed at him. Though he was a Twix for the eyes, he was still a detective, which meant he came with a motive like the fat calorie side of that same Twix.

He returned her stare, waiting for her to object. "I just have a few questions."

Raleigh wiggled her bare toes on the cool cement steps. She had a preference for being barefoot, but she wished she'd had a fresh pedicure right about now. She'd intended to walk barefoot through the garden as she'd done as a child, but now she had someone actually seeing the chipped polish. At least he'd come before they were covered in dirt.

He waited and when she didn't reply, he continued. "How did you know that the car was in the canal?"

Raleigh stared into the midnight of the barn. It had been one of her favorite places as a child. She had loved to hide in the cool crevices where sunlight never reached. The image triggered another one, and Raleigh blinked against the memory, pushing it away where all the others lay. "Let's just say I had a feeling."

Again, his forehead wrinkled. "A feeling?"

Raleigh sighed. Why couldn't Joey do this part? "I just knew."

She could feel him staring, though she didn't look at him. Oh well, Paul, she was failing miserably again. She didn't want more practice either as he would advise. "Where were you when you had these feelings?"

"I live in Baton Rouge."

"So you were there this morning?"

"Yes."

"What time did you get here?"

They were going to get nowhere like this. A different approach was in order. She finally looked into his face and met his expectant green eyes. Again, his focus stunned her and nearly derailed her thoughts. She gathered herself together, and put on her poker face. "You can stop the interrogation. Claudia was immersed in the canal at six-thirty this morning, at which time I was still in bed in Baton Rouge. I had breakfast with my roommate at six forty-five in Baton Rouge. What you need to do is talk to Joey first, so that maybe you can come back with some questions that will get you closer to finding my sister."

His olive face went blank of emotion and he drew his shoulders in tight. He must be a good detective, good at hiding his emotions. That didn't make for a good relationship, though. She'd tried that flavor in a man before. It had left a sour taste in her mouth that tainted every nibble after.

She needed to stop thinking about how attractive he was. He was a Barbeaux detective, for heaven's sake. The police had made her senior year of high school hell. She hadn't come back in eleven years because of people like him.

He straightened up and his shirt pulled against his arms. "Why did you leave the scene this morning before I could take your statement?"

Raleigh shrugged as she rubbed her toes against the cement. "My family needed to know."

"We have people who do those things."

"Those people aren't family. Do you have any idea where Madison is?"

He studied her nose, her forehead, and her cheeks. She felt him linger over those three freckles on her bare cheek. Her face burned under his scrutiny. She knew from her job as Paul's assistant that he was looking for a tell. Something to indicate she might be lying. Raleigh always wondered if she had one. She'd worked very hard on her poker face.

"I was hoping you had one of those feelings."

Raleigh frowned, wishing she'd grabbed a sweater before leaving this morning. At least she could be warm for this conversation, even though she'd like to strangle him with it more than wear it. "It doesn't work that way. The living are way too complicated. She's alive, though, if that's what you're asking."

He stared at her, a vein twitching in his neck. She was getting under that thick skin. Confusing him and avoiding giving him anything he could use. Raleigh would enjoy it if she didn't need him to find her sister. The police had once twisted her into knots, made her cry, and then had kept coming back for more. She should enjoy giving one of them a difficult time, but she didn't feel it.

"Are you claiming to be one of those psychics?"

A bang crashed through their silent stare down.

Voices from inside grew louder, but Raleigh was unable to figure out who or what was being said.

She stood, hesitating to release the quietness of the outside to return to the den. Then came the crescendo.

"It's all your fault. All Madison's fault!"

She wheeled around and yanked on the screen door. She felt Max's body heat behind her, warming her backside. A warning in her head that he shouldn't be there was firing, but she hurtled ahead.

She stopped short in the kitchen nearly stumbling into the middle of Uncle Camille and her father's face off.

"Gone all hours of the night, running around with your daughter. Should've known something was going to happen. Look at what your other daughter did. Madison's just following in her big sister's footsteps, and my baby is the one dead. No good…"

Raleigh felt as if her head were on fire, and then a soft wail trickled in from the living room, Me'Maw.

"That's enough!"

The two turned toward her and the burning kindled her body. "This won't bring back Claudia or help find Madison."

Uncle Camille stumbled forward. His pupils were swimming and overbearing whiffs of alcohol emanated from his skin. "You, you should have saved my baby. You could have tried. You know what happened to her. You need to tell them."

Had a person ever been able to evaporate? She'd really like to do it right about now.

Detective Max sidestepped her, and slowly approached Uncle Camille. "Sir, how about the two of us talk out here? You can tell me anything you know, and I'll help you find out what happened to your daughter."

Uncle Camille stared at Max, his eyes unable to focus, but he allowed Max to lead him toward the screen door. Raleigh stepped out of the way, wondering how he'd managed it so easily.

The screen door snapped behind them, and Raleigh looked toward her dad, wondering what had started it.

His face was gray, but it was his dull, tired eyes that spoke. She'd seen those eyes before. It was the day Raleigh had realized that they'd let her go. "Maybe you shouldn't have come."

Ouch. A screen door snapped down against her chest as it had once smashed her fingers as a young girl.

She turned away from him and went in search of Me'Maw.

Somehow, this would be all her fault. One mistake and she'd be blamed for everything the rest of her life. It didn't help that she seemed to be only good at finding the dead. If she could actually save people, maybe they'd appreciate what she did more. Then again she'd been responsible for one of those dying people. They would never forget or forgive that.

Damn small towns.

Chapter Six

Rolling to a sitting position on her parent's sofa, Raleigh groaned as a pain shot through her back. Her body ached, her shoulders were tight, and her legs were cement blocks.

This sleeping arrangement wasn't going to work.

Her old bedroom had been turned into a five-year-old dinosaur fanatic's playroom/bedroom. The only evidence that she had once claimed the room was a box of mementos stored in the top of the closet, marked in her mom's handwriting. She'd considered Madison's room for all of three seconds, but it was too creepy. She couldn't bring herself to sleep in her missing sister's bed.

Raleigh repeated it again. She was missing. Not dead. There was a chance she would show up on the doorstep, unharmed, with a story to tell. Madison had always been one for stories. Her voice would swell in excitement, she would wave her arms around, and her eyes would twinkle as she described each drawn-out detail. Of course, this story wasn't too exciting with Claudia dead, but maybe she could just tell it in that quiet, expressive voice she'd used when she'd called to say she was pregnant.

This was all going to be okay. Somehow, it would end better than it started. And if she said it to herself enough, she might actually begin to believe it.

A loud banging in the kitchen caused the nerves to jump in her neck. Mom was awake. Her philosophy was that it was a waste of the morning to sleep late. The teenage years had not been pretty on this point.

Not that sleeping late was a problem on this lumpy sofa.

Raleigh stretched and dragged herself upright off of it. It was a good thing Cassie had flung a small duffle bag of clothes at her before she'd raced out the door yesterday. Otherwise, she would have been sleeping in jeans. Not that Cassie had actually thrown in pajamas, but her velour tracksuit would suffice. Cassie must not have had many sleepovers as a kid. Knowing Cassie, she'd probably had none.

Mom leaned against the counter, tapping a spoon as the coffee pot dripped its dark liquid slowly. Her dad sat at the kitchen table drinking his first cup. Nothing had changed here. They'd been doing the same thing eleven years ago when Raleigh had carried her boxes out to the old car on her way to college.

Raleigh strolled to the cabinet on the side of the fridge. Inside were boxes of cereal, crackers, potato chips and the grand prize, chocolate. She sifted through the basket. Apparently, Mason's favorite candy was M&Ms, but several others were mixed in. No Twix. Damn. A Hershey bar would have to do this morning.

"I can fix you some grits or oatmeal."

Raleigh twitched as she closed the cabinet. Why did everyone want to make her eat their breakfast food? It wasn't as if she was stuffing candy bars down their throats. "I'm okay."

Her father shook his head in disapproval, but he remained quiet. Typical Dad behavior.

Mom pulled the coffee pot out and poured her second cup into her favorite blue, extra large coffee cup. Raleigh's eye traveled over the white chip on the handle. "When do you plan on going back home?"

Raleigh bit into the chocolate and felt it coat her mouth before she swallowed. Her body began to tingle awake. "I'm going to stay awhile. At least until we find Madison."

She didn't miss the look her parents exchanged.

Her mom stared into her coffee cup. "We thought you would go back home until the funeral. You don't need to work?"

She was going to need a Twix for this conversation. The Hershey bar didn't fire enough happy neurons for a "you need to go away" conversation with her parents. "I have a few days I can take. Besides, I think it's more important to be here."

Her dad's coffee cup tapped the table. "Your mom and I were thinking that it may be best if you go home and return for the funeral."

The chocolate was leaving a thick, sour taste on her tongue. She set the package down on the counter. "Why?"

Her mom stared out the front window instead of looking her way. "It's just that people will remember the incident and they may not take Madison's being missing seriously."

Her father looked at her and then averted his eyes. "It's not that we don't want you here. We just want to find Madison, and we think this is the best way."

Raleigh breathed in a deep breath, but only old resentments filled her insides. "Were ya'll concerned this much when I was missing for over twenty-four hours? Oh, that's true, you didn't even notice."

Raleigh's heart immediately skipped. Why had she said that? What was she? Twelve?

The chair scraped the floor as her father stood. "We're not going to rehash the past. Right now, the most important concern is finding your sister, and if you stay here, people will think it's her fault. Because... well, because, it was your fault."

Raleigh crossed back toward the living room, but turned as she reached the doorway between the two rooms. "Madison is the most important concern right now, and she is why I'm staying. You know, maybe if you had supported me eleven years ago, you wouldn't be worrying about it coming back to bite you in the ass now."

"Raleigh!"

Her dad's lips thinned and his jaw stiffened. "You will not speak that way in this house."

Raleigh's face was burning in anger, with more than a little bit at herself. She just couldn't seem to stop this morning. It was as if someone needed to gag her with a sock. "I guess I won't be staying here since I'm not needed. At least Me'Maw has always wanted me home."

Raleigh stomped out the house. She was burning up. Her forehead scorched her hand as she rubbed it.

Outside on the front steps, the sun washed over her, only increasing the heat.

What was it about parents that could make a twenty-nine year old feel twelve again?

Raleigh stretched, feeling the soreness in every muscle. She needed a walk. She needed to clear her head.

She took one step down the cement steps when Detective Max's Caprice pulled into the front lawn. Damn it. What was it now?

Raleigh continued her walk down the steps and headed in the direction of the street. He could find someone else to talk to this morning.

Unless… he might have news on Madison. After twenty-four hours, she was officially considered missing. Oh, God, twenty-four hours. Her experience with Paul wasn't giving her waves of good vibrations right now.

He nodded her way. "Good morning. Just the person I've come to see."

Raleigh bit down on her lip, conflicted. His hair was neatly in place and his gray shirt was wrinkle free. He had a fresh cleaned gleam to his face, and a spicy smell tingled her nose. He definitely wasn't having her morning. She hadn't brushed her hair or her teeth. She didn't want to know how unpolished she looked. "If you want to talk, you're going to have to walk."

She passed close to him and shivered, even through the heat still burning her skin. She couldn't do this now. He was a detective on her sister's case. She shrugged it off and continued her pace.

She turned to see him only one step behind. He must really want to talk.

"Where are we going?"

She bit her lip. "Walk off frustration. It could take awhile."

Silence. He adapted to her pace and walked on her left. She gave her Uncle Camille's small rectangle shotgun house a quick glance and then returned her attention to the black top road.

"So, I talked to Joey last night."

Raleigh's face flushed. "Yeah, did he give you the right questions to ask me?"

"I'm not quite sure of all of…this. I don't usually buy into stories like yours. It's my job not to believe everyone that comes my way."

The heat rose again, burning the back of her neck. "What would you like? For me to prove it?"

His hand tugged on her arm. "I'm willing to go on a little faith if you'll help me."

A shiver traveled from the touch of his fingertips. Raleigh stiffened herself against it. "What do you need my help with? I told you Madison's not dead. By the way, do you have any idea about her whereabouts?"

His eyes on her created a prickling feeling behind her neck. What was with her?

"Getting details has proven to be very difficult. I haven't known everyone in this community my entire life, and they're very guarded when answering any real questions. Consequently, I have been unable to narrow down the two young women's whereabouts before the disappearance."

Raleigh frowned. She understood better than he knew. She'd grown up here her entire life, but she was responsible for the death of one of their own and blamed for the death of another. She'd been cast out by half of the town, which meant they weren't eager to have a slumber party and share all their deep, dark secrets with her, either.

"How would I be able to help?"

Max stopped in the middle of the road, and she hesitated but stopped with him. She couldn't help but admire the focus in his eyes. She'd always been an eye person. It's how she decided to trust someone even after Paul had told her it was ridiculous. "You know these people. They will talk to you, maybe tell you things that will lead somewhere, and then I could question the ones that you think might know something."

Raleigh burst out laughing, the sound bouncing around the street. She flung her hand to her mouth to muffle the sound. She hadn't meant for it to escape. She really needed to get it together. She had found Claudia dead, and cracked up all in one day.

Max tilted his head and his forehead crinkled in concentration. He must believe her to be completely insane.

"Raleigh, Raleigh Cheramie, is that you?"

Raleigh looked over at the green house to her right. A small grayish-white picket fence surrounded the front yard, and several trees shaded the house, already casting shadows in the morning sun. Under the tree, nearly out of view of the road, Ms. Margaret sat swinging on her weathered wooden swing. Raleigh groaned inwardly. Of all the people to want to see down the street, Ms. Margaret came last on that list. She didn't even make the list.

Raleigh shaded her eyes with her hands and squinted to see her, wanting to make sure she hadn't imagined that rough voice. "Yes, Ms. Margaret, it's me."

Ms. Margaret pulled herself up with a walking stick and wobbled closer in their direction. She stopped when she reached the edge of the shade. Her thin flowered cotton duster floated around her hunched frame, and her slippers were the color of the dirt and grass. Raleigh ran through her memory to determine how old Ms. Margaret was, but all she could remember was that she was older than Me'Maw, and Me'Maw was eighty-two. Every year had marked Ms. Margaret's face with another crease.

"I heard that you were back. It's nice to see you."

Yeah, the nice old woman act. The question was, who would she call first to confirm that indeed Raleigh Cheramie was on the bayou and being questioned by the police in public no less?

"It's nice to be back, but not under these circumstances. How have you been doing?"

She laughed a harsh laugh, and then a cough rattled her chest. "I'm old and feeling it. Not like those young people traipsing through that house these days."

Ms. Margaret gestured toward Aunt Clarice's house. Raleigh looked toward the white house with its sweeping front porch and heavy brown French door. The grass grew up to the bottom of the windows, and considering the house was built on cinder blocks, the grass was tall. The carport was empty of any cars, and no lights could be seen from the uncurtained windows.

She looked back toward Ms. Margaret. "Someone lives there?"

Ms. Margaret's chest heaved through another round of coughs. "I don't think Claudia or your sister live there, but they sure do throw parties there."

Raleigh looked back toward the house. She remembered now. Madison was supposed to buy Aunt Claurice's old Acadian house after

45

she'd died last year. She'd never heard that she'd saved enough money and actually bought it, though.

Ms. Margaret coughed again.

Max stepped closer to the road's edge. "Do you know when their last party was Ms. Margaret?"

"A few nights ago, Beb. I believe it was Saturday night. I called the police that night. I couldn't go to sleep with all the noise."

Raleigh resisted the urge to laugh. It was more like she couldn't stay up any longer to watch what they were doing.

"It was nice seeing you, Ms. Margaret, but I need to get going now."

Ms. Margaret leaned forward. "I hope you stay long enough to find that missing girl this time. Her poor mother has been waiting for you to come back."

Raleigh's neck grew hot until she felt as if she was sunburned. "I've come back to find my sister. I don't know what happened to Katherine, Ms. Margaret."

"All the same, it would be nice for Bethany to find her daughter."

Raleigh pivoted, turning toward Me'Maw's house. "It was nice seeing you, Ms. Margaret."

She walked, nearly sprinted, in the direction of her house. She could feel Max's presence behind her.

"I'm not sure if you fully understand the situation, but I can't help you."

Max's pressed shirt brushed against her arm. "She did tell you something, though, which is more than I would have gotten from her without you. I'm not asking you to do my job. I just need to have an inside view of your sister's life."

Raleigh laughed. "Anyone can get something out of Ms. Margaret. She's the gossip queen. Probably has a tiara in her living room to prove it."

Max tugged on her arm to stop as they neared his car. "Look, you were right about the time of death. I don't understand it, but you were. I've just got a lead to follow up from someone you had a three minute conversation with. If you truly want to find your sister, you're going to need to help me."

Raleigh frowned. The guilt card. Pretty low, but a good move to make on his part. "I don't trust the police, especially the Barbeaux police."

His eyes gazed down into hers, and she squirmed under their intensity. "Is it stemming from the incident eleven years ago?"

"Incident?" She flushed, that sunburn giving her sharp pains by this point. "How do you know about that?"

"I pulled the report last night. I like to know about the people I'm dealing with."

Raleigh's face surely was the color of the cotton candy at the festival. "You know what, Mr. Pyles, I'll find my sister myself. I don't work with people who don't trust me."

Raleigh stalked in the direction of Me'Maw's house, leaving Max standing in the driveway by his car.

He called out, "Don't go too far, I'm going to have more questions for you."

How could someone be so tantalizing and annoying at the same time?

How could two people in the span of thirty minutes make her feel like a teenager again, and certainly not in a good hormonal lust way? That might be welcomed right about now.

Chapter Seven

Sheri's shop was once an older square home, though Raleigh didn't comprehend how since it could have fit into Cassie's living room. Apparently, people liked to keep their family close a hundred years ago. Someone in her family would have gone missing a long time ago if her family had to live that close. The shop lay to the left of the Cheramie (no relation) grocery store and across the highway from the radio/newspaper/television studio where Mike worked.

Though Detective Max had left her frustrated, he'd also left her with an idea. Who else would know all the town gossip but Sheri, a hair stylist? Luckily, Sheri was a friend from high school. Raleigh had let the friendship slide, just like every relationship in Barbeaux, but she was counting on Barbeaux's insatiable need for gossip to help her out.

Raleigh pulled in next to a Lexus. The town had really blossomed in the money department. Well, more like the spending the money department. The money wasn't new, just the showing it to the world. A black Ford compact car was parked in the back. Raleigh assumed it to be Sheri's car. One customer, not bad.

Raleigh strolled to the door, noticing the stillness in the area. The sign to the left of the door read *Sheri's Creative Image's* open Tuesday through Saturday. Not very creative, but it got the job done. Raleigh turned the doorknob and a jangle tickled her ears. Sheri stood over an older woman Raleigh didn't recognize, tweaking her short, red-streaked highlighted bob.

"I'll be right with you."

Sheri hadn't yet glanced toward the door.

"I have the time to wait for an old friend."

Sheri looked in her direction and popped her gum with a smile spread across her face. "It can't be Raleigh Cheramie back on the bayou."

A movement to her left drew her attention sideways where another woman sat with perfect posture. She looked familiar, yet Raleigh couldn't place her. Raleigh glanced back toward Sheri, who was taking the cape off the woman in the chair.

Raleigh watched Sheri fold the cape. "Yes, imagine that and no one chasing me away with pitchforks or paddles yet."

Sheri's lips dropped, and her eyes widened. "Ms. Mimi, are you ready?"

Mimi? As in Mimi Blanch?

Raleigh felt the need to fall through the floor or perhaps rewind time. Again, where was that ability in her gene pool?

The woman in the chair stood. Her dyed blonde hair was neatly pulled back into a twist, and gold chandelier earrings dangled from her ears. "I don't feel the need to have my hair done today and perhaps never here again. If you're ready, Dory, we'll be leaving. I don't want to associate with this sort."

Raleigh's cheeks burned and her body felt feverish, but all she could do was step to the right as the two exited with their noses high in the air.

Sheri gushed, "I'm so sorry, Raleigh. The thought didn't even dawn on me at first."

Raleigh waved her hands in the air. "It's my fault, really. I should have called first."

Sheri twirled the chair before throwing herself into it. There were two chairs facing mirrors, and several chairs lining the front wall. Raleigh could see a sink to the back, and a small table in the corner with nail polish. Sheri had done well for herself.

Sheri looked up from her fingernails, popped her gum, and squinted at Raleigh's hair. "Who cut your hair?"

Raleigh patted her hair down, self-conscious. "Twelve bucks."

Sheri popped her gum once again. "You can tell. Sit down in this seat, and I'll fix it. Your hair is too coarse for that style."

Raleigh did as she was told and was greeted by her own reflection in the mirror. It did look worse than usual this morning, since Cassie had not thrown any gel or hairspray into her bag.

"I'm sorry you lost the customer."

Sheri waved the scissor in the air. "She'll be back. No one else will listen to her ridiculous commands. But I guess that means she hasn't stopped blaming you for her son's death."

Raleigh frowned, worrying about what Sheri was pinning up her hair for. "I was responsible in a way, and I imagine it isn't easy to let something like that go."

Again, the popping gum. "Still, this is your town, too. People believed your side then."

"Not everyone."

Not the people who really mattered to her.

A shiver ran down Raleigh's neck as Sheri snipped at her hair. She hated haircuts. They never came out as she hoped, and then she was left to figure out what to do with it, having absolutely no skills in the hair department.

Sheri glanced up. "You can't win everyone. So, what's up with your sister and Claudia?"

Some of the tenseness eased in her neck with the change of subject. "I was hoping you could fill me in on what those two have been up to, so maybe I can figure out what has happened."

Sheri laughed. "Come to the hair stylist for gossip, have we?"

Raleigh smiled, feeling guilty for her motive. But her sister was missing... wasn't that enough to ease her guilty conscience? "It's the best place in town. At least for me, and see, I get a haircut served with a side order of gossip."

Sheri laughed, her chest shaking. "Looks like you need both."

Sheri was not what you'd call slim. She was rounded in all areas, including the bust. Her strawberry blonde hair was a perfectly smooth flip, not a hair out of place. Her eyelashes were coated as thick as fur with black mascara, and she preferred deep maroon lipstick. Anyone else would look like a clown, but Sheri pulled the look together and somehow managed to look classy.

Sheri worked on her hair for a moment, and then looked at her in the mirror. "The two of them have made a reputation for themselves. They hadn't even graduated high school before Eddie was talking them into a job. I guess he figured they might as well get paid for dancing on the bar since they were doing it already."

Raleigh's heart throbbed in her chest. Madison was twelve when she'd left. She still saw that cute twelve year old pouting on the front steps as she'd pulled away. This wasn't right. "Eddie, as in Eddie's ladies?"

Sheri frowned. "The one and only. Anyhow, Madison got pregnant a few months after working there, and I thought that would be the end of it, but she went right back to work after having Mason."

Raleigh swallowed the lump of guilt building in her throat. She hadn't called Madison but once every other month. No one had mentioned any of this. Why not? When Madison had told her she was pregnant, and she'd asked about the father, Madison had only answered that he was out of the picture. "Any gossip concerning Mason's father?"

"All kinds of gossip. I don't believe any of it. Madison refused to tell anyone, including your mamma and daddy. I don't think anyone knew the truth there."

Did they want her to know any of this? The two hadn't been close, but over the years, some of this should have found its way to her. A nagging inner voice reminded her that she hadn't asked, either. Never ask what you didn't want the answer to was what Paul used to tell their clients. Had she done that?

"What about Claudia?"

Sheri shook her head; not a strand of hair moved. "At eighteen Claudia began making her way through every married man who would stray, and of course this is the bayou, so many did."

Raleigh released a deep breath. "So, any wronged wife or ex-wife could be responsible for Claudia's death. That wouldn't explain why Madison is missing though."

Sheri continued snipping, but Raleigh couldn't see the back. "About a year ago, Madison quit dancing, got a normal job, and I thought she would marry Alex as they'd planned."

"Alex?"

"Alex Thibodaux. You remember him from high school?"

"My junior prom date? I think so. He's a bit older than Madison. He was our age."

Madison was six years younger than Raleigh. How had that happened? And she didn't even want to think about the nauseating factor of her sister dating her ex.

"She was happy until a few months ago, when it was over. Again, she wouldn't talk about it." Sheri pulled the flat iron from its hook. Raleigh felt the heat on her neck as she pressed it through her hair. "Though Madison was wild, she was also private."

"I still don't know what the two were doing in the last week or so."

Sheri laughed as she twirled Raleigh's chair around. "I can't help you there. She was due for her cut next week."

"Thanks, Sheri. At least you've given me a better idea of where to start."

The Velcro crunched as Sheri pulled the cape off. "What do you think about your hair?"

Raleigh stood and moved her hair side to side, watching it swing with the movement and then fall back into its place, brushing her back. She'd added a few layers and it now fell neatly instead of puffy. "Definitely the best haircut I've ever had. Let's hope I can keep it up."

Sheri smiled as she folded the cape and popped her gum. "You know where to find me."

Raleigh said good-bye and left with the bell jangling in her ear. In the car, she watched the empty highway, considering her next move, and then she crossed the highway. She pulled the rent-a-car into the T.F. Delacroix Communications parking lot. The building was a simple two story white brick box, but Raleigh knew there was a metal building jutting out from behind, where much of the station was located. She noticed the nearly empty parking lot as she pulled into a front row parking space.

Raleigh's steps felt lighter as her hair bounced against her shoulders and again fell back into place. There really was something in a haircut making you feel good. She'd been missing out by getting cheep cuts from people fresh out of school with plenty of creativity, but no experience.

She strolled to the receptionist, whose eyes were glued to her computer monitor. She wasn't even sure if Mike was in the office, but Ms. Betty Marjorie, as her desk plate read, should be able to tell her where he was.

"Excuse me. I'm looking for Mike Simmons."

Ms. Betty Marjorie glanced at her, but then returned her eyes to the screen. She looked as though she should have retired a few years ago, and her crinkled brow and shaking hands hinted at an anxiety from one more day on the job.

"He's in the back finishing up for the deadline. Does he know you're coming?"

Raleigh smiled, studying Ms. Marjorie's computer screen. She was entering classifieds, something Barbeaux had many of. "I'm an old friend. If you just buzz me in, I can find him. I once worked for David."

The receptionist continued typing, but then reached over mid-thought and pressed the buzzer. Raleigh strolled toward the door and pulled as the buzzer released the lock. Not much security these days.

Behind the door, four large cubicles greeted her. She remembered from high school that these belonged to the paper side. Two for advertising copy and two for news copy. David's office was to the right, the first of several offices. To the left was the radio station, two rooms, and straight to the back was the television studio. All housed in the same building, all owned by a different member of the Delacroix family. It might be considered a monopoly if they actually got along.

The first thing Raleigh noticed was the quiet and the second was the lack of people. Did Ms. Betty Marjorie say deadline?

Just as she was about to turn around and ask for assistance, a chair squeaked. Raleigh strolled around to the other side of the cubicles, and there was Mike leaning back in his desk chair and reading his computer screen.

"Hard at work?"

Mike glanced up and smiled. Mike was one of those men who still looked like a boy. His shaggy blond hair, angular face, and green eyes all added to his charms. Not to mention the thick eyelashes that brushed his eyes. "Finishing up my copy. Do you have some news on your sister?"

"Not really, but that's why I'm here."

Mike sat up in his chair. His legs still reached the end of the cubicle. "I haven't been able to find out much yet. That detective is holding out, but I think I've managed to add my name as a person of interest."

Raleigh smiled, squinting her eyes in a way she knew he'd recognize. "How would you like to be my date to see some naked women tonight?"

Mike chuckled and the sound filled the open area. "I can't say I've ever had that request before."

She stepped closer, wondering if anyone else was here. From the dimmed lights, she couldn't tell. "I want to check out *Eddie's Ladies,* where Claudia and Madison worked. I thought you might enjoy coming with me."

"Would I be risking my life?"

"Only if you touch one of the women."

Mike chuckled again, and a door to the right opened. Raleigh watched as David peeked his head out his door.

"That you, Mike?"

Mike stood in his cubicle and stretched upward. "Yes. Do you remember Raleigh Cheramie?"

"Raleigh?" David strolled closer. "As in the Raleigh who would chase down a story for me faster than reporters twice her age? Always asking the tough questions?"

Raleigh's cheeks burned, but she couldn't help but smile. "It's good to see you again, David."

David stopped three feet away and peered at her above his thick lenses. He spent way too much time in front of his computer screen. "It's nice to see you. We've missed you. Are you visiting us or staying?"

Raleigh squirmed. She had been waiting for that question, but the answer didn't surface as she thought it might. "Not quite sure yet. I'm here for a while though."

David rolled forward and backward on his feet. He had never been one to keep still. "If you stay, we definitely want you here. As you can see, we are on skeleton crew right now. We could use some of your old skills."

Was getting in trouble a skill? Raleigh would have listed it on her resume if she'd known. Would she stay here after they found Madison? It wouldn't be so bad working here, but Paw would probably not approve. He'd think it was just another way for her to get in trouble.

Raleigh smiled. "I'll give it some thought."

Mike moved out of his cubicle, pressing a few keys on his computer keyboard. "Raleigh's helping me with the dead slash missing woman story."

David smiled and nodded his head. "Good, good. Keep me updated. Well, let me get back to paper layout. Your last story in, Mike?"

Mike grabbed his coat. "All done and emailed. I'm heading to the town council meeting right now."

David strolled away. "Good, good."

Raleigh looked up into Mike's face. He was so tall. "So, we're working together? You would dare try that again?"

Mike smiled; his green eyes twinkled under the fluorescent lighting. "Of course, what guy would turn down a date that was taking him see naked women?"

Chapter Eight

The wind pounded against the soft cover of the Jeep and the roar in her ears vibrated her body. Mike's Jeep brought back many memories of their high school senior year. Saturday nights of riding around until curfew, blaring the radio, riding to the Island, and the first real sunburn she'd thought she'd die from. She looked around her bucket seat. Quarters and dimes were strewn beneath her feet and newspapers were stacked a foot tall on the back seat.

In high school, she'd kept a mirror in the glove compartment, along with a brush and a bag of extra clothes in the back. Back then, they'd stuff the high school newspapers under the seat so they could chauffeur their other friends around.

"Sometimes high school doesn't seem that long ago."

"Nice times," Mike said as he swung the Jeep onto the highway. "Did you give any thought to sticking around here after we find Madison?"

Raleigh allowed the passing lights to blur her vision into a splinter of white lights. "It would be great if I wouldn't keep walking into my mistakes. I just thought people would have let it go by now."

Mike glanced her way with a grin. "You just need to give them a chance to forget. If they see you every day, eventually they'll see you and not the gossip."

But she wouldn't forget. The overwhelming diesel stench, the blood dripping into her palms and then down her fingertips, the sound of the gun firing and echoing so loud it deafened her, and then sinking into the water dark as mud; it still caused her heart to pulsate and her lungs to burn as if it were happening again instead of almost eleven years ago. When she looked around at the bayou, she felt the memory creeping around the edges. It caused an indescribable panic that she wasn't proud to admit to.

No. Forgetting hadn't been any easier for her.

Mike seemed to be faring well, even though their past was shared. He'd been down in that boat lying at her feet. How had he managed to get on like nothing had happened? Or were there signs that she'd missed? He seemed to be doing well these last few days. Was it always like this?

Raleigh returned her attention to her surroundings as the tires kicked up gravel.

A neon sign blinked Eddie's Ladies with the i and s burnt out. From the outside, the peeling, dingy purplish building looked like any normal building. Raleigh scanned the parking lot and counted nine cars. At least she wouldn't have too many witnesses.

The tires ground to a stop, and Mike swung his door open. He popped out, and then back inside, mumbling "wallet".

Raleigh tried to relax one last time with a deep breath pushed out through her lips and then swung her door open as well.

She was admiring her hair in the passenger side mirror when she heard the familiar guitar strums of Skid Row's *Eighteen and Life to Go.* Strange music for a strip joint. She would have thought it more sleezy and up beat. Music to throw themselves at the fellas. She shuddered again. She was feeling like a prude.

Raleigh closed the door as the front door of the place swung open, and some techno mix blared into the open air.

She stopped and listened. She could still hear the old song as the front door swung closed. It was faint, as if it were traveling far. There were no buildings for two or three miles on this stretch of highway. They were essentially in the middle of nowhere.

"Mike, do you hear that old song we used to listen to by *Skid Row?*"

Mike stopped in front of her. She could tell from his wrinkled temple that he didn't hear it, though he was trying.

"No, what's going on?"

Raleigh shook her head and straightened her posture. "I'm sure it's just a crossed signal."

What she didn't say aloud is that she remembered singing this song at the top of her lungs with Katherine. It had been one of their favorites, though Mike had grown tired of hearing them sing it, especially when they'd stand up in the Jeep with the top off and blare the music as loud as it went.

Mike's eyes stared at her in a way that told her she didn't have to explain it. Yeah, their past was shared for better or worse.

Raleigh forced herself to move forward. She didn't want to go inside, but she didn't want to stay and listen to her past in the form of an old song stepping up to center stage instead of remaining backstage in the wings where she liked it.

Mike pulled the door open, and a bouncer propped against a stool blocked their path. The sound from inside was ear shattering.

She pulled her ID out of her back jean pocket and handed it over. She had to lean in to hear him say the cover charge was ten dollars. She pulled out a twenty and pointed to Mike. It was easier than trying to yell it.

They made their way past a black wall, and she felt with her fingertips where she was going, cringing at the rough texture of the surface. The wall opened into an open area with light pulsating, spotlighting areas of the open room.

Raleigh avoided the center stage with its two stripper poles. She'd told herself she was an adult and this wouldn't be so bad, but seeing another woman naked was causing her flesh to burn, and it wasn't in a good way.

Several men lounged at the back, having a drink at the tables. There was a crowd of hooting and hollering men near the stage. Raleigh glanced away as one customer moved, and she could see a woman in a fuchsia pink thong giving a rather rumpled guy a lap dance. She could have lived the rest of her life without ever seeing that.

Her Me'Maw would probably have a heart attack if she could see her now. Thank goodness, she'd told her she was grabbing a bite to eat with Mike, though Raleigh suspected she hadn't believed her. Me'Maw did have a way of seeing through her. Of course, she hadn't asked when Raleigh told her, which meant she really didn't want to know.

She turned toward the bar since it seemed likely this area would be clothed, but even the long brunette bartender wore a sequined bra. Sitting in a bar stool watching the room was Eddie; Crazy Eddie as some called him after a motorcycle stunt he'd attempted in his youth. The stunt had left a burn scar on the left side of his face. Some said the scar extended much further down. Raleigh had no interest in validating those rumors.

She glanced at Mike, who was squinting under the pulsating light, and jerked her head in Eddie's direction. Mike hovered over her as they crossed over to him.

Eddie looked her up and down as they approached, which did nothing to ease her awkwardness. She slid into the barstool next to him, and Mike sat to the other side. It would be difficult to have a conversation with the noise, and the bass was causing her stomach to churn.

He stared at her, making her squirm on the stiff seat. "You Madison's sister?"

Raleigh nodded. "I've come to ask you a few questions."

He set his empty glass down and nodded his head in the direction of a darkened doorway. His bald head did nothing for that scar.

Raleigh stood and followed him, still avoiding eye contact with Eddie's ladies who were within smelling distance with their cheap, heavily alcohol-scented perfume.

The music dulled to a roar as they passed through the doorway, and as they passed through the next doorway, it became a vibrating thump-thud noise. They entered an open room with dressing tables and a couch. The room held little in decoration except for photographs pinned or taped to the walls. Raleigh stopped not too far from the entrance as she noticed one of the women sitting at a dressing table adjusting her false glitter eyelashes.

"Get your ass out there, Jenny."

A strong disgust for Eddie burned through her throat, warming her ears. Who did he think he was? He wasn't shaking his perfectly glittered boob job body out there. No, he was just profiting from it.

Raleigh forced herself to breathe. No use burning the bridge before she got any information from him. Now, after...

For her part, Jenny just narrowed her eighties blue eye-shadowed eyes at him, and made a face before crossing through the entrance. As she walked past Raleigh, she stared for a moment and then paraded out in her skimpy attire with glittered chest.

From a small, uncluttered corner, Eddie hefted a box that he thrust in Mike's direction.

"This is those bitches' stuff. I don't want anybody asking questions around here, you hear? It scares the customers off, so tell the police we don't have nothing for 'em."

Raleigh bit her tongue against the string of insults she could fling his way. Some that Me'Maw would wash her mouth out with soap for. "So, Madison was working here as well as Claudia?"

Eddie stared at her through narrowed eyes. The scar made him look like the serial killer in a horror flick. After a minute of this had passed, she didn't think he was going to answer. But finally he released the stare and rolled his eyes at the room. "When the bitch needed money, she'd show up. I know she was talking to my girls about her little business. She thought I didn't know, but I know everything about my ladies."

Mike's serious expression contrasted sharply with his normal fun-loving attitude. "Was Madison seeing anyone? Maybe a customer or someone who'd show up to see her?"

Eddie's laugh didn't reach his burnt brown eyes. It caused the skin on his left side of his face to stretch tight and appear more translucent. Raleigh shuddered. "Madison wasn't like she used to be. She wasn't quite the tramp she was five years ago. Claudia was the tramp. Had three guys buying her things, and then taking money from customers for private dates. She was a real piece of work."

Raleigh felt dizzy, and it had certainly grown hotter in here. "Do any of these men have names?"

"Yeah, I'm sure their wives know 'em," Eddie gritted out. "The only one I remember is Kyle Allemande. He hooked me up with some good bait for my fishing trip. He runs Allemande's Lures."

As he walked toward her and the doorway, she knew the interview was over. "Was there any problem with a customer recently or a boyfriend or even one of the girls?"

"They were bitches, there was always a problem. I think our chat is over now. I'll have Rodney show ya'll the way out."

Mike sidestepped closer to her. "I'm sure we can handle it."

"What? You're the bodyguard now?" Eddie laughed and shook his head. "Have it your way."

Raleigh walked back through the doorway, trying to keep her pace even instead of sprinting for the exit. Her uncomfortable meter was maxed out. The music pounded against her body as she again entered the room of pulsating light. No one seemed to have moved in their five minute absence. Raleigh still avoided looking directly at any of the people in the room.

Jenny was entertaining the rowdy group of men, but Raleigh felt her eyes the moment she began looking their way. As she rubbed against some enthusiastic male, she watched Mike and Raleigh exit.

Strange. Friend or enemy or just curious?

Outside in the parking lot, Raleigh's ears were ringing. Though it wasn't a comfortable feeling by any standards, it made hearing a song that wasn't really there impossible.

Mike kicked at the gravel with his Sperry shoe. "Nice guy."

"Do you think he had something to do with it?"

Mike shook his head. "I'm not saying it's not possible, but Eddie's known for changing his women weekly. None of them have ever gone missing."

She leaned against the Jeep, admiring the full opal moon. The night was still. She'd missed the stillness, hearing the frogs and the crickets at night. Texas and Baton Rouge had their own night sounds, but it wasn't the same as here.

The click of Mike's door opening drew her back to the parking lot. She could never get that moment of complete silence, could she?

In the Jeep, Raleigh leaned back in the seat and closed her eyes. "How did Madison or even Claudia end up here? How did they get to this point?"

Mike swung the Jeep back onto the highway, and Raleigh opened her eyes to oncoming headlights. "The two should have never been allowed to be friends. It was just a volatile combination."

"Mom and Dad were so strict when I was in high school. What happened?"

Mike laughed. "I don't think Madison gave them a chance. I think the two were dancing before they graduated high school, and they moved into an apartment right after. They were known for their partying habits.

Madison was never arrested, but Claudia was in the arrests section of the paper a few times. Disturbing the peace, disorderly conduct. Nothing serious."

"They were such good kids." Raleigh shook her head. "And Madison had Mason at eighteen. I couldn't have handled that at that age."

Mike looked over at her. "We're going to find her."

Tears burned her eyes. Damn. How could Mike still know her so well? "She's alive. I know she is."

"And we are going to find her."

They rode the rest of the way to Me'Maw's house in silence. Not an uncomfortable silence, but the familiar silence of two people who'd known each other forever, which was almost true. In kindergarten, they'd been sent to time-out the second day for knocking their tower of blocks down on Katherine. She'd cried and Raleigh had called her a tattletale. Mike had gone to make nice when they'd been released from the chairs. It had all worked out. They'd become friends and had remained that way through high school.

Except they were missing Katherine from that back middle seat, where she'd always sat. Katherine would never sit in that seat again. She'd died the same night as Ross, but only Raleigh had ever seen that body. And of course, whoever had hid it later.

As they pulled into Me'Maw's front lawn, Raleigh smiled at the front porch light on, but then she noticed Paw rocking in his rocker with Spencer, the old Labrador, sleeping by his feet.

Raleigh's insides twisted and frissons traveled down her legs. She immediately thought of Madison.

She sprang from the Jeep and bounded toward the front porch. "Madison?"

Paw shook his head and rubbed his bristly chin. "No. No word on Madison."

A pain throbbed through Raleigh's head. Paw never stayed up past nine o'clock. It was already after ten. Raleigh suddenly felt tired.

"What are you doing up?"

Paw pointed out toward the car parked under the old oak tree. "Someone busted up your windshield earlier. Joey came out and took pictures, but since no one saw anything, he can't really do anything about it."

Raleigh looked at the car. Broken glass twinkled in the moonlight. "Why would someone do that? I haven't even been here forty-eight hours."

Paw stood, and Raleigh noticed his hunched back and his stiff legs. "Someone wanted to give you a message, and I'd say the message was received. I'm going to bed. Lock up, will you?"

Raleigh turned back to her car, which Mike was now walking around. The glass-strewn grass glittered like stars under the moonlight. Who had she managed to offend in less than forty-eight hours? They could have at least waited until she had screwed up first, or was it because she had screwed up eleven years ago? When would she be done paying for what she'd done? She definitely hadn't missed this.

Chapter Nine

Raleigh stretched, feeling herself sink into the goose feather mattress. There was nothing like sleeping in this bed. She inhaled deeply and the faint feather smell lingered. This bed had belonged to Me'Maw's mother, a woman Raleigh had never met. It was Raleigh's favorite, and everyone had known when she was little that this was her bed for sleepovers. Me'Maw hadn't even asked which room she'd wanted. She'd simply told her she could stay as long as she liked and then had put clean sheets on this bed.

Raleigh rolled over to the glaring sunlight peeking in through the sheer mother's lace curtains. Of course, she couldn't stay in bed all day. Too many problems and worries to deal with.

First would be the car windshield.

Raleigh bit down on her lip, rubbing her eyes.

It was a rental. Her old Chevrolet had finally gone beyond repair a month ago. The garage repairman had told her it would cost more to do the engine overhaul than she could sell the car for. She'd put off buying another one, wanting to make sure her income would remain steady. She hadn't been too sure about her new job, as she'd had to take a drastic pay cut upon hire. When she'd picked up and left Texas, unfortunately she'd had to leave her job behind, too.

Now, she hadn't gone to work since Monday, and she didn't have vacation time because she hadn't even worked a full six months. She'd probably be fired come Monday.

That would mean dipping into her savings. She wondered how much and if she'd be able to save to put it back. It wasn't likely in her current situation. To think a year ago, she'd thought she'd be able to stop worrying about money. Of course, a year ago she'd thought she'd be married by now. That was until her fiancée became the prime suspect in the pesky murder case of his secretary/secret lover. Raleigh drew in a long, shallow breath. The windshield. The windshield would be easier to deal with than all that suppressed anger and betrayal.

Of course, there was also the problem of who broke the windshield, and if they intended to stop at the windshield.

It could be a warning to stop asking questions about Claudia and Madison, but Raleigh thought it more likely they were just telling her to go away.

Mimi Blanch had many friends, and they didn't have to worry about resorting to their savings over a windshield. They could reach down into their Coach or Channel bags and pull it out of their spare change. Raleigh guessed it would be insensitive to ask for any of them to dig. Besides, would they really stoop that low? When you had money weren't there other ways to seek revenge?

Barbeaux did have its wealthy crowd. Most of the town barely scraped by on thirty thousand a year for a family, but the boating industry also had created another side outside the shipyard or oil rigs. A side with money to throw away. Mimi Blanch fell into this side. Even in high school, Ross had burned through three brand new vehicles in a year, totaling each in an accident of his own making. Ross had bragged to anyone who would listen about his mom's total lack of reprimand for the accidents.

Sometimes money didn't change people.

A pungent odor drifted through the cracks in the door. Me'Maw must be cooking.

She reluctantly pulled herself from the mattress and sifted through her clothing. Two jeans, a pair of dress pants, a halter top (which Raleigh thought belonged to Cassie), a pullover, and a polo. She definitely needed more clothes.

She pulled on a pair of jeans and the polo and checked her hair out in the mirror. It wasn't quite as flat as yesterday, but it definitely wasn't as puffy as before. A hint of lip gloss and mascara did the trick. The three freckles on her cheek seemed to be especially dark this morning, but she refrained from concealing them. She definitely wouldn't win any Barbeaux beauty pageants, but she wouldn't win a most ugly contest, either.

As she drifted down the hall, the pungent smell of onions and shallots blended into a sweet, heavy aroma. Me'Maw must be making fettuccini. The smell of the ingredients blending together was heaven. Raleigh's mouth watered as she imagined tasting that first rich bite.

Raleigh found Me'Maw stirring her concoction in her big magnalite pot. The sound of the ventilation overwhelmed the small kitchen.

Me'Maw turned around as Raleigh stumbled into the kitchen. "Good morning, sunshine. I hope you slept well."

Raleigh smiled. She'd asked the same question the morning after every sleep over. "It was wonderful. Any news this morning?"

Raleigh reached into the top cabinet and pulled out a glass. The smell of sweetness had her yearning for orange juice.

Me'Maw continued stirring. Raleigh leaned over to smell close up. The butter was melting and blending with the seasonings into a yellowish hue.

"Detective Max was here this morning to bring the news that we could bury Claudia tomorrow. They are sending her body to Sam today."

Sam was the local manager of the funeral home. Me'Maw had played cards with his mother for forty years. Raleigh remembered her as a quiet, stiff-postured, lots of red rouge woman.

Raleigh stopped with the orange juice in her hand. "That soon?"

Me'Maw nodded. "It's best if we begin to grieve now. Everything will settle down."

Raleigh knew she was referring to Uncle Camille, who'd been drunk more hours than not in the past two days.

Then, Raleigh's heart skipped. Madison had been missing for two days. Where was she?

Me'Maw glanced sideways at Raleigh, and Raleigh knew she had felt her thoughts. "I'm preparing a few things for tomorrow. All the family will be here."

Raleigh leaned over the laminate counter. "Yes, but everyone will bring something, Me'Maw."

"It keeps me busy."

She also loved to cook. Loved for people to comment on how much they enjoyed it, though she'd wave them off as they complimented her cooking. Proud, but modest.

"Is there anything I can do?"

Raleigh made a mental note to visit the grocery store later and pick up Twix. Many, many Twix.

Me'Maw shook her head. "You're doing what you should do. You need to find your sister."

"Are you sure Paw is okay with me staying here?"

Me'Maw smiled. "He's definitely not okay, but the two of you will mend this bridge in time. Don't you worry about *tete dure*."

Hard Head. Me'Maw's favorite way to describe Paw.

Raleigh turned and looked out the windows that faced her parent's home. A navy blue Caprice waited in the driveway.

Me'Maw had said he'd come early this morning. What was he still doing here? Or had he returned?

Me'Maw continued stirring, her spoon occasionally scraping loudly against the metal bottom. "Why don't you go out and talk to him? He may tell you more."

Raleigh laughed and shook her head. She supposed she better watch what she thought around Me'Maw. No hot detective thoughts.

She pulled open the back screen door and stepped into the sunlight. Out on the back porch, she could see Paw in the back garden walking down his rows, inspecting his crop. What was it this time of year? Raleigh wasn't sure what Paw would be growing in October. Was it pumpkins? She'd never really paid much attention to it growing up. She'd eaten what it yielded when it was given, but what did months mean to a nine-year old?

Raleigh walked across the yard to her parents' house. When she was younger, the distance had seemed greater. Now, it felt like such a short walk.

As she approached Max's car, he stepped onto the front stoop of her parent's home, shutting the door behind him. He ran his fingers through his dark hair and squinted at the sun. Raleigh noticed the slight crinkles in his khaki pants as though he'd been sitting for awhile.

She smiled uncomfortably. Their last meeting hadn't ended with a smile, and she did not feel like an apology this morning.

He noticed her standing near his car and walked toward her. "Good morning. I thought I'd see you at your parents' home this morning."

Raleigh looked toward the window of the living room. "I'm staying at Me'Maw's house. I just wanted to check with you and see if there was anything new."

Max cocked his head to the side and studied her face. Raleigh was intensely aware of her tingling neck. "Are you considering my offer to help?"

Raleigh studied her pink flip flop. She really should have packed other shoes besides her boots. At least she wouldn't have to stare at her unpolished toes when avoiding his eyes. "I will agree to pass on any information I discover that may be useful, but I'm not going to interrogate people for you."

Raleigh saw a light flicker in his eyes. It could have been the glare of the sun, it was gone so fast. "What do you know about your dad's job?"

She stared at him a moment, her brain rushing to keep up with the switch in topic. "He's worked in the shipyard since he was eighteen. He works long hours under difficult conditions. The same as most men in town."

"Would you say he's ready for retirement?"

Raleigh stared at him, waiting for him to blink. She'd seen a master detective at work and she recognized the strategy. "Isn't everyone when they reach my father's age?"

"Is he set for retirement? I mean, financially?"

Raleigh crossed her arms over her chest. "Why is that any of your business, Detective?"

Max looked away from her stare and back toward their house. "I'm just looking at every angle. Your parents purchased a life insurance policy on Madison only a few months ago."

Raleigh stared at him with her mouth open. She was conscious of the blaring silence in her ears as the sun beat down on them. "What the hell is wrong with you? My sister is missing and Claudia is dead, and the best you can do is look at my father for a life insurance policy?"

Max frowned. "As I said, I'm just studying all aspects of the case, but I understand why you're upset."

Raleigh turned in the grass. She wasn't upset, she was furious. Her face was scorching under it. She turned her head over her shoulder, unable to see his eyes in the sun. "Maybe people don't talk to you for other reasons than you're just new here. You may want to work on what normal people call tact."

Raleigh crossed back over to Me'Maw's house, numerous degrading insults she could have yelled at him running through her thoughts. She would never say them aloud, but they caused her anger to dissipate. Then, she thought of all the questions she did not have answers to and wished she'd controlled her outburst a little while longer. Damn. Why did that man make her feel like an uncontrollable tween?

Me'Maw had said she could help by finding her sister. It was about time she got serious about it. She crossed to the old barn. Paw's truck was still parked inside.

She looked out over the field, shielding her eyes from the sun.

She yelled, "Paw, I'm going to borrow the truck for a little while."

Paw looked back at her and waved his hand and nodded his head.

It shouldn't matter to him anymore. He couldn't drive these days, but she needed to have the rental fixed. Raleigh didn't even know where to begin.

Raleigh stepped into the cool darkness of the barn and shivered. The packed mud floor emanated a strong rotting smell. She'd always been comfortable here, but right now her hair prickled. Strange. She slid inside the driver seat of the old Ford.

She laughed as she looked around the old truck. Paw kept the interior spotless, though it still had a lingering old smell. Its grey seat covers were stiff against her body and the steering wheel felt as though she would be steering a ship, but it held its appeal.

The engine sputtered and started on her first try, and she backed up into the yard. Paw stood staring at her from the field, hands on hips. He really loved this old truck. He'd had it for over thirty years, refusing to buy another one. A case of nervous jitters wriggled into her stomach. If something happened to it, it would be her fault. She really needed to get her windshield fixed. It definitely needed to get moved to the day's to-do list. Scratch that. She never finished a to-do list. She needed to just do it when she got back.

She pulled into the street and crawled toward the highway. Ms. Margaret was again sitting out front. She waved, and Raleigh waved back. She wondered if the windshield incident had been released yet via Ms. Margaret's PSA.

Back to the matter at hand. Where was Allemande's Lures? She'd gone there a time or two with her dad before going fishing. It had been a while, though. The last thing she remembered doing with her dad was riding down to the police station for the third time. It had been even longer still since the last father-daughter trip. Preteen years, maybe?

At the street stop sign, Raleigh took a minute to remember the town's layout. Allemande's Lures was down Petite Oak, only ten or so streets to her left. It struck her how easy that was. She had difficulty remembering what direction to turn to get to the grocery store in Baton Rouge, but here, it all came back in a flash.

The old truck eased onto the highway, the accelerator harder to push than her compact car. It only increased her discomfort with the truck. An old blue Mustang passed her. Frustration and the anxiety welled inside and her neck burned. Ten Twix bars would not have delivered euphoria this day. Though right about now, she wouldn't mind giving them a try and to hell with the waistband of her jeans.

Minutes later, she turned onto Petite Oak. Allemande's Lures was painted in white script on a shed-sized building, second building on the left. And not an airplane hanger shed. A golf cart would have difficulty parking inside. Okay, maybe that was a stretch.

Raleigh maneuvered the large truck between a Chevrolet pickup and a cement fish statue. She held her breath, hoping she didn't scrape the side of the truck. Her rent-a-car was one-third the size of this truck, and she shuddered at the idea of explaining any mishap to Paw.

A bell jangled on the door as she pulled it open. She blinked, adjusting to the dim lighting. When her eyes adjusted, she found she was staring at an aquarium of minnows on the back wall. To her left were three white wire spinning racks of bait and several fishing lines hanging on the wall from brackets. To her right was a wooden cabinet with an old black metal cash register on top.

Behind the counter stood an average size blond man with a chiseled face and wide forehead. He had been working in his ledger and a pencil was still poised in his hand, though his green eyes were now squinting her way.

"Can I help you?"

Raleigh smiled, noticing his roving glance. "Are you Kyle Allemande?"

"I sure am." His face brightened, and he leaned closer in. "Were you looking for me?"

"You could say that." Raleigh stepped forward. "I'm Raleigh Cheramie, sister of Madison and cousin to Claudia."

His face paled and he pulled back, tapping his pencil on the spreadsheet. "Who sent you here?"

"Not exactly the reaction I'd hoped for, so I'll just get to the point." Guilty. Some people were just not great at covering their guilt. Of course, she supposed that didn't usually pertain to murderers. "I've heard you had a relationship with Claudia."

He looked around at the empty store as if someone were hiding behind the one shelf of tackle boxes. "Look, I don't want to upset my wife. This isn't exactly the best place for this conversation."

"I'll make it quick." Raleigh smiled, stepping closer. "When was the last time you talked to Claudia?"

Kyle stared at her. She could see an argument with himself going on behind those eyes. "I spoke to Madison Friday. She invited me to a party she and Claudia were throwing. I passed on the invite."

"What kind of party?"

Kyle stared at the door. "Those two threw wild invitation-only parties. I went to one with Madison and one with Claudia."

Raleigh pursed her lips as her head gave a small throb between her eyes. "You were with Madison as well?"

He grunted. "Only a few times. She was weirded out by my wife."

Imagine that. Raleigh was weirded out just by him, and she hadn't met the wife yet. "Does your wife know about your affairs?"

Kyle studied the numbers scribbled in his notebook. She could see his face reddening under her stare. "She knows some, but we're working through it for the children."

Raleigh's stomach churned in disgust. "Is your wife the jealous type? You know, would she want to get rid of the competition?"

"Leave my wife out of it." His face darkened. "Those girls were crazy. Go question the others- Luke Comeaux, Davey Griffin, and all the rest. I got myself away from them. They were the ones harassing me. I think I've answered enough of your questions. "

His all-American good looks had taken on a dark tinge during his tirade. He definitely had a temper. Maybe he could have snapped if they'd threatened to go to his wife with all the details? She needed to check into him further.

Raleigh pushed the door open, the bell ringing in her ears. "I'll be in touch, Mr. Allemande."

Raleigh settled into the truck and scanned her surroundings. A short, dark-haired plump woman stared her way with her hands on her hips. She'd been trimming some overgrown bushes in front of her small box house next to the shop.

Wife, maybe?

Raleigh wouldn't normally shy away from finding out, but common sense ruled, for once. So did her headache. No one knew she was here, and someone had killed Claudia. Raleigh would want to kill her husband and love interest if he were attending these parties.

She backed into the road slowly and headed up the street. Cheramie Grocery was just a few minutes away, and they were sure to have Twix and maybe a few other things Cassie had neglected to throw into the bag.

Five minutes later, with no mishap, Raleigh parked the truck in the parking lot and headed in. The brown front of the store looked dingy and worn; it hadn't changed much since she was a girl.

Inside, a young blonde teenage girl stared at her from her register, and a young man leaned over the service counter. There wasn't anyone else visible from her vantage point. Raleigh walked by, feeling self-conscious, but scolding herself for being paranoid. These two teenagers couldn't possibly know who she was. They probably just didn't have any customers right now.

Raleigh oriented herself and located the candy aisle. Thankfully, there were several packages of Twix. Raleigh grabbed a handful and then went in search of hygiene products. Apparently, Cassie hadn't thought of things like soap or toothpaste, either.

She was grabbing a toothbrush when she cringed at a familiar laugh from the end of the aisle.

It was Mimi Blanch, pushing a loaded shopping cart and holding a shiny red cell phone to her ear. Raleigh quickly glanced back and pulled toothpaste from the shelf. She hurried up the aisle, grabbing shampoo on the way out.

Raleigh threw her arm full of items onto the black conveyor belt of the lone girl checker whose nametag read Ashlie. Ashlie's green eyes stared at her through the strands of hair covering them before she heaved a loud sigh and scanned the items.

The clunk-clunk of a basket came from behind and Raleigh glanced back to see Mimi Blanch push her cart into the lane behind her.

Ms. Blanch frowned, her whitish makeup wrinkling by her thin, frosty pink lips. "You're still here?"

Raleigh stiffened. Why couldn't they just have had a silent exchange? "I'm here until we find my sister."

Mimi shook her head. "I'm sure she's just in hiding. Most murderers try to escape capture, only some are able to lie their way out of it."

Ashlie paused mid-scan and looked from Raleigh to Mimi. Raleigh's cheeks burned and anger burned her throat. She'd like to throw herself on top of her and strangle her. She could probably take her; Mimi Blanch was much older.

Raleigh yanked a roll of money out of her pocket and nodded to the cashier. Ashlie frowned but continued scanning, flashing black painted fingernails.

Raleigh looked back at Mimi, and her fingers trembled. "Do you go to church?"

Mimi's eyebrows rose. "Of course I do."

"It's none of your business to be doing the judging. My sister isn't a murderer, and even if she were, it wouldn't be up to you to pronounce judgment. Maybe you should worry about praying for all your son's sins before his death."

Raleigh handed the cashier a twenty, grabbed the bag, and walked toward the exit, feeling Mimi Blanch's glare all the way.

She finally inhaled as she stepped outside, but guilt rushed in, replacing the anger. She should have remained silent. Who knew how the incident would be replayed? And of all the conversations she'd had in her mind, that had never been one of them. Why that? It reminded her of another conversation, but she couldn't quite pin point which one. Of course, that was probably due to her quivering body.

It was time to get back. There was less chance of running into people if she were tucked away at Me'Maw's house.

Chapter Ten

Raleigh was waiting in traffic at the bridge on the way back to Me'Maw's house to hide, when she had one of those ideas that in hindsight she should have dismissed. Of course, hindsight was a pain in the butt; it always made her feel like an idiot.

She signaled and drove back to the canal. It was just as quiet as it had been on Tuesday morning. The same picturesque scene of the bayou that had cradled death within it awaited. It was the kind of scene they filmed for those movies that made South Louisianans all out to travel by pirogue, to wear white shrimp boots, and to speak in a language foreign to the rest of the world. Those were sights most of the locals never saw these days, and for the record, Raleigh had never worn shrimp boots. Raleigh noticed that the grass was flattened in spots, and a yellow police ribbon fluttered in the light breeze.

Her heart jumped as the bayou water came into focus. No one spoke to her from its murkiness. That was a plus.

Except that's what she'd come for. She'd wanted to see if she could feel that connection again.

Raleigh closed her eyes and breathed in deeply the scent of stagnant water, the sugar cane, and a hint of something she couldn't identify.

Behind her eyelids, all she saw was darkness.

She was filled with disappointment.

What had happened before Claudia had woken up only to drown? Had Madison been here? Had she tried to stop whatever had happened? Had she gotten hurt?

She opened her eyes, blinking against the brightness of the sun. She couldn't make the connection. She hadn't tried since she was eleven, and even then she hadn't understood what she was doing. Me'Maw had cradled her head in her lap and had tried to pretend it was a game.

Hold your breath and count to three. Please tell me what you see.

Me'Maw had brushed her hair with her fingers. Raleigh's heart had steadied, though her lips had chattered from cold. "What is the girl doing now?"

"She's scared, Me'Maw. She can't see, and the mattress is rough under her back. She's crying, and her arms hurt. She wants to go home."

Raleigh had felt Me'Maw's breath on her ear. It had tickled, and she'd felt as though she were standing in the middle of two worlds for a moment. "What does little Emily see?"

"It's dark, but it smells like paint and bleach. Her foot touched something cold and rough when she felt on the side of the mattress. It's a large room. His footsteps echo when he walks."

"He's coming, Me'Maw. She can hear him whistling."

What she'd ended up seeing was a seven year old girl being raped and smothered, because she'd been unable to describe in enough detail where the girl was for anyone to save her. She understood that it wasn't her fault, though for months she'd dreamed of it every night, and she'd felt his hot spearmint breathe on her neck and his rough fingers scratching her legs. She'd bury her face in her pillow until she could breathe again. She'd come to understand that knowing you weren't guilty and feeling it were two different things.

She'd never tried to reach the dying since. She'd let *them* reach her several more times, but she'd never gone deliberately to that place again.

She didn't even know how to try. She sighed. How would she find Madison? Would she be too late and only find a body?

Coldness pumped through her, and she struggled to keep her breathing even. She couldn't feel Madison die. It was unthinkable. She wouldn't be able to live through that.

Maybe that was her problem. Maybe Madison had already died, and Raleigh had blocked Madison from reaching her.

She looked around, studied the road, the trees, and an old tin dilapidated boat shed falling into the canal. Nothing. There was nothing around to trigger a memory. No, not a memory exactly, at least not one of her own. She'd hoped to see what Claudia had seen right before going into the water.

She needed some proof for herself that Madison was still alive, that she hadn't missed something. She couldn't help feel that Madison might not have reached out to her. Maybe she was the last person Madison wanted to reach when she was dying, since she hadn't wanted to connect to her alive. Claudia had tried, though. Of course, Claudia didn't hold a grudge against Raleigh for deserting her as a kid.

She was startled by the wings of a bird bursting out a nearby oak tree moments before the quiet hum of a car crunched onto the shells.

Raleigh blocked the sun with her hand only to see Max's Caprice easing to a stop on the side of Paw's truck.

Did he have Low Jack on her? How could he know she was here?

He stepped out, and she could see his forehead crinkled in concentration as his eyes scrutinized her. "What are you doing here, Raleigh?"

Raleigh turned from him. His gray cotton shirt pulled just right over his chest, and he stood in the open door of the car as though he were totally in charge. Why did it have to be so damn difficult? "I came to see if I missed something."

There, that was pretty generic. Not a lie, but not exactly the whole truth.

He slammed the car door and another bird's wings fluttered above the tree, this time with a squawk, chiding them for disturbing their quiet. "Our guys went over every inch of this place. There's nothing left. Anyway, this isn't the scene of the crime. She was just dumped here."

"Oh." The word stung Raleigh's jaw and her face stiffened. Not the scene of the crime. There was a someplace else. A someplace that Madison and Claudia would have been together before Claudia was knocked out. She should have thought of that, but she'd been focused on Claudia waking up in that car alive.

"Raleigh." He paused, studying her. She could see conflict twisting his jaw muscles. Did he still think she was crazy? Well, it probably ran in her family, along with the other talents. "You can't come to crime scenes and snoop around. It's going to make you look like a suspect. This was called in, and now I'll have to fill out a report."

"Someone called you because I was out here? I've only been here five minutes at the most."

Max nodded. "I was down the road when I received the call."

She shook her head and breathed deeply. Barbeaux's gossip engine must have had an upgrade since she'd been gone. She scanned the trees, the gravel, the long grass, the water lilies, and the yellow tape. Not the scene of the crime. So there would be no connection to the car here. She'd need to look somewhere else. But where?

"I just want to find my sister."

Max's voice was soft as though he were trying to be gentle. "Did you consider the possibility that she may not want to be found?"

"Why wouldn't she?" she snapped, surprised, but then his words sunk down like an anchor. Anger gushed through her. Something in her head grew warm, and words struggled to find their way to the surface.

Max held up his hand as if to calm her. "We don't know what happened yet, and it's my job to look at all the possibilities."

"You keep saying that," she snarled.

"Hey, I'm not the enemy here. I want to find your sister just as much as you do."

"To blame her for Claudia's death?"

He sighed. His eyes had a heavy deepness to them. She knew it wasn't easy for him, but only part of her wanted to see it. The other part wanted to blacken one of those eyes, though she'd probably just hurt her fist. "It's not like that. I have to work on theories. There isn't much physical evidence to lead me in one direction, so I have to consider every possibility."

Raleigh glared at him. She wished her body would get as angry with him as her head. It would certainly make things less complicated. She couldn't handle his nearness. Her body yearned to be near him, to feel his heat. Her mind just wanted to spit and scream at him.

"Any ideas on the crime scene?"

Good. She'd managed to spit that out without her voice trembling. Maybe self-control was within her reach after all. There was always a first time for everything, as everyone said.

"I can't discuss the case with you."

On second thought, self-control sucked. Everyone was usually wrong, anyway.

"I'll be going now." She turned from him. It was easier when she didn't feel his eyes on her. "I'll let you know if I stumble across the crime scene."

"Raleigh, don't be like that," he called after her.

She sank into Paw's driver seat, started the engine with trembling fingers, and didn't glance back as she heard the shells flying from her tires.

How was that for an exit?

Chapter Eleven

Uncle Camille and her dad's voices, loud and angry, traveled to the front porch from the backyard, filled with all the emotions that followed death. They rose and fell, magnified in the darkness.

Raleigh closed her eyes to the stars, but the voices and the frogs still vibrated through the front porch boards. Where was the peace of the Bayou?

Her dad and Uncle Camille were at it again. Uncle Camille's pores were leaking alcohol, so he was in the right frame of mind for a fight. Her father was tense and scared about the terrifying possibilities surrounding Madison's disappearance. It was like putting two alligators together with only one snack.

She bounded down the front steps, heading in the direction of the street. It was a good night for a walk to clear her head. Yeah, as if the night air could magically take all the stress away. She hugged her arms around her chest as the chilly night air surrounded her. She would have liked a sweater, but that would mean going inside and looking once more into the sad and heavy faces of Me'Maw and Paw. She'd rather suffer from hypothermia.

Spencer bounded down the front steps behind her. Though he limped on his back right leg, he was still quick. He also suffered from high self-esteem. He believed he was younger than he was, so that limp was not getting in his way. Raleigh rubbed his ears as he settled in on her side.

The street slept, unaware of the turmoil. At least she hoped no one else was hearing this. Me'Maw had said that Great Uncle Francis still lived in the yellow shotgun house three houses up to her right, and the brick house that was built next to it was Cousin Jolie's, but besides Uncle Camille, everyone else wasn't part of the Cheramie family. Most had been brothers or sisters or cousins of Paw, but they were gone now.

Raleigh shivered. She didn't want to think about that, since Paw and Me'Maw were old as well. How much longer would she have them? If she left after Madison was found, would they still be here for her next visit? Who knew when that would be, considering how long it had taken for this one. It all made her sad. So instead of mourning, she focused on the light streaming through a side window in Great Aunt Clarice's house, Madison's former pleasure party location.

Her heart fluttered as possibilities flooded her thoughts, but she managed to steady herself. She approached the shell driveway, trying to be nonchalant, opening the front gate careful to close the latch without a sound. The weeds licked at her knees, and she tried not to think about what could be hiding in there. Spenser fell in stride behind her. She assumed neither Madison nor Claudia knew how to operate a lawn mower. Not that she was being judgmental. She'd specifically lived in apartments so she wouldn't have to cut grass, and even Cassie paid someone to take care of it for her. Nope. She wasn't judging.

Raleigh padded up the steps and across the porch, holding her breath, hoping that the porch boards wouldn't creak. Spencer's nails tapped on the weather beaten wood before he settled onto the steps. She twisted the knob and the door pushed open. That was one thing about Barbeaux; most people still didn't lock their doors. Raleigh would probably be the only one who had to lock the doors here, and they wouldn't be coming to steal what was inside the few cardboard boxes that she lived out of these days.

Raleigh entered the darkened room, anxiously trying to remember the house's floor plan from her childhood. The only light pouring in from a window cast confusing shadows. She blinked as her eyes adjusted to the dim light from the windows, and she could make out a sofa to her left and an empty room to her right. Nothing hung on the walls, and the furniture was sparse, consisting only of a sofa and two dining chairs. Raleigh inhaled stale cigarette smoke and lingering booze. She remembered Saturday's party and assumed it was leftovers, although there was no trash lying about. No signs that someone lived here.

Raleigh tripped and stumbled over a rug as she stepped further inside, and then bumped against a wall. She froze, her heart hammering in her chest, waiting for a sound from within. She could hear rifling and something being dragged on the floor from the back of the house.

Someone was obviously here. Was it Madison? What would she be doing here?

She tiptoed along the floor to the back. She left behind the living room, feeling along the wall of the dining room and entered the kitchen. A man in paint- splattered blue jeans was bent over, rifling through a box among several stacked in the corner.

Panic clinched down on her. Stupid. Stupid. Stupid. She'd come into a house where a stranger was going through her sister's things. How did she know this wasn't the person who'd murdered Claudia? Isn't that why she hated horror movies? The characters were usually stupid enough to walk into a room unarmed when a murderer was on a killing spree. She contemplated easing back the way she'd come, but her legs weren't listening to her logical reasoning. This person could be a link to Madison, and she knew that time was important in missing person cases. She'd worked a few with Paul. Come to think of it, they'd never turned out that well for the missing. How much time did she have left to find Madison? It seemed to tick in her ear.

Raleigh cleared her throat. "Hello." The man jumped, jerking around. "I'm sorry. I didn't mean to startle you."

He ran his hand through his short, chestnut hair and laughed. "I guess that wasn't too macho. For a moment there, I thought you were Madison. I had forgotten how similar your faces were."

Raleigh studied him, noticing that he was a little edgy, never looking directly at her eyes. "Were you looking for Madison, then?"

He frowned, leaning against the outdated stove. "You don't remember me, do you?"

Raleigh studied him. His face had seemed familiar, but she had been sure he was a stranger. She looked closer still. His green starburst eyes were soft around the corners and rounded. Take off thirty pounds and the facial hair. Was it Alex Thibodaux, her junior prom date and Madison's ex-fiancée? Raleigh attempted a smile as she shuddered again. "Alex?"

Alex nodded. "I know I look a lot different. You're still the same, though."

"God, I hope not." Raleigh laughed. "I'd heard you were dating Madison."

Alex's lip trembled, and he looked toward the washroom. He'd still not met her eyes for longer than a few seconds. She had a feeling that she

82

was making him nervous. It had been the same in high school. Weren't they supposed to get past those things? "For awhile, until everything went to hell."

Raleigh cocked her head. "What happened?"

He shrugged. "I truly don't know. We were going to buy this house, get married, and maybe have another baby. And then bam, just like that she refused to see me, talk to me. She wouldn't even explain."

"Did she maybe think you were cheating?"

Alex shook his head, looking at the pine wood floor. "I tried talking to her. I even showed up at work. She would only say that she couldn't see me anymore because of the past. I had no idea what she was talking about."

"Your past or hers?"

He shook his head. "I don't know. I think it had something to do with that club. She started doing things... Things she would have never done before. She was a good person. I think they had some kind of control over her."

"You mean like blackmail?"

"I know it sounds crazy, but why else?" He breathed in deeply, rising to his full height. "I just wanted to understand what was going on with her."

Raleigh glanced down at the open boxes. She couldn't make out anything but a jumble of clothes. "Were you looking for a reason in here?"

"No, these are my things. Madison had packed up some of my things when we were moving in, and I just couldn't bring myself to move the boxes back. I needed clothes for the funeral tomorrow, so I figured the house would be unlocked."

He looked so pitiful and sad with his hands in his pocket and hunched shoulders, Raleigh couldn't help but feel sorry for him, though it still kind of weirded her out that he had been her prom date and then her sister's boyfriend, um, fiancée.

Raleigh looked around the house. Other than the smell, there was no sign that there had been a party here Saturday night. Everything pointed to the house being abandoned. Not a single item was left out in the kitchen. Aunt Clarice had had the cabinets filled and the counters overflowing. It felt unfamiliar, as though it wasn't the same house she'd spent many days in after school chatting with Aunt Clarice. She couldn't imagine this being the party place, whatever kind of party her sister was throwing. Though she hadn't heard any specific details, it didn't sound like a party she'd accept an invitation to.

"I need to get going." Alex grabbed a few items from the top of one of the boxes. "How is Mason doing?"

Raleigh smiled as she followed him out. "He's dealing. He has Madison's tough attitude, so that helps." She hesitated, but then figured why not. "Are you Mason's father?"

Alex paused, leaning against the front door. "I would like to have been. Mason is a great kid, but I didn't know Madison back then."

"Did Madison ever tell you who his father is?"

He shook his head. "It was the one secret I agreed to let her have. I always figured that in time she'd tell me. I sure hope none of this has to do with whoever he is. I don't think anyone knows his identity but her."

Raleigh followed him out back through the house into the chilly night air. The light shining through the window was now extinguished, and the moon had settled behind the dark clouds.

"Get out of here!"

A loud shout startled them, and they both turned to see an old, stooped over man next door brandishing a cane in his hand. "This isn't a brothel. I'm calling the police."

He turned around and limped back toward his house, mumbling under his breath about human decency, and there are children in this neighborhood, and other words Raleigh couldn't make out.

Alex pushed the door closed and released a heavy breath. "Rumors are that the parties were a little more risqué than Barbeaux has ever seen. The old people's tongues are flapping on this one."

Raleigh cringed as she walked down the stairs into the creaking night, Spenser limping behind her. She wished she could find her sister without hearing any of the seedy gossip. One thing Barbeaux did well was gossip. If she were to talk to enough people, she'd be caught up on the last eleven years. She didn't want to hear about Madison that way. She'd rather sit on the front porch of Me'Maw's house, shuck some peanuts from Paw's back porch, and have Madison tell her story. Madison wasn't here though, and more and more she felt the gossip might hold the information she needed to find her.

Raleigh walked back down the street toward Paw's porch light. Spenser nuzzled her fingers a few times with his nose, but he kept up with her quick stroll. Maybe he had a little more life in him yet.

The wind hitting against a vehicle caused her to turn and see a Jeep hurtling down the road. Mike skidded to a stop on her side, and she leaned into the topless Jeep. Spenser whined at her feet. Raleigh patted his head, rubbing behind his ears before he leaned in against her, pushing his body into her leg.

Mike turned the volume down on the stereo. "I hope you're not out here by yourself."

Raleigh frowned, but her eyes crinkled in a laugh. "I misplaced my bodyguard tonight, and I still managed to survive." She pointed up the street. "I ran into Alex Thibodaux. I was just getting back."

Mike shook his head but laughed. "I just had a date with Suzy, who works at police headquarters."

Raleigh's eyebrows rose. Date? So he was dating. She wondered if it were a first, second, or double digit date. "How was it?"

Mike shrugged. "Pretty boring, except I was able to get out of her what the document was in the car."

Raleigh bit her lip. Okay, maybe she could lecture him on his insensitivity when she didn't want the information. Maybe this was why he was still single. "Document?"

Mike's eyebrows squinted together. "It was an act of donation. Your sister was donating the house and land to an unnamed person. It wasn't filled out completely."

Raleigh stepped back and looked back toward Aunt Clarice's house. Paw's head would have exploded. "How could she do that?"

"I don't think she could. I'll need to wait until tomorrow, but I don't think your sister owned the house. If she didn't, she couldn't donate it."

Raleigh rubbed the scar on her wrist, feeling the rise and fall. "Alex thinks she was being blackmailed by someone at the club."

Mike strummed his fingers on the steering wheel. "Maybe. Let me check into the house issue tomorrow. Then maybe we can see who drew up the document. It may lead somewhere."

Raleigh sighed. "The funeral's tomorrow."

"I'll be here tomorrow morning to pick you up. Ready escape if you need it."

"I'm going get some sleep." Raleigh smiled, feeling tired and achy. "Try not to break any more hearts in your search for information."

Mike laughed. "I'll try not to. Always difficult, you know."

He certainly wasn't single from lack of confidence.

Raleigh stepped back with Spencer as Mike turned the Jeep in the road. She watched him crawl slowly up the road, taking a moment to realize he was waiting for her to finish her walk to the house.

She turned and walked briskly to the house, with Spencer's moist nose at her fingertips, such a loveable coward.

As she neared the front porch, she took in the sound of the crickets. Uncle Camille and her father must have given it up for the night. Maybe if they would just hit each other and get it over with, it would be better. Raleigh thought it might be one of those twelve year old macho things that would work. She'd like to hit them herself right now, but she'd probably hurt body parts she couldn't even name. She hated what it was doing to Me'Maw and Paw.

Raleigh let herself in. Spencer curled up on his worn, braided rug and rested his head on his paws, watching the front yard. If she could talk to the dog, maybe he could tell her who broke her windshield. On second thought, that talent might make her more of a freak.

The house was dark except for the faint glow from a lamp in the living room. Raleigh switched it off and then padded quietly to her room.

She threw herself down onto the bed and sunk into the mattress. The moon shone through her window like a shaded lamp.

Three days and no clue to Madison's whereabouts. No leads, no witnesses, not even a theory. What was she going to do? She could see it in Me'Maw's eyes. They were waiting for Raleigh to find her. The soft as clouds mattress didn't ease the tension in her body.

She had to be honest with herself. Mimi Blanch and Max had touched a nerve. Many people were probably thinking the same thing. It was plausible that Madison would be hiding if she were responsible for Claudia's death. Their wild ways wouldn't make that story so far-fetched. But for what reason? Her work with the detective had always taught her to look for the motive. How would Madison benefit?

Raleigh would need to dig farther. The idea didn't make her feel better. Madison wasn't just a client, and Raleigh might not want to know the truth.

A tingle spread down her neck and her body stiffened against the creepy prickling.

She turned her head against the balled pillow, a faint cinnamon tickling her nose. A tingling awareness crawled through her chest, up her neck, and into her scalp. *Someone was in the room.*

The form flickered like a hologram near the edge of her blanket-covered toes. As her eyes adjusted to the darkness of the room, the shadows slipped away, revealing the feminine features of a teenager. Water beads trickled down her mud-tangled hair. Her blue lips, the only color in her face, trembled. Mud splattered the drenched silver and green cheerleading outfit. Her battered arm reached toward Raleigh, pushing a blackened Polaroid in her direction.

Raleigh squeezed her eyes tight as her heart hurtled against her ribs. She gasped before throwing her eyes open and sitting up.

The room was empty. The moon still shone through the window, but the red numbers on the clock displayed 11:14. Two hours had passed.

She must have fallen asleep. Had it been a dream? Raleigh shuddered. Her thumping heart didn't think dream.

She knew it had to be Katherine. Katherine had been a cheerleader, and she'd been in water the last time Raleigh had seen her. But what did it mean? Did it have to do with Madison, or was everything going to come back at her?

She needed to wash the dirty feeling away. She could feel the mud clinging to her, the fear still pumping through her body. Raleigh jumped out of bed.

Chapter Twelve

Father Lucas's voice droned in a continuous rumble, only to be absorbed by the border of white tombs. His Adam's apple barely rose and fell with his words, and his lips barely opened. Raleigh was concentrating on his pious figure standing before her so hard that she could count the stitches in his vestment. It could really use some mending along the seams.

If her eyes slipped to the graves around her, messages would transmit through the concrete and marble, nauseating her and drilling her scalp. Graveyards were filled with the dead. Most were settled, only their bodies crumbling within the walls. But some reached out and transmitted their feelings, which could cause an overload of emotions and chaotic memories to pound her senses. Her body ached from her statue pose.

Cassie squeezed her arm. Raleigh smiled, though it barely touched her lips. Cassie had driven down this morning dressed for the funeral, Raleigh's cardboard moving boxes loaded in her small Mercedes. She'd really loved Cassie this morning when she'd shown up with funeral-appropriate black clothes. It was something Raleigh hadn't thought of until this morning. Tongues would have wagged if she'd worn her tracksuit.

Finally, Father Lucas ended the ceremony, and Uncle Camille stepped forward with his red rose. He placed it on the maroon coffin, and Raleigh saw his face droop and his shoulders sag under the heaviness. He'd sobered up some this morning for the funeral. It had eased his temper, but it had aged his face even more.

He reeked of the dying. She recognized the clinging odor. It always smelled like mud and decay to her. Definitely not minty fresh. Raleigh stiffened, relaxing a little to allow the feeling to enter.

His liver and spine gave a faint wisp of decay. She could sense the cancer eating him away, rotting his insides like death.

Raleigh wondered if he knew. More importantly, did Me'Maw know?

She looked to her left, past Cassie to Me'Maw. Me'Maw clutched a pale blue handkerchief tightly to her mouth. Her grayish face stared off, looking past the tomb to somewhere Raleigh couldn't see. She stood strong against the sorrow as an old oak tree in a hurricane. She wouldn't give in now, but how much could she take?

Raleigh choked up and glanced behind her shoulder. A few rows of people behind her stood stripper girl from Eddie's Ladies. Her blond hair was slicked back into a bun at the base of her neck. Gerbils could have jumped through her hoop earrings, and her black skirt could have been a napkin. Other than that, she didn't look much different than some of the other mourners. Raleigh had definitely noticed a distinct difference between family and friends.

People greeted each other, approaching Me'Maw to offer their condolences. Uncle Camille was now hunched over near the tomb bawling, while Uncle Jude comforted him.

Raleigh turned and stepped toward Jenny. Her heavily black outlined eyes widened, and she stepped back. Two, three, four steps and then Jenny immersed herself into the crowd. She was gone. Strange. Raleigh studied the people around her, conscious of a burnt paper smell tingling her nose, a soft music box ting, ting, tinging in her ear, and a numbness creeping up her arm.

She'd lost her concentration. Death was slowly crawling into her senses. She shuddered and attempted to breathe through it.

She caught a whiff of Mike's subtle cologne and seconds later, he was leaning into her ear. "Why don't we get back to the house and get everything ready?"

Raleigh looked up, remembering how tall he was up close, and smiled. "Sounds perfect right about now."

Raleigh followed Mike out with Cassie close behind her. Raleigh stiffened as they walked near Katherine's marble gray tomb, but then she eased her shoulders as she reminded herself that Katherine wasn't in there. Wherever her body was, it had been unable to reach her. At least, not anywhere but a dream. Raleigh shivered at the memory. Flowers in various stages of dying filled the length of the ledge. Someone, Raleigh figured Ms. Bethany, visited here often.

They were nearly out of the tombs when Ms. Bethany rounded the corner with an arrangement of day lilies, Katherine's favorite.

Raleigh jerked in surprise.

Ms. Bethany smiled hesitantly, her eyes lingering over her face, pleading with her. Raleigh looked away. Damn. Why did she have to see death? Why did people want her to see it?

"Did you come to see Katherine?"

Raleigh's throat constricted and her neck muscles clenched. She never visited a cemetery. She didn't need to come here to visit with the dead. They thought her brain was the best social function in town.

Mike cleared his throat. "Ms. English, we buried Claudia today. We're just leaving the funeral."

Ms. Bethany shook her head, her eyes losing focus. "That's right. I'm sorry. I wasn't thinking. It's Katherine's birthday and I was just absorbed... well, it doesn't matter to ya'll."

Raleigh felt awful. Ms. Bethany looked lost, unsure of herself. "I'm really sorry that I couldn't do... that I couldn't do more."

Ms. Bethany stared at her blankly. Something seemed off about her today. Had losing her daughter done this to her, or was it something else? She'd looked better only a few days ago.

Mike nodded. "We'll see you around, Ms. English. We need to get things ready for the reception."

Raleigh stumbled after Mike, unable to look back to see if she were staring after them. She felt sadder about Ms. Bethany than about Ms. Mimi, and she'd actually been responsible for Ross's death. Well, he'd been just as responsible. He'd tried to kill her first. Sounded like a round of tattletale on the school yard, but still, she'd been the one successful in her attempt.

Finally, she climbed into Mike's Jeep, Cassie in the back seat. Raleigh briefly thought, Katherine's seat, but she allowed the thought to flutter away. It was only eleven-thirty in the morning, and she was exhausted.

Cassie leaned forward. "That was the strangest funeral I've ever attended, and I'm not even talking about me not being Catholic. Did you see the woman with the leopard dress, or the dude who thought he was a character from the movie *Grease*? Are you sure this was your relative?"

Raleigh laughed and some of the tension in her taut muscles eased. She'd found the guy with the shirt unbuttoned to his midriff to display his chest hair quite unique. Not to mention the one in flip flops. "Apparently, Claudia led an interesting life."

Mike swung the Jeep onto the highway. "The best was Davey Griffin, showing up with his wife. Makes you wonder if the rumors of a threesome were true."

Davey Griffin. Davey. Kyle Allemande had mentioned him. A boyfriend of Claudia's. Apparently, another married boyfriend of Claudia's.

"Did Claudia ever date single guys?"

Mike laughed as he tapped the steering wheel. "I don't think Claudia actually dated much. That would be too tame compared to the parties she hosted."

Cassie gripped the seat. "What kind of parties? The kind we went to in college?"

Mike shrugged, though Raleigh noticed he didn't look her way. He could never lie to her and look at her at the same time. "I was never invited. Not right for that crowd, I guess, but rumors began a couple of months ago. From what I picked up, they were having what they nicknamed pleasure parties. Of course, I never attended to find out, but some of the guys bragged."

Raleigh cringed. Pleasure parties? She certainly wasn't feeling any pleasure at the idea. What had happened to her sister? What had she gotten herself into? She certainly wasn't the same girl who wouldn't try makeup at the time Raleigh had left for college. Madison had only been twelve then, and a hopeless tomboy. My, how things had changed.

Back at Me'Maw's house, Raleigh fiddled in the kitchen, warming and setting out the various dishes that people had dropped off at a continuous pace this morning. There wasn't much to do, though, so her mind wandered back to Madison's life so unlike her own. Wasn't that an understatement? Raleigh hadn't had any casual dating experience, much less what could be found at a pleasure party. She wasn't even sure what could be found at a pleasure party, but she was pretty sure she didn't want to know.

Mike and Cassie had gone out to carry the rest of the boxes inside from Cassie's car, leaving Raleigh alone. She sat down at the table and stroked the top of Me'Maw's worn deck of cards. The blue background on the backs of the cards were faded to white on the bottom right corner where Me'Maw's thumbs handled them. Card reading. Me'Maw didn't show anyone she could do it, but Raleigh had watched her since she could see over the table. She used a plain deck of cards, so Raleigh had come to believe over time that it wasn't the cards that gave the reading.

Could she find Madison through a reading?

She doubted it. Me'Maw would have done one already. No, Me'Maw had said it was her job to find her sister. It meant that a reading hadn't worked.

"I'm sorry to disturb you."

Raleigh looked up to see Detective Max standing in the doorway. His black cotton collar shirt had the first two buttons loosened, and his black pants were slightly wrinkled at his knees. His grayish green eyes focused in on her, but not as harshly as she'd seen before, and his brow was crinkled in a look of concern or what she imagined was concern. She couldn't read him very easily, so she ended up guessing.

"Do you normally attend funerals for all your cases?"

He approached. She saw his eyes travel over the cards her fingers rested on. She covered them instinctively with her palm. Hah, as if Mr. Intuitive hadn't seen them already. "It's a way to look for suspects. How are you doing?"

Raleigh studied him, trying to decide if he were serious or just going about investigating her again. It's not as if the two-step they were doing was going smoothly. Yesterday, she'd wanted to run him over with the truck. "I usually try to stay away from cemeteries. Otherwise, it's been a great day so far."

He gazed at her for a moment, and she felt the hold of his gaze. She didn't look away, though her body was beginning to warm in response. He looked away first. Then, he crossed to the table and pulled out a chair. Raleigh heard people coming in through the front door. Feet shuffled and stomped into the living room, and somber voices filled the silence. Guests had made their way here from the cemetery. She had set up a table with food and refreshments in the living room, counting on most visitors to have come for lunch. She'd thought she could hide out in the kitchen and keep busy. Apparently, she needed to find a better hiding spot.

"I wanted to apologize for offending you the other day and yesterday." She focused back on his face. His eyes had softened, and he wasn't afraid to keep looking at her now. "I've just been treating you as if you were another detective investigating. It's been too easy to forget that this is your family."

Raleigh studied his eyes. She couldn't figure him out, and his eyes were just as guarded as his words. He certainly was attractive, but his personality was bristly. "Do you have doubts about what I can do?"

"Some days it's easier to believe than others." He shrugged. "What can I say? I'm a contradiction."

They stared at each other, searching for something Raleigh couldn't put her finger on. She thought they were probably looking for the same thing. They seemed to be on opposite sides of this case, but they both felt the attraction. They both were trying to understand where it came from.

Feet shuffled behind her. She turned as Father Lucas approached, a smile twitching his thin lips. Raleigh noticed that his strawberry blond hair had thinned and his spotted complexion had deepened. His boyish looks were maturing to reflect his slow approach through his fifties. When she was a little girl, she could remember him turning the heads of more than one parishioner.

"I was wondering if you were trying to avoid me, Raleigh Cheramie."

Raleigh stood and allowed him to embrace her in his hug. He smelled of incense. Not the kind that smelled good, either.

"It's nice to see you again, Father Lucas. It's been too long."

She pulled away, noticing the crinkling of his eyes as he squinted at her.

"I imagine it hasn't been an easy time for you. Today must have been especially rough. How are you coping?"

"Better than some."

Father Lucas had Saturday afternoon meals once a month with Me'Maw and Paw for the last twenty years, and he knew more about what she could do than her parents. Me'Maw had seen to that. Me'Maw had a talk with God or Father Lucas before she approached anything, including counseling Raleigh on her talent. In fact, he had lectured her about final judgment after she'd been responsible for Ross Blanch's death. She supposed it would be childish to blame him for her loss of control yesterday. Probably not real Christian of her, either.

Father Lucas bobbed his head with his hands behind his back. "God works in ways we're unable to understand. We are only left with our faith. Some take a little longer to realize it."

She felt a lecture coming on. "Me'Maw said you were moved to a different church?"

"I would never refuse Me'Maw a service." He paused and smiled. "How long do you plan on remaining 'ere?"

Raleigh glanced back toward Max, who was openly listening to the conversation. Well, what was he supposed to do? Pretend to stare at the refrigerator? She guessed she could give him this one. "Indefinitely. I'm here until Madison is found and until Me'Maw is okay."

Father Lucas stepped closer, his head still facing down. "What has God told you about Madison?"

Raleigh smiled. It always surprised her at how seriously he took her when most thought she was insane. "She's alive. I just don't know where."

Father Lucas and Me'Maw both believed that it was God who allowed her to see. Raleigh wasn't always so certain. Did God have that much of a sense of humor? Had she done something wrong that she should be punished with death? She sure would have liked a second chance then.

He bobbed his head, his smile returning. "I'll go and see if Me'Maw needs me. She was occupied earlier. I hope to see you again, perhaps at a reunion of the Cheramie sisters."

Father Lucas shuffled back into the living room.

Raleigh sank back into her chair. She looked across the table again, her fingers brushing the deck of cards. Why didn't they work? If Madison was alive, why didn't Me'Maw see her?

"I went to church every Sunday during my childhood, and I was never that close to the priest."

Raleigh frowned, wondering what he meant by it. Was he implying something inappropriate? Was she going to do this for every conversation they had? It was exhausting. "Me'Maw treats most of the congregation."

"Huh?"

"Me'Maw is a traiteur. Surely you've heard of it? You're from Louisiana."

Max's brow crinkled. "Of course I've heard of it. I just never met one before. Is that where you get it?"

Raleigh shook her head. "I can't do what she does."

Raleigh could see the questions forming behind his murky eyes. He didn't ask, and at the moment Raleigh respected him for it. A nagging thought was beginning behind her temple. Something she wanted to push away until later.

"It's not Madison's fault! It's Claudia's fault!"

Raleigh jerked in her chair as the yell roared through the living room.

She was up and had crossed into the living room before she could place the voice. Alex stood in the middle of the living room, squaring off against Uncle Camille.

"Madison was fine! Claudia kept dragging her into more trouble. It's probably Claudia's fault that Madison is missing, so don't go blaming Madison."

Alex's face was red and his hair stood up as he pumped his fists by his side. Uncle Camille rose to the occasion, his face blushing with anger. He was half of Alex's size, though, with his emaciated frame. If they were placing bets, Raleigh's money would be on Alex.

She dashed across the living room, grabbed Alex by his taut arm and pulled him with her. "Come on, Alex, we need some air."

At first, he stood unmoving against her tug, but then he glanced around the room at the faces all staring, hanging onto his words, and he relented. Why again was she always rushing into situations with absolutely no self-defense skills?

Outside, he slammed his fist against the front porch post. "I'm sorry, Raleigh. I really meant to stay away from him today. But I've heard what he's been telling everyone in town. He started today, and I just lost it."

Raleigh released a deep breath, trying to push her exhaustion out with it. Maybe she should have majored in psychology instead of English. It sure would have come in handy lately. "It's okay. Uncle Camille has been quite the pain recently. He's not dealing with Claudia's loss real well."

"And I get that." He stopped pacing and pain clenched his facial muscles. "I'm really sorry about her, but it's not Madison's fault. Claudia wasn't an angel."

Raleigh didn't say that Madison didn't seem to be an angel, either. She didn't believe it would help him cool down, and she certainly didn't want to make him angrier. She could see the blood dripping from two of his knuckles and he didn't even seem to notice. She'd be sobbing like a baby right now.

Everyone was falling apart.

Why couldn't they just cry?

It couldn't possibly be as exhausting as the temper tantrums.

Alex walked off the front porch and headed in the direction of Aunt Claurice's house. Could Madison have meant to donate the house to him? Give it to him as a way of telling him to get on with his life? That didn't make any sense, though. He wouldn't want to live there without Madison. Talk about living too close to your ex. But who could she be donating the house to? Had Mike discovered that piece of information, yet?

The screen door snapped, and behind her Mike walked toward her. He stared off in the direction of Alex just approaching Aunt Clarice's house.

"I guess he's not a fan of Uncle Camille?"

Raleigh shook her head. "Uncle Camille needs to keep his mouth shut. He's going to make finding Madison harder."

Mike stepped closer. "I just spoke to a friend at the bank. Your grandparents own the house. Well, they don't own it outright. They're paying a small loan back. I have a call into a lawyer to help explain the donation document."

The screen door creaked. "How do you know there was a donation document?"

Raleigh and Mike looked back toward the door. Raleigh's face burned as Max's intense gaze honed in on them.

Mike put his hand up and an innocent schoolboy expression appeared instantly. "Hey, I get paid to find out these things, just like you."

Max's hand went to his hip, crinkling his shirt even further. "The two of you seem to know more than you should. In my line of work, we call that suspicious."

Raleigh rubbed the indention of her scar. It seemed like only this morning she'd sat in that hard wooden chair at the metal table in the interrogation room being grilled about her story of why she'd shot Ross Blanch. An intense hatred for Barbeaux police swarmed through her, stinging her flesh. She wouldn't go back to that place again. "If you'd have found my sister already, we wouldn't be trying to find her ourselves. Why should I expect any more from the Barbeaux police, though?"

Raleigh pivoted and jumped off the porch, heading toward Paw's garden. Her face burned from shame. She'd allowed her emotions to control her once again. What was it with him? She was like a teenager every time he came around.

She walked to the edge of the garden and was startled from her self-condemnation by Paw standing behind the old barn with a red and white beer can in his hand.

She squinted against the sun. "I thought I'd get to hide out here."

Paw took another swig. "You're welcome to it. Only problem with hiding is someone always stumbles across your spot."

Raleigh frowned as she walked down the rows of dirt, greens, and deep purple. Paw always had a way of cutting to the truth. Of course, he was a man of few words, and the words he chose were always the truth. He'd once talked more to her than he did anyone else. She'd secretly thought everyone else was jealous. That was of course before everything had gone to hell.

She walked down the row, feeling the uneven dirt under her shoes. She could feel her anger and frustration seep into the dirt, but no matter how far she walked, she couldn't release it all. Me'Maw couldn't sense Madison, and she couldn't, either. Me'Maw was always listening to her talent. Raleigh, not so much. Did that mean that Raleigh had missed something? She couldn't help but feel that she had.

After awhile, a whistle sounded from the front. She looked up to see Cassie waiting with her arms crossed across the chest of her black skirt suit. Her hair was still slicked back, not a strand out of place.

Raleigh sighed and made her way back to the front.

Cassie watched as she approached. "I'm going to drive back now. I have an open house tomorrow I want to get ready for."

Raleigh leaned in and gave her a stiff hug. It wasn't exactly one of their specialties. "Thanks for coming. I don't know when I'll be back."

Cassie smiled. "Take your time. You may find what you're looking for here. By the way, Greg called yesterday morning again."

Raleigh felt her spine stiffen involuntarily. "You didn't tell him I was here, right?"

Cassie frowned and stared down at her. "Of course I didn't. I just think you need to talk to him and tell him to give it up."

Raleigh looked away from those reproachful brown eyes. Greg was supposed to be her husband right now. The wedding had only been two months away when she'd packed up and gone. He'd come under investigation for the murder of the woman he'd been seeing on the side. Not exactly the picture perfect marriage she'd dreamed about as a girl.

Cassie cleared her throat. "Just think about it. Maybe you should give that detective a shot or hell, even Mike. Both options are looking pretty hot."

Raleigh laughed skeptically, then walked toward the front of the house with Cassie.

Chapter Thirteen

The stench of cooked cabbage besieged the kitchen. It was worse than the smell of Paw's old gardening boots, but at least Me'Maw didn't allow the shoes inside. She only hoped that the smell would come out of her clothes one day. Me'Maw stirred the cabbage and then banged the spoon on the side of the Magnalite pot.

Raleigh pulled the utensils from the drawer and began placing them around the table. "So Madison didn't even tell ya'll about Mason?"

Me'Maw shook her head, dragging her slippers on the laminate floor as she trudged to the rocker. "Madison was real close-lipped about that business. Of course, your mom cried for weeks, and your dad thought she didn't say anything because she was scared of him."

Raleigh turned to her, watching her raise her legs. Blue and purple streaked like shattered glass through her legs. "What did you think?"

"Why don't you cut up those cucumbers on the counter?" Me'Maw leaned back in her rocker as Paw banged in from the back screen door. "I think Madison was afraid of the father finding out. She loves that boy like anything, but I think whoever his father is could take it all away from her."

Paw pushed the screen door back open. "Call me when it's ready, Lou."

The screen door snapped back behind him and Raleigh sighed as she pulled the cucumber from its position near the window.

Me'Maw raised the lid on the cabbage and a strong odor puffed through the room. Raleigh resisted breathing into the sleeve of her shirt as she pulled a knife out of the rattling drawer.

"Did you ever have any idea of who his father might be?"

The metal spoon scraped the bottom. "Someone important. Not like those boys she sees now. He has to be someone who wouldn't see Madison too much to not know about Mason." Me'Maw paused. "Girl, rub the ends of those cucumbers."

Raleigh rolled her eyes, but rubbed the freshly sliced ends of the cucumber against its other half. "Remind me why we do this again?"

Me'Maw smiled. "Takes the bitterness out. Can't forget where you're from child."

No chance of that. Anyone else would need a manual to visit the bayou. It was like coming to a foreign country and not speaking the language.

"It's not that bad."

Raleigh laughed as she finished with the cucumber. She really needed to watch her thoughts, but she'd missed that, too.

She slid into a chair and went over it in her head. Someone important. Definitely not the strip club-pleasure party crowd or he would know. How would Madison have met him? Had he found out about Mason and taken it out on Claudia and Madison? But then why not come for Mason?

Her head throbbed. The smell wasn't helping.

The screen door creaked open again, and Raleigh looked up to see a strange dirty blonde, frizzy haired woman blocking out the sun.

"Excuse me, I'm sorry to drop in like this." She said in a soft voice. "I'm Denise, Madison's boss at Creative Celebrations."

Denise looked unsure of herself in her gray pantsuit as Raleigh flashed her a smile. She wasn't quite sure what she was assuring her about, but Denise looked as though she needed someone to hold her hand or maybe carry her inside. Denise allowed the screen door to snap behind her, though she remained standing in the doorframe staring down at them and biting her lower lip.

Raleigh tried again. "I'm sorry if no one contacted you about the situation. We've just been handling, well dealing."

Raleigh thought given the circumstances she'd put it the best she could. She certainly didn't know who was in her sister's life to make phone calls.

Denise frowned again. "It's just, well... I was sort of hoping for some news. Madison is my only full-time employee and I miss her..."

Me'Maw gestured toward the chair as she moved herself slowly into her rocker. "Have a seat, Beb. Madison spoke of you often. She sure loves her job."

Denise hesitated, but then crossed to the chair. She still looked uncomfortable. "I just can't do the work all by myself. I can't keep up. I didn't realize how organized Madison kept me until I've had to plan this party without her."

A light blinked from the fog of her brain. Madison had mentioned once, a while back, last year maybe, that she was working for a party planner. At least she wasn't only stripping and hosting pleasure parties. That was a start.

Raleigh ran her thumb over the uneven table surface. "We haven't had any word on Madison yet."

Denise sighed. Raleigh hoped she wouldn't cry. She supposed tears would be better than another temper tantrum. She may not know how to deal with the crying though. Not like throwing yourself in front of a crying person couldn't bring danger she supposed. She might drown in tears. "I don't want to replace her, but I'm going to have to. I have three upcoming parties, two of which are big deals, and I don't know what to do."

Me'Maw shook her head. "I hate to hear that. Madison sure loves the work."

Raleigh looked up as Paw filled the door again. He was staring down at them, narrowed eyes, frown on lips. Something else for people to talk about was probably what he was thinking. "I'll do it."

Denise looked her way, her face blank. Raleigh had to wonder what kind of business Denise could be running. She seemed pretty slow on the uptake.

"I'm here until we find Madison anyway. I'll fill in until she's back. At least then she'll still have her job."

"That's great. That would work out perfectly." Denise's smile grew. "But, uh, have you ever done this kind of work before?"

Raleigh smiled. "I'm a personal secretary right now to an insurance agent. This has to be more interesting."

How difficult could it be? They planned parties. *Parties.* It couldn't possibly involve as many forms as insurance claims.

Besides, it was the first smile she'd seen on Paw's face all week. At least that she was responsible for.

Denise stayed for a cup of Me'Maw's coffee that she fiddled with, drank half, and then left saying she needed to get back to the office.

Me'Maw shook her head as she picked up the coffee cup from the table. "The girl could have just said she doesn't drink coffee."

Raleigh laughed and Me'Maw joined in. Me'Maw picked up the strangest information sometimes. She'd told Raleigh once it was like a voice whispering in her ear serving as the commentator at a big football game.

Raleigh thought her own head was crowded enough without the sportscaster. At least the dead didn't come with a narrator.

Small footsteps thundered through the living room toward them. Mason bounced into the kitchen, his eyes dancing with excitement and a smear of dirt on his cheek.

"Nanan, Nanan, You need to come see."

Paw's voice thundered through the kitchen, and Raleigh held her spine stiff against a jump. She'd definitely felt like she was five just then. "Boy, what did I tell you about running through this house?"

Mason's excitement only dulled for a moment. "But really, Paw. Someone put letters on Aunt Raleigh's car. Come see!"

The chair scraped against the linoleum floor, and Raleigh followed the bouncing Mason out the front door.

From the porch, Raleigh could make out black markings on the rear side. She hopped down the front steps, and as she approached, she could make out six-inch black letters, Go Away or Die. Raleigh's heart sank. How did they do this with no one seeing? Why couldn't Spencer have barked or at least bit whoever it was? At least with a bite, she could have DNA evidence. Probably a lawsuit against her too, but still it might be worth it. He really was getting old.

Paw's boot scraped against the front porch as he squinted at her car. "Call that detective friend. It may be important."

Raleigh stared at the car another moment. Between the black garbage bag covered windshield and the dust, and now the letters, the car looked as though it belonged in a scrap yard. Did rental insurance cover this? Had she even purchased the insurance? She couldn't remember the contract.

She pulled her cell phone out and begrudgingly called Max.

He seemed confused by her request, but agreed to come out and see. She couldn't help but notice his warm, smooth phone voice.

What was wrong with her? How could she be attracted to him and be so frustrated by him at the same time?

She sat down on the front porch watching Mason kick a soccer ball around. Had anyone even been watching him? He was staying with her mom and dad, but she'd only seen her mother out of the house for the funeral. Did anyone even know where he was all day? She guessed this is what they meant by families falling apart during a tragedy.

The neighborhood was quiet. She and Mason were the only two signs of life on the street. She noticed Alex's truck in Aunt Clarice's old house's driveway. She imagined it must be difficult for him to deal with the gossip and not knowing where Madison was. He was probably using the house to hide out. Ms. Margaret was again sitting out on her swing; the oak tree in Me'Maw's front yard blocked the top half of her body, which Raleigh didn't think was all that bad.

It wasn't a bad place to live if you didn't count the car vandalism and of course, the murder and disappearance.

Max pulled up about twenty minutes later. Raleigh remained sitting on the porch, not liking the vulnerable feeling that had crept up. Why did she need to keep calling on him? Had she turned into a helpless, hormonal lunatic?

Mason excitedly ran to the car, pointing to the letters as he bounced around Max's legs. At least when Mason begged to know what it said, Max told him it said Go Home. Maybe he knew a thing or two about children. That would shed some doubt on Raleigh's theory of no tact or social skills.

Max pulled out a few tools and dusted around the letters. He shook his head as it came up empty for any prints.

Raleigh watched his eyes scan the area, lingering over the oak tree her car was parked under, her parent's home, the nearest house, which was Uncle Camille's, and finally her.

"Someone doesn't seem to want you here. Have any ideas?"

Raleigh smirked and stifled a laugh. For a detective, he wasn't putting the facts together quickly. "Anyone who was close to Ross or the

Blanchs, which since they are Barbeaux royalty, we're talking a long list. Or maybe someone who doesn't want me looking for Madison. If all of that isn't enough, maybe it's Suzy Leblanc from sixth grade because I slammed her in my slam book."

Max sighed as he ran his fingers through his disheveled hair. From the slight gray tinge to his face and the dark circles under his squinting eyes, he didn't appear to have had a stress-free morning. He crossed over to her and sat down on the porch. "I haven't had a real easy time since you've come to Barbeaux. Not that I think it's your fault, but things just keep getting stranger."

Raleigh noticed the creases in his forehead, his dark eyelids, and a slightly wrinkled pant. He was exhausted. She wondered why he didn't have anyone taking care of him. She noticed the absence of a wedding ring. She guessed maybe he was in his mid-thirties. Most people were married young in Barbeaux. Divorced young as well, but married at one time… or two. Some she'd graduated high school with were already on marriage number three. She hadn't managed to make it down the aisle for number one.

"I wish it were easier. I wish Madison would drive down the driveway and say she'd decided to take a vacation, but I know that's not going to happen."

He studied her. She could feel his eyes scorching hers and then her cheeks and her lips. "What do you think happened?"

Raleigh shuddered even in the sunlight, and she caught the flicker of his eyes as he caught the gesture. She needed his attention off of her. Did she not despise the hormonal teenage self? It wasn't quite convincing right now with him near her. "Apparently Madison and Claudia were hosting pleasure parties. I don't have a clear picture of it yet, but I've heard from several people that it was going on. Maybe something went wrong. Alex thinks she was being blackmailed, and maybe that document is part of it. I just don't know, but it's been too long."

Max remained quiet. He seemed to be staring at her forehead, but she noticed the far off glaze to his eyes. "How do you know she's still alive?"

Frustration churned inside her. How was it useful for her to know about the dead if no one believed her? Was he really looking for her as if she was alive or did he think she was already dead?

Raleigh swooped down off the porch and yanked a clump of grass out. Her heart was pounding, and she felt lightheaded. How would they ever find her if he didn't believe her? "This grass is dying. It only registers as a small blimp in the whole scheme of death, but as I tore it out of the ground it began to die. I can *feel* it. I can feel the cancer killing Uncle Camille's cells but he doesn't know it yet. When Claudia was under the water, she didn't want me to leave until she'd been brought to the surface. She was afraid to be left alone and not to be found. I can feel it all. Madison is not dead. I would know."

Raleigh was huffing by the time she finished, and her cheeks were scorching.

Max seemed taken aback, openly staring at her. Why had she done that? She'd always refused to explain it to anyone. She was filled with anger at herself, spreading quickly through to her thundering heart.

"I need to get back." Max stood up and looked toward the street. "We were compiling a possible suspect list. I'll let you know if anything comes up. Meanwhile, I'd maybe park in the back yard and be careful not to go anywhere alone."

His lack of response stung, but she nodded her head coolly and let him gallop off to his police buddies.

No doubt she'd freaked him out.

Hey, what could she say? Feeling the dead was a pretty freaky thing.

But she still didn't know who was trying to get rid of her. Ruining her car wasn't a good way to get rid of her either. So it had to be someone with questionable intelligence.

Raleigh looked around the neighborhood. It was still quiet as if it were the calm before the storm. Spencer stopped near her feet and shook himself off. Raleigh bit down on her lip. Spencer was a loyal dog, but not much of an eyewitness. Apparently, not much of a guard dog either.

The trees rustled in the breeze and again the quietness eased through her, calming her. An extended cab black truck had pulled up in front of Aunt Clarice's house, but Alex's truck was still there. She hoped it was someone checking on him. She didn't need any more attacks or outbursts or whatever else came with anguish. Her gaze lingered over the empty yards until she fell upon Ms. Margaret's legs contrasting against the darkness of the shade trees.

Ms. Margaret sat on that swing most hours of the day.

Raleigh gritted her teeth and released a haggard breath. Whose karma was this, hers or Ms. Margaret's?

It would have to be Ms. Margaret then.

Raleigh walked up the street; Spencer's nails tapping on the black top at her side. He'd followed her around as a puppy fourteen years ago as well. She guessed he hadn't forgotten her in the last eleven years. Even the dogs in Barbeaux had good memories. Some forgetting would be nice sometimes.

In minutes she'd reached Ms. Margaret's gate. She fiddled with the latch as she felt Ms. Margaret's eyes on her. Why did it have to be Ms. Margaret? Everyone would know that someone was trying to scare her away by nightfall, if even that long. They'd probably be calling in an hour to hear a full report.

Raleigh called to her as she crossed the yard. "How are you doing, Ms. Margaret?"

Ms. Margaret coughed and the swing creaked as she leaned forward. "I'm still alive. What else can an old woman ask for?"

Raleigh smiled and eased herself down onto the swing next to Ms. Margaret in her pink tulip flower duster that Raleigh hoped was not see through. Still, Raleigh decided not to look close enough to see. "Come on now, at least you get to relax and enjoy the quiet."

"The quiet is lonely." Ms. Margaret cleared her throat. "I see you're still here, so I guess Madison is still gone."

"Yes, we still haven't found her." Raleigh gritted her teeth. "I was wondering if you had seen anyone recently near my car."

Ms. Margaret glanced in the direction of Me'Maw's house, squinting her eyelids, wrinkles crinkling tighter at the corners. "I can't see like I used to. I'm afraid that's too far these days."

"What about any strange cars coming down the street?"

Ms. Margaret raised a trembling finger in the direction of the black truck. "Mais, there's been so many strange cars these days at that house; I couldn't tell what is familiar anymore."

Raleigh glanced toward the black pick-up. Was that truck's driver responsible? She'd never seen it down here before. As if she knew what was usual in all of her five days here. "Not too many have visited in the last week though, right?"

"Really, just that nice young man." Ms. Margaret coughed and cleared her throat. "He hadn't been around for awhile until this week. That black truck was at those horrible parties. Such bad business, I tell you."

Raleigh forced her lips down from a smile, as Ms. Margaret did the sign of the cross. "Do you know what was going on there?"

"Lots of people were talking." Ms. Margaret performed another shaky sign of the cross. "All poor taste. Drinking, drugs, young people making a ruckus. I just know they were loud, and I would lock myself in the house when they would bring it out onto the front porch. They could scare an old woman."

Raleigh stared across at the front porch of the old Acadian. The old stairway to the second floor leaned to the left, certain to tip over in a storm. The paint was peeling to reveal a dirty gray wood, and the grass still reached the porch boards. The house was one of the few on the street that had a carport. Raleigh could remember when Paw and several others had built it. She'd been really young, maybe six. Aunt Clarice had been a lean, well-kept woman. She'd lived alone her entire life and had been more modern than any of Me'Maw and Paw's relatives. She'd smoked her Virginia Slims, kept her short bob perfectly groomed, and had played her music so it filled every room of the house. It was the first time Raleigh had ever heard blues and jazz. She'd admired Aunt Clarice though she hadn't understood why.

Raleigh sighed. "Things sure have changed."

Ms. Margaret raised her bruised legs. "People just get old and die, and the young people take our places. Your Aunt Clarice wasn't tame as I remember it. She probably wouldn't even blink at what is going on in that house."

Raleigh smiled. That was certainly true. She'd heard some stories of Aunt Clarice as a young woman. She was definitely a woman ahead of her time. "Well, let me get back to Me'Maw. I told her I'd help her around the house today."

Ms. Margaret nodded. "I liked the company. Sorry, I couldn't help you with the car. I'd say I'd keep an eye out, but my eyes don't do much good these days."

Raleigh had to smile and nod. Maybe age had done Ms. Margaret some good. Maybe she was trying to cleanse her karma. Who wasn't these days?

She crossed over to the gate and was latching it, when a scuffle behind her caused her to look toward Aunt Clarice's house. Kyle Allemande slammed onto the front porch boards, shoulder thudding against the wood, but had picked himself up before Alex stormed out the front door.

"HOW DARE YOU!"

Kyle stood and glared at Alex face to face.

Raleigh hurried across the street and unlatched yet another gate. She could see Alex raise his fist as she bounded through the tall grass.

Alex's face was red and his brows were furrowed into a straight line. Kyle's shirt was disheveled and perspiration dripped down his forehead. She bounded up the steps as Alex drew his fist back.

"Alex, stop!"

Alex glanced toward her, but returned his glare back to Kyle.

Kyle edged closer. "Yeah, Alex. Why don't you stop?"

Raleigh advanced closer. "Kyle, shut up. You need to leave."

Kyle sneered down at her. "And who do you think is going to make me?"

"My Paw's shot gun might do it." Raleigh met his glare, unflinching. "You know I know how to use it."

He glared down at her a moment and then threw his hands up. "I'm outta here. You people are crazy. To think Madison was the sane one."

Raleigh stood still until he gunned the engine of his truck, and then her body began to tremble. He was right about one thing. She certainly felt as though she'd gone crazy since coming back to Barbeaux. She was supposed to see death not have a death wish.

"What was that about?"

Alex ran his fingers through his hair and paced the front porch. His face was still flushed in anger. "People are talking, Raleigh. They're saying things. What's going to happen when Madison comes back? Her reputation is ruined."

Raleigh released a breath feeling it ease the trembling in her upper body. Her legs still felt like weeds in the wind. "Alex, as long as we get her back alive it doesn't matter. We can fix anything else. My life wasn't ruined because everyone was gossiping."

"But you didn't stay here. Madison loves it here, and it would kill her if she had to leave."

Raleigh felt that familiar ball in her throat. Why did everyone have to know so much but so little? She hadn't stayed away because everyone was talking. Her reasons hurt more than what they were saying. "I'm here now, and it's okay. Alex, you need to stop losing your temper. It's not going to help Madison."

Alex leaned against the house and closed his eyes. "I know you're right, Raleigh. I just hate not knowing."

"We all do."

Wasn't that the understatement of the week?

Raleigh's legs began to steady. They were beginning to feel like something that could carry her home. Spencer snuggled up next to her legs, and Raleigh reached down and patted his head. She'd nearly forgotten about him. He may not be a guard dog, but he certainly stuck around.

She gave Alex one last look, turned, and headed back toward the gate. She felt as though she was no closer to solving her car problem or finding her sister than she was when she walked up the street. Maybe she should look for her sanity at the same time. It seemed to have gotten lost on Cheramie Lane with everything else.

Chapter Fourteen

She fiddled around the kitchen with Me'Maw the rest of the afternoon. Me'Maw commented that she'd wanted to clean out her cabinets, but she couldn't get down on the floor anymore. So for the rest of the afternoon Raleigh pulled out pots, casserole dishes, serving dishes, and numerous containers. Me'Maw wiped them down, and Raleigh cleaned the cabinets, all in a perfect rhythm.

Paw came inside a few times during the afternoon and watched them work, but he would then go back outside and sit on the back porch or walk along the garden rows shucking peanuts and popping them into his mouth. They looked like a perfectly normal family from the outside. That was, of course, if you didn't look too close that these were her grandparents, and she didn't know where her parents were.

At six o'clock Raleigh was placing the pots back into the cabinet when Mike rapped on the back screen door.

The screen door snapped behind him, and he filled the doorway. "Well, you don't look as though you're ready for our date."

Raleigh looked his way, scrutinizing his wide smile. She knew she would have remembered a "date", and they definitely wouldn't have called it a date. She was sure of that. "I don't recall you asking me for a date."

Me'Maw laughed as she leaned back into her rocker. "If I wouldn't be so tired, I'd take you up on that."

"C'mon now," Mike grinned. "Paw would probably bury me in the back garden with the radishes."

Me'Maw laughed until she coughed.

Raleigh stood up from the cabinet, shaking her head, but with a grin.

"I thought we'd go down to Nick's and have a drink." Mike grinned. "I have it from a good source that Davey Griffin will be down there tonight, and I thought it might be a good time to ask him about his relationships."

Raleigh looked down at her grimy hands and dusty clothes. "I need a shower."

Mike nodded. "I'll wait. Don't take too long though. Me'Maw might whisk me away to go dancing."

Me'Maw laughed and her eyes twinkled.

Raleigh strolled down the hall with a smile twitching at her lips.

After ten minutes of washing away the dust in the shower, Raleigh, feeling clean again, stared at the boxes stacked in the corner. She'd simply moved her problem from one room to another. Three times if she was keeping an accurate count. Cassie had brought nearly every box from her room in Baton Rouge, and Mike had stacked them three high for her in this room. All she owned fit in fourteen boxes. She was tired of looking at cardboard boxes. She needed to find a place where she could unpack.

Raleigh bit down on her bottom lip. It was the finding a place that was giving her trouble. And of course by place, she meant a town she wanted to stay. Houston had been okay for awhile, but she wasn't going back now. Baton Rouge may not welcome her back anymore since Cassie had brought all of her boxes here. Had she meant that as a message? But where then? Where would she go now?

She yanked open one of the larger boxes and stacks of folded clothes greeted her. She fumbled through, upheaving the neatly folded stacks, (Cassie must have packed this box) until finally she found a pair of jeans and a sort of dressy maroon button down shirt in a satiny fabric.

Not too bad. She didn't know how people in Barbeaux dressed to go to a bar these days, but this wouldn't be too dressy or too casual.

After fifteen minutes of fiddling with her hair, she gave up and allowed it to go in a wavy do. Maybe she needed to ask Sheri if she offered Hairstyle 101. After a little make-up, she was ready to go. She slipped into her comfortable old friends, her black boots, and made her way down the hall.

Paw was now sitting at his old ladder back chair at the table, and Mike thumped his fingers on the table across from him. Me'Maw leaned into her rocker cushion, and they were talking about the parish council's latest decision to use money to try and repair sections of the bayou side that were caving in. Raleigh gathered that Mike had just covered it for the newspaper, and Paw was asking about it and commenting that they needed to spend the extra money to do it right.

It was more than Raleigh had heard him talk since she'd come in Tuesday. She stopped a moment and listened in the hallway before emerging into the kitchen.

"Ya'll enjoy yourselves." Paw leaned back into his chair. "Don't just cause the misere. I'll leave the front lamp on for you."

Raleigh smiled, though she wasn't sure if she should feel insulted or complimented by him telling them not to cause trouble. She could certainly say he knew her well though. She hated to tell him that in her experience the warning didn't usually do much good.

Mike held the screen door open, and Raleigh hurried into the crisp air. The weather had been up and down in temperature for even October, and today had been a particularly windy day. They hurried to the Jeep Mike had parked near the old barn. She could feel her hair twisting in the wind. So much for attempting to fix it. She supposed teased hair still hadn't come back in style. Raleigh climbed in the passenger side as she glanced at her parent's home. No lights spilled into the yard from the windows. She hadn't heard from them all day. Well, she hadn't spoken to them yesterday at the funeral either.

Mike started the Jeep, and Raleigh strapped herself in. "I think Nick's will be crowded tonight. There's no party this weekend, so the party crowd will be there."

Raleigh shuddered as she flattened her hair with her hand. Who was she kidding? She'd need something better than her fingers for this job. "So, what's the plan? Hello Davey, did you have a threesome with Claudia, and oh by the way do you have anything to do with Claudia's death?"

"No, I think we should be a little more subtle." Mike chuckled as he pulled into the street. "Although, if he's had too many drinks, that approach may work."

Raleigh stared through the side window as they stopped at the front of the street. It was already dark outside. "Did you find out about that donation document?"

Mike's tires skidded as he pulled onto the highway. "John, the lawyer we consult for the paper, says that it was a do it yourselfer. A lawyer would have phrased it differently and filled in all the information."

Raleigh touched the window, side lights spraying small specks of lights everywhere. Trick of the eye. She couldn't help but think that they needed a different perspective on the situation. "So Claudia died in Madison's car with a phony document that would have donated a house she didn't own to someone who was possibly blackmailing her or them. Does any of this make sense to you yet?"

Mike shook his head. "We're missing too many puzzle pieces. For instance, if they were being blackmailed, what for? If we knew what for, it would narrow down the suspects. Or like if they were blackmailing Madison, why is Claudia dead? Or why would they want to keep Madison? There are just too many unknown variables right now."

Raleigh leaned her head against the seat. What if it was Claudia blackmailing Madison? She tried to pull back that thought, singe it from her memory, but instead in five seconds she'd connected some of the points. Madison still alive somewhere, but Claudia found dead in Madison's car. Madison and Claudia operating a pleasure party business. So many things could have gone wrong. One could have got greedy. They could have had a falling out. Raleigh could conjecture all kinds of scenarios.

She didn't want to think about it. She released a slow breath trying to push the tension out through her pores. It didn't work. She'd have to meditate for days to release the tension she felt balled in her head.

Ten minutes later, Mike pulled the Jeep into a tight parking space in the side parking lot of Nick's. It was a large wooden building that Aunt Clarice had said was built when she was a girl. It had been a dance hall back then. Aunt Clarice had told many stories about when it was a dance hall. As Ms. Margaret had said, Aunt Clarice would not have flinched at pleasure parties. There were probably thirty-five to forty vehicles in just the side lot of Nick's. Raleigh didn't want to think about the number of people inside. She patted down her hair again, and then hopped out the side of the Jeep.

Mike squeezed her shoulder as they walked toward the entrance, and Raleigh noticed for the first time his striped cotton shirt's top few buttons unbuttoned with the sleeves rolled up. She wondered if he was trying to impress anyone tonight. He certainly smelled and looked like it.

The music suffocated her ears the moment Mike pulled the blackened glass door open. Raleigh stepped inside to a den of people. Nick's bar and grill (mostly bar) was in the shape of an L. To her left was a bar, a pool table, and several booths, but to her right was open dance space, currently packed with people, and at the back was a small stage where a band was spitting out early nineties rock music.

Mike's hands on her waist guided her to a small space at the bar where she spotted Sheri. Sheri patted the stool next to her, and Raleigh slid onto it. She peered at the other patrons above her eyelashes to see if anyone was watching her. She needed to get over this self-consciousness. It was beginning to even annoy her. No one seemed to be openly gaping at her.

Sheri leaned over and winked her heavy blue eye shadowed eye. "Nick's isn't usually so full. I guess there's no good party going on tonight."

Raleigh looked up as a young blonde bartender moved in front of her. He looked as though he still belonged in high school. But, hey, if he could mix a drink, who was she to judge? "I'll have a mudslide."

Sheri held two fingers up. "Bring us two shots, the same as before."

Raleigh stared at her a moment and then shrugged. As she turned to the right, she spotted Max at a table huddled with two other men who looked just as authoritative as him. She guessed they were cops or detectives as well. She was going to need reinforcements in the form of that drink.

Mike rubbed her back, and she looked up into his eyes. He pointed toward the dance floor, and Raleigh recognized one of the men from Claudia's funeral. The long, dark haired woman in a turquoise mini dress dancing to his right in his group with several other women had been attached to his arm at the funeral. Her dress for the funeral had covered more of those long legs that seemed to be taller than Raleigh. She guessed that this was Davey Cheramie and wife. At least they hadn't been runner-ups for the weirdest funeral attendee awards.

The bartender set the two shot glasses down in front of them as well as the smooth mocha mudslide. Raleigh picked up the shot glass, briefly thought that it should be called regret in a glass, and swallowed. She coughed against the burning sliding down into her insides, coating her chest. It did not deliver instant comfort, that's for sure.

Mike leaned in and tickled her ear with his lips. "How about I introduce you?"

Raleigh looked at him skeptical. "We can try it, but you know me."

"I hope he's had a few drinks." Mike grinned.

She glanced at her Mudslide, but the shot still simmered in her chest. She picked it up and slid off the barstool. No reason to leave it waste here when she may need it later.

"I'm not missing this conversation." Sheri slid off the barstool. "Gossip is so much juicer when you get to be the spectator."

Raleigh groaned, but followed Mike toward the dance floor with Sheri on the heels of her boots. Raleigh noticed the moment she caught his ogling eye. His eyes darkened, and his face stiffened even with the smile licking his lips. She knew that her naturally dark chocolate hair and amber eyes set her apart from most of the dyed blonds in the bar, but these two features were shared with Madison. Madison was two inches taller than Raleigh, but they were both slender. Of course, Raleigh had more curves on her shorter frame since Madison probably weighed one hundred pounds wet with her clothes on. She could see his eyes deepen further as he looked her over, and his lips curled into a half grin. His eyes met hers, and the alcohol churned in her empty stomach. If she were going to be sick, she wished it would be on him. Those nice, expensive shoes would make a great target.

Mike stopped in front of the slightly balding gentleman in a sports jacket standing at Davey's side.

Mike reached out and shook the two gentlemen's hands. Raleigh felt as though she should cross her arms over her chest to protect herself from his creepy ogling. "John, Davey, you remember Raleigh Cheramie, right?"

John nodded his balding head with a silly grin. "I worked with the two of you on the paper for awhile. How've you been, Raleigh?"

Raleigh smiled. He'd been the pimply-faced boy who'd carried the high school newspapers printed at the *Barbeaux Gazette* in his mom's van. They'd handed them out as everyone came in the doors in the morning. "I'm doing okay."

Raleigh looked to Davey, who was gazing down on her with what she supposed he thought was a smoldering gaze. She wanted to tell him that there was no way he was undressing her with his eyes or any other part of his body, but she hadn't found out anything useful yet. No use offending yet. "Unfortunately, I was a bit younger than you. I knew Madison though."

Raleigh nodded her head, sipping her drink. The cold chocolaty feel seeped through, calming her. That was way better. Raleigh looked up toward him and tilted her head in what she hoped was an alluring way. "I was hoping to talk to you about that."

The music changed into a slow rock ballad. Davey stepped in closer. Raleigh could see the perspiration on his forehead. She needed to add that to her list of turn offs. "How about a dance, and I'll answer a question or two."

Raleigh looked to Mike who she could see had stiffened his normal relaxed stance. She knew she also had Max sitting in a back booth with a perfect view of the dance floor. Ugh. Maybe she wasn't being paranoid that people were always watching her. What the hell? Mike had gone on a date for information. She could surely manage one dance. She'd try not to think about the touching part.

She gave Mike a smile with a raised eyebrow expression she knew he'd understand. Gesturing toward the dance floor with her mudslide free hand, she stepped toward Davey. His clammy hand grasped her free hand and reeled her forward. Raleigh gripped her drink tighter so it wouldn't spill. He certainly was persistent. He finally stopped when they were surrounded by dancing couples and out of hearing distance from Mike and his wife. He cinched her close, but Raleigh nudged herself further away from him to see his face.

"I've heard you were a guest at Claudia and Madison's parties."

"You're beautiful." Davey smiled. "Do you have anyone telling you that?"

Raleigh frowned as she maneuvered her drink to his shoulder so as not to hit the couple dancing inches from them. They looked as though they'd learned their moves from *Dirty Dancing*. "I'm sure there were enough beautiful girls at the parties for you."

He laughed. Raleigh's stomach churned at the mixture of his sweat and overpowering cologne congested her nose. "Madison resembles you. You know my type is the dark-haired woman."

Raleigh yearned to drain her glass to flush out the shudder running through her, but she didn't see how she could maneuver it without spilling it or being rude. She was definitely not numb enough for this conversation. "Claudia was a blonde."

He laughed again. It was a low, throaty sound, and his eyes would not look away from hers. She shifted even further away from his clammy body. "She wasn't my choice."

He gestured with his head to his brown with subtle blonde highlights wife. Raleigh felt her cheeks flush. Nope, not numb. "What about Madison?"

His head leaned in closer to her neck. "She was off limits."

Raleigh's muscles clinched, yearning to pull away from him. Ten feet might cover it. On second thought, maybe twenty. "Do you know where she's at?"

She could feel his breath on her neck, and she clinched her jaw.

"If I find her for you, what are you going to do for me? I can show you what I do like."

Raleigh's head flushed with a heat that caused light-headedness. She reached and grabbed his shirt with her free hand and yanked him closer as her lips went near his ears. "Listen you rude, sexist prick, I don't know who led you to believe you were a gift for women but you are far from it. When I find Madison, and I will, you better hope you had nothing to do with it because if you did, so help me you will wish you would have considered me off limits, too."

Raleigh released his shirt and stepped back, and he released his grip from her, stunned.

Someone brushed against her from behind, a familiar touch, and Raleigh looked up into Mike's cold eyes.

"Is there a problem?"

Raleigh stared back at Davey, who was gazing at her with eyes that were a mixture of anger and respect. He seemed incapable of speech as his neck grew red.

"I think I'm just feeling a bit stuffy. I'm going to visit the ladies room."

Raleigh edged to the left, brushing against Mike and squeezing his arm. She weaved her way through the crowd of unfamiliar faces to the restroom in the front to the left of the stage. Once there, she stared at herself in the mirror and a paler, shakier version of herself stared back.

She'd never considered herself prudish. A little modest, maybe. Apparently, her limits were being tested and she was failing miserably at every turn. She was crazy and a prude. Who said you couldn't discover who you were by going home? What was next? She wondered how many acts this show was going to have.

Davey Cheramie seemed to be a first class asshole, but Raleigh doubted he stopped worrying about his sex drive long enough to blackmail or murder someone. She wasn't sure if she were willing to get close again to find out anymore.

Raleigh drank down her mudslide and was touching up her lip gloss when Davey's wife peeped into the restroom, spotted her at the mirror, and came in.

She advanced toward Raleigh and gushed in a melodious voice.

"I'm Christine, Davey's wife. I wanted to apologize for Davey. He's just upset right now. Normally, he's very laid back and sweet. I want to get a divorce, and he likes the way things are between us. So it's causing him a great deal of stress."

Raleigh nodded. Was there a camera in this restroom, one of those confession cameras on a reality TV show? "He likes being able to have sex with other women while he's married. Many married men would love that arrangement."

Christine frowned, studying Raleigh with a thoughtful expression. "It's really me. I like women. I thought he was going to make me happy, but then everything got twisted. You know he had a thing for your sister. She didn't play though."

Raleigh shook her head, feeling the alcohol prickling her forehead. Maybe numbness was finally coming. It needed to arrive before she died from shame or embarrassment or whatever her modesty was doing to her heart right now. "She didn't go for the threesome?"

Christine twisted her fingers, pulling at her wedding ring. "No, but Davey didn't have anything to do with Claudia or Madison and whatever happened. He wouldn't do that."

Raleigh slipped her lip gloss back into her pocket and reached for the door. "All the same, I'd rather if he stayed away from me and my family."

Christine smiled and then bit down on her brandy stained lips. "I'll let him know."

Raleigh emerged back into the clatter of the bar noise, instruments, and buzzing of voices.

Christine had tried to make things better, but she'd only succeeded in making him look guilty. Eliminate the competition, keep your wife. Or was that what Christine wanted Raleigh to think? She was supposed to narrow down suspects not add more to the pool.

Raleigh couldn't get a grip on her thoughts any longer between the thumping drum and clatter of voices. Mike stood waiting at the edge of the wall with a clear view of the restroom. Raleigh directed herself toward him, but she looked beyond him through the crowd, and she could see Max's intense eyes following her, scrutinizing her.

Maybe another drink and things would look better or at least a little fuzzier.

Mike grasped her elbow and steered her toward the bar. "What was that about?"

Raleigh leaned in close, though she still had to tilt her head up. Had everyone she'd known had a growth spurt but her? "We had to reach an understanding. He now understands that I'm not one of the party girls for sale or lease or whatever they were."

Mike glared back toward Davey, whose arms were draped over the shoulders of a group of young women near the dance floor. Raleigh guided him forward with her fingertips on his waist.

Sheri sashayed toward them, flanked by two long haired blondes with pierced navels. They were the kind of beauty that stepped out a magazine. Raleigh avoided those magazines. She didn't need the blow to her fragile self-esteem, or was it her thighs? The two towered over Sheri, who was not a short woman at five foot nine, by at least two inches. Raleigh glanced down at their stiletto heels. She'd be afraid to hurt her butt on the way down.

Sheri clutched her amber drink close to her chest as she squeezed her way through the crowd to stop in front of them. "Raleigh, Mike, I thought you'd like to meet Summer and Winter."

Raleigh leaned in closer to hear. She felt as though she was going to be deaf from the noise decibel, and who named children Summer and Winter anyway? You weren't even supposed to capitalize seasons. How confusing would that be? She guessed she couldn't say much since her mother had got their names from an old Atlas lying about in Aunt Clarice's house. Her mother had thought they sounded interesting, and Aunt Clarice would have probably named them Virginia or Martini.

The blonde with the long, stick straight layers stepped closer. Her shirt came inches from the line of her low rider jeans and her bare arms were visibly toned. The blue eyeliner on her eyes caused her contact blue eyes to glow in the dim lighting. "I'm Summer. You look so much like Madison that we noticed you earlier when you walked in."

"You knew Madison?" Raleigh glanced at Sheri. She supposed it shouldn't irritate her so much that it should be Madison taking after her since she was the older sister.

Sheri leaned in closer. If it weren't for the noise, they would all be too close for comfort. "They worked for Madison and Claudia."

"Oh," Raleigh took in the other one whose tank top brushed her navel. Her arm was wrapped with at least twenty silver bangles. Her skinny jeans tapered down to her black stilettos. This one's brown eyes were coated in black eyeliner, and her blonde hair was in soft perfect waves. Disgusting.

Winter laughed and threw her head back, and the waves cascaded around her face. Were they filming a hair commercial? Couldn't be or Raleigh would be banned. "Don't look like that. It was loads of fun and good money. I wish there was a party tonight because it beats this place."

Raleigh flinched, but kept her head up and her eyes level. It must be a generation gap. "When did you see Madison and Claudia last?"

"Sunday night." Summer looked at Winter frowning. "We all worked together, and we had planned to sleep all day Monday. It had been a long weekend."

Mike stepped closer. "What time did you'll work until Sunday?"

Winter smiled up at him, her eyes glistened with interest even in the smoky room. Raleigh noticed the cleavage erupting from the top of the tank top. She wondered if Mike noticed it, too. Really, it was impossible not to notice. "We left at about three o'clock to go home. We had two bachelor parties that night which was odd for a Sunday."

Raleigh noticed Summer's eyes flicker around the bar. She seemed unable to focus on one thing. "Did Madison or Claudia mention any problems with anyone? Someone suggested that they may have been being blackmailed."

Winter eased closer to Mike. Raleigh kept waiting for her to reach out and touch. "Madison's ex was like stalking her, and Claudia had some problems with some old guy at work the other day."

Summer waved at someone across the room. Raleigh couldn't pick any one person out from the crowd to tell who she was waving to. "And Jenny was giving them trouble. That girl is nuts."

"She's just young." Winter frowned, pinching Summer on the arm. "Some of the guests were unhappy the last couple of parties. It's always difficult to please everyone."

Raleigh nodded her head. Her thoughts were swimming around, paddling through the fuzziness. Just moments ago she'd wanted fuzzy, now clarity would be welcome. "You haven't heard from Madison since Sunday?"

Winter shook her head. "She usually scheduled on Wednesday. She was the brains behind everything."

Summer frowned. "Claudia was smart, too."

Winter shook her head again. "Claudia was crazy. There's a difference."

Summer rolled her eyes. "Anyway, I see Davey. I'll catch ya'll later. I hope you find Madison. It won't be the same without her."

Summer waltzed off with her shoulders high, and her hair bouncing with each step. Several men openly stared at her tight butt as she crossed the floor. She didn't seem to notice.

"Summer's attention span is as long as a Jack Russell." Winter laughed. "But seriously, Madison and Claudia were really tight. They didn't really tell anyone else anything personal. I can't imagine anyone we know actually killing Claudia."

Raleigh fought to keep her thoughts straight. It would be easier without the band playing *Fuel*. "And you haven't heard of anyone who talked to them Monday?"

"I slept until 3:00 PM that day. It had been a long weekend, and it was my day off." Winter shook her head, looking up at Mike again. "I'm going to go make sure Summer doesn't get into trouble. She tends to need a babysitter. If you need anything else, Sheri knows how to find me."

She smiled again at Mike and sauntered away. Half-way toward Summer, Winter turned to see if Mike was watching while looking him up and down. Wow. Not a fan of subtly. Raleigh couldn't help but laugh, and Mike glared at her.

"At least I didn't have to dance with her."

Raleigh laughed and shook her head. "I don't think you would have gotten off as easy as a dance."

"That was good, right?" Sheri edged closer. "I remember them talking at one of their appointments about working the parties. I thought it might be useful."

Raleigh nodded. "It's more than I found out from Davey."

Mike shook his head. "Still, we don't know who saw them on Monday or what they were doing. With how public they were, you would think someone would know."

Sheri shook her head. "Madison wasn't really public, and like Winter said, Claudia was crazy, but even still, she didn't talk about the things she did. People just saw her do them."

Mike's lips twisted into a frown, and he smoothed his hair with his hand. "We need to find someone who saw them on Monday. There has to be someone."

Raleigh looked around the crowded bar. She could see Max through the crowd holding a beer bottle and looking their way. She moved on to the men standing around the pool table as a tall bald man leaned over and shot at the eight ball. The clatter of voices was just as loud as the metallic guitar solo from the other side, but as she watched them talk and several move around shaking hands, the noise took a back seat as she searched each face. Which ones attended these parties? Who could have seen them Monday?

Was it the bald man with a dragon tattoo on his neck? Maybe the young guy who really needed to find smaller pants because he didn't even look like he had a butt much less one she wanted to see. There was a room full of people that she didn't know, but maybe had known Madison.

There was a group of young guys standing in a group. Each held a beer bottle in his hands with nice pressed collar shirts hanging over baggy jeans. From their smooth faces and intact hair, Raleigh figured they were young. Maybe Madison's age. Were they regular guests?

The freesons traveled up Raleigh's spine. She didn't want to meet every stranger in Barbeaux, and wonder if they'd had the pleasure of Madison's parties.

She most definitely had more modesty than she had thought.

"Earth to Raleigh."

Raleigh looked up at Sheri and Mike who were smiling down at her.

Sheri laughed and popped her gum. "You need another drink."

Raleigh scanned the bar again. Someone here could know where Madison was. How could she find that person among a crowd of over one hundred?

Sheri pushed a shot glass into her hand. "Relax just for one night."

Raleigh stared down at the amber liquid. What the hell? She couldn't find that needle in this crowd even if she were sober. Her prospects might look better if things were a little fuzzy.

Chapter Fifteen

Raleigh shook her head against the clutter and heavy weight crushing down on it. Her body was cradled by the feather mattress, but her head felt as if it rested on the wooden floor.

What had awakened her?

The familiar chords of her cell phone drilled through the heaviness sending waves of discomfort jutting down her body.

Ugh, what time was it?

She reached over to the nightstand and felt around for the smooth plastic of her phone. The chords vibrated through her body again. She really needed to change the ring tone. Had she ever even liked it, or had she figured she'd actually answer it to get rid of the annoyance?

Finally, her hand clasped the phone, and she brought it to her ear. She wasn't quite sure since she couldn't feel it there with the lead in her head.

"Hello."

"Raleigh? Is that you?"

Raleigh groaned, wishing she'd looked at the caller ID before answering, but no, she hadn't even opened her eyes yet. She must really deserve punishment after those drinks last night. "Yes, Mr. Grabert, I'm here."

Mr. Grabert, her boss at the most boring job in the world. At least that's what her consensus had been last week when she'd decided she needed something else. He'd be the only person calling on a Sunday. In Barbeaux people would just show up at the door with no warning for you to at least brush your teeth.

"I'm calling to see if you'll be in tomorrow. Cassie informed me of the funeral on Friday. I was sorry to hear about, umm…was it a cousin?"

"Mr. Grabert, we still haven't found my sister."

He cleared his throat. "I'm sure the police are doing all they can. These things tend to work themselves out."

"Still, I'll be staying here until we find her."

Would she? What if it took years? Raleigh shook her head. That was too deep before she'd had chocolate.

Papers ruffled in the background. He must be keeping his usual Sunday morning hours. Every Sunday from seven until eleven he went in, and though she was off, she could expect at least three calls to tell her what he needed her to do on Monday. "I need you back here, Raleigh. You know I don't know how the police are down there, but I'm sure they are capable of finding her."

She allowed an awkward silence to fall into the phone. She'd known this was going to happen with his stickler for routine, but still it didn't stop a cold nervousness creeping into her stomach. It was difficult to be out of a job again and unsure of when you'd get your next paycheck. "Mr. Grabert, I won't be in for awhile. I understand if you need to replace me."

Another silence came through the phone. Anything out of his routine took time to sink in. She could imagine him staring blankly into space and reality slowly registering on his round face. "I'll expect you at work tomorrow. If you can't make it, I will have to replace you."

"I understand, Mr. Grabert."

Raleigh hung up the phone and flung it toward the end of the bed. Now she had no home or job, and still those cardboard boxes. She may have to literally live in those boxes if things didn't start looking up.

This was going to be a great day.

Raleigh reached up and clutched her head. Twix or Tylenol? Maybe she should do both this morning. It couldn't hurt, right? But that's what she'd said after her second mudslide, too. This sure felt like pain this morning.

Her head pulsated as a banging followed by a rattling of glass came from the front of the house. What were they doing? Couldn't they wait on the construction or whatever it was until later? Much later.

Oh, wait. This was Sunday, and Me'Maw and Paw would be at church in their third row pew.

Raleigh heaved herself up, and her head throbbed as she became vertical. The only person waiting on the other side of the door that would be worth getting up for would be Madison, and then Raleigh would be fussing for a whole list of reasons besides the waking up.

She dragged herself to the front door thinking as she approached to peek down. Okay, she was appropriate. Somehow she'd managed pajamas last night.

Cousin Joey stood on the other side of the door, and a tow truck stuck out against the empty street behind him. Raleigh's eyes strained against the sunlight, sending whole new waves of unpleasantness through her. She was going to get her chocolate from her Twix from now on. Its yummy goodness only came with the thigh side effect.

He nodded at her. "Morning, Raleigh."

"Morning, Joey. Me'Maw and Paw are at church this morning."

He nodded again. "Me'Maw talked to me about your car. I think if I bring it in to the rent-a-car company and talk to them about the car vandalism, maybe we can get you out of paying for it. At least we can try."

Raleigh bit her lip. She knew she hadn't taken the rental insurance. She remembered something about trying to save a little money. Her insurance deductible was pretty high. "You're going to bring it all the way to Baton Rouge?"

Joey smiled. His face wrinkled and his balding head shined in the sunlight. It made her think that he was only four years older than she, but thankfully she'd aged better. He looked so much like the Uncle Jude from her childhood, including the balding. Were they becoming their parents? Definitely too much thinking this morning. "I'm on my way to Baton Rouge anyway. I'll just bring the car at the same time."

Raleigh nodded. "Let me just get the keys."

She stepped back inside the cluttered living room with its side tables, rockers, two sofas, a coffee table, and many knick knack items and grabbed the keys from the side table. She hesitated a moment. The keys were, after all, her way out of Barbeaux. A place she'd sworn at eighteen never to return to.

Where would she go, though? It wasn't like she had a lease to get back to or even a job at this point. Cassie didn't seem to be pinning away waiting for her roommate to return. She shrugged and walked back toward the door. The car wasn't much use with a cracked windshield and a message in permanent marker to announce she was coming. It wasn't as if she were going to this unknown destination with this vehicle. Maybe it would be easier not to have a target for the vandals.

"Raleigh, I hope you don't take this car vandalism as a reason to leave. Me'Maw loves having you here, though she may not have said it yet. I'm sure Uncle Burt and Aunt Beth will come around."

Raleigh frowned. The family must be talking. Did everyone know that her parents thought she shouldn't be here? Her head throbbed again. "Joey, I'm not leaving until we find Madison."

Joey's hands went to his hips, pushing up his light police windbreaker, but his eyes were such a light brown, they looked yellow as they stared at her. "I mean even after. It's nice to be near your family."

Raleigh smiled, leaning against the doorframe. She could remember him playing Superman in the back yard behind Paw's old shed. He had always tried to rescue Claudia, Madison, or sometimes even her from the bad guy. She guessed this is what the superheroes grew up to be. At least he didn't have to wear that red, star printed cape. "I'll think about it."

She watched from the doorway for a moment as he loaded the car onto the tow truck, but the cranking sound reminded her of pulling Madison's car from the Bayou, and the drawn out waiting to see who was inside. She retreated to the stillness of the kitchen for a Twix and Tylenol search.

She was reading through the medication in the medicine cabinet in the kitchen, when her dad came in the back screen door. Raleigh turned as the screen door snapped behind him. His brown hair was combed down this morning, but the dark circles around his eyes were extending into his cheeks, and the whites of his eyes had shoots of red through them. Raleigh would bet that he wasn't sleeping or eating much.

"I saw Joey leaving with your car."

Raleigh nodded and popped open the top on a bottle of aspirin. "He's going to bring it up for me and try to get me out of paying for the damage."

He stood in the doorframe staring at the empty table. Me'Maw's carnations had died, and for the first time Raleigh could remember, she hadn't gone out into the yard and picked more. This just made her sad.

She couldn't help but think that if she could fix things, the sadness would ease. "When you're ready to leave, I'll bring you up."

Raleigh pulled a bottle of water from the fridge door. "I'm not leaving until Madison is found."

A silence followed, and Raleigh did not look at him. She would keep her cool this time. She was an adult, damn it.

"It doesn't have to be now."

Raleigh looked at his grayish tinge face with the coal grey circles under his eyes. He looked like a sapling in the middle of a break in a scattered storm. He had aged ten years in the last few days. Would the years erase when Madison was found or were they to be etched forever in his face?

"She's alive and out there. I just need to find her."

Her father sighed, and his shoulders sagged. "Why must you always try and save the world?"

Raleigh shook her head. It felt as if something had clamped down on her chest. "Not the world. Just Madison, but I guess that's your world."

Raleigh clutched her Twix to her chest and padded down the hallway. She'd kept her cool. She hadn't yelled, but she still didn't feel any better about the exchange.

She was definitely going back to bed. She had a blanket she could hang over the curtain rod to block out the sun. It didn't have to be Sunday morning yet. She didn't have to be jobless and without transportation until later in the day.

She knew sometime had passed as she swayed side to side, the feeling lulling her into a suspended calmness. She felt the water lapping against her, but it was dark, and she couldn't see the water's edge. Raleigh turned to search for the water, and she met a soft, sticky wall.

The feeling of not being able to breath seized her. Panic bounced around her chest, racing her pulse.

Raleigh blinked her eyes, the darkness seeming to stick and blur her vision. She couldn't move, or breathe, or see. What was going on?

A slow realization seeped through her panic. This was a dream. She sat up in bed, greeted by the light pouring in from the thin strip not covered by her makeshift curtain.

Cardboard boxes stared at her again. Geez. Did anything ever change? Could she possibly dream of the mountains or an open grass field and wake up to a room without brown cardboard boxes?

She blew her hair out of her face and rubbed her eyes so she could read the alarm clock on the white side table.

1:00 P.M. She'd slept through lunch. Hell, she'd slept through half the day. Me'Maw must be fretting in the kitchen watching the clock tick away the minutes. She rose and pulled on the clothes Me'Maw had folded and placed on top of the nearest box. She stopped to peek in the mirror and immediately grabbed an elastic to pull her hair back. She'd washed it last night when she'd got in at two o'clock, and it had dried as she slept. Puffy was a nice way to describe it right now.

As she opened the door, voices drifted down the hall. She bit down on her lip and considered going back in to fix herself up a little, but figured it was just Uncle Camille or her parents visiting after church. It would be nice if her mom had come out the house.

As she entered the kitchen six sets of eyes turned to greet her. Me'Maw was the only one who smiled as she came further into the room. It was as if she'd walked into a séance instead of the spirit they'd called. She was conscious of Max staring at her, but even more conscious of what she looked like right now. She immediately regretted not fixing herself up even the slightest.

She looked away from him, and her eyes fell to the table where a black kit rested. Raleigh lingered over the inkpad and the black fingerprints stamped on the white cards spread across the table. A heat rose up her bare neck.

"What's going on here?"

Her father rocked back in his rocking chair. "Detective Max is here to help find Madison."

Raleigh searched Me'Maw's pale face, Paw's grim stare, and Uncle Camille's vacant gaze. It only looked as though he'd brought the plague. "How?"

Paw frowned as he gazed directly into her glare, something Raleigh had noticed the others were avoiding. "There were some fingerprints in the car. The detective here is trying to eliminate the family so he can focus on the others."

Raleigh focused on Max. "And we're not trying to prove it's one of us again?"

Uncle Camille slammed his fist down on the table, and Raleigh jumped. At least she wasn't alone. Everyone except Max jumped, too. "If you'd just tell him what you know, we could solve this. What are you hiding girl?"

"Shut up, Uncle Camille." Raleigh's legs trembled in anger. "If I'd know what happened, I'd have told you already. What do you want to hear? All I know is that Claudia woke up in the car as the water began to come in. She didn't know how she'd gotten there, and all she remembered from before waking up was being angry. She drowned. End of story."

Uncle Camille glared at her. "Some talent."

Raleigh glared back. "And how exactly have you used yours?"

"Raleigh, that's enough." Her father stood up. "This is why I wanted you to go home. This is only making things worse."

"Are you going to send Madison away after we find her?" Raleigh's face flushed in that not so good, black out from overheating kind of way. "Should I expect a roommate in the nonexistent home you want to send me to?"

Paw's voice boomed through the breathless room. "Raleigh Lynn."

Raleigh studied Paw's tightened jaw and knew she would not win this argument. "Excuse me, I need some fresh air." She turned away from Paw and glared at Max. "I don't think you need my fingerprints, Detective Pyles. After all, they're on file."

She allowed the screen door to snap behind her with all of its momentum, causing her heart to thump harder.

Today had to be the worst day of her life. Of course, as soon as she'd thought it, all the other days she'd thought were the worst came back to her. Didn't that just make today all better. Yeah, right.

"I'm sorry about that, Detective. Our family is dealing the best we can right now."

Raleigh flinched as her father's voice drifted through the screen door.

Max's voice was smooth like liquid. "It's understandable, but Raleigh has been nothing but a help to me. She's definitely not making my job difficult."

A chair scraped against the linoleum, and Uncle Camille's hoarse voice leaked through the screen door. "She's a troublemaker, and she's killed someone before. I say this is retribution for what she did."

Raleigh heard Me'Maw's slippers drag on the floor. "Ya'll never gave her a chance. Ya'll speak as if it would've been better if it was the other way around, and she'd be dead. Shame on ya'll."

Tears dripped down her cheeks. So much for being tough. She couldn't even turn and say, yeah, Me'Maw, you tell them. They'd rather it was her dead. No, she stood eavesdropping, crying. So not being the tough one. Raleigh jumped off the back porch unable to listen any longer. She could at least do that much. She wasn't a complete moron.

She felt drawn to the old shed she'd spent so much time playing in as a kid. With her first step into the darkness, she shuddered. The coolness prickled her flesh, causing it to rise. Upon the second step, she choked on the stench of rotting animal as the mud whirled around her feet. An image of worms and bugs flashed through her consciousness, and Raleigh stepped back, the heat of the outside warming her neck again, easing some of the discomfort. Raleigh's feet trembled, and she couldn't bring herself to step back inside though she kept telling herself to try again.

Strange. The shed had been her favorite place as a child. Raleigh peered into the dark. What was there? Had she gone mad? An idea slowly twisted itself through her conscious and wrapped itself around the crevices of her mind.

Raleigh took big steps back, her chest burning under her shallow breath. Someone was buried in mud. Was it Katherine? Was it Madison? Did she really want to know?

Raleigh leaned against the weathered wood of the shed's boards. It was rough against her skin, and its harshness brought back feeling to her limbs. She blinked against the sunlight beating down on her, and didn't notice Paw until he was standing in front of her, squinting down on her.

"Girl, you ahright?"

Raleigh looked up and squinted at him. "Yes," She inhaled deeply. Her body feeling lighter with the fresh air. "Yes, It was just...nothing. I'm alright."

Paw stared at her a moment, and then continued walking toward his garden. "Well then, come for a walk."

Raleigh hesitated, knowing that it meant he had something to say that he didn't want to. The garden is where he did his thinking, what he called tinkering, and if someone wanted to tell him something, they did it there. It was his territory. She'd be at the disadvantage, but she followed him anyway. He was her Paw.

She chose the row next to his, watching her footing between his neat rows. She'd chosen a neat hill of bare dirt. She wondered if something was planted below, or if he was waiting for a new season. She didn't want to ask him since she was mentally stiffening herself against whatever he might say, but as a girl she would have never not asked.

Finally, when they'd walked about seventy feet in, he stopped and looked around. "Girl, do you plan on staying here?"

"I'm not sure yet." She met his gaze. "I really don't have anywhere else to go right now."

Paw began walking back to the front, and she hastened to keep up. "Then you may want to start smoothing things out. Ruffling everyone's feathers isn't going to make you any more welcome."

Raleigh stopped. "Do you think it's my fault then?"

Paw stopped and stared at her. "What I think is that you put yourself in business you had no business being."

Raleigh frowned. "So you think it's my fault."

Paw shook his head. "It doesn't matter whose fault it is. It happened, and if it was him or you, I'm glad you're still here, but when we put ourselves in other people's business, it shouldn't be because we're trying to stir up trouble. When you stir in a pot of live crabs, they're going to bite you."

Raleigh bit down on her lip. "But, isn't that what we do? Stick ourselves in other people's lives."

Paw began walking again. "Raleigh Lynn, I know you have the answer to that."

Raleigh watched him walk to the front a ways, and then she kicked at his perfectly formed hill. Dirt sprayed everywhere. Of course, then the indention looked out of place with his neatly molded rows. The bright side was that this day could only go up from here. She stooped down and dug her fingers in the smooth, crumbling dirt, and then patted it back into place.

It didn't look as perfect when she'd finished, but it was fixed.

Now if her life would only be that simple. Maybe Paw had the right idea with gardening; its problems had solutions.

Chapter Sixteen

The phone slipped from Raleigh's shoulder and ear grip once again. She grabbed it with one hand and held her place in the file cabinet with the other.

"Yes, I'm sorry. I need to confirm the menu for the Christen Scott boat christening Wednesday."

"It's through Creative Celebrations, right?"

Raleigh flipped through the files. Blanchard wedding, Cantrell family reunion, Dantin Wedding, and Christie bridal shower. Where was the damn folder? "Yes, Ma'am."

"I'll fax it over again, and you can call back if there are any changes."

"Thank you very much."

Raleigh put the phone back down in its cradle and groaned in frustration. Why couldn't her sister file things in a logical order? C for Christen Scott or C for christening would be easy. Too easy for Madison, she supposed. She had to have her own system. A system Raleigh couldn't decipher though she'd been trying for a few hours.

The phone rang again. Raleigh gave up on the file cabinet. It was as useless as firewood.

"Creative Celebrations. How may I help you creatively celebrate today?"

Raleigh rolled her eyes at the corny greeting. She'd fought a laugh when Denise had told her it this morning, but after fifteen times in the last hour it was no longer funny. It was topping her top ten list of most annoying expressions.

"I wanted to change my 2:00 P.M. meeting this afternoon to later in the afternoon."

Raleigh grabbed the calendar and scrolled down the list. Was it only 12:30? My how time stalled when you wished for warp speed. A Ms. Marsha Crosby was penciled in for a two o'clock planning. She wondered if she was related to the Crosby boat company. She'd bet yes, since everyone here seemed to be related to everyone else.

"Denise has a 3:30 opening and a 4:15. Which would you prefer?"

She was quiet on the other end, but Raleigh could hear papers shuffling. "I can do the 3:30. It will give me just enough time."

Raleigh erased and wrote her in at the later time. "We'll see you then."

Raleigh replaced the phone and again searched her sister's work area. She'd already turned the picture of Madison and Mason face down on the desk. After an hour of looking at their candid smiles, it felt as if Madison was accusing her of not looking hard enough for her. She didn't need any more family members looking to her to fix this. There were more than enough of them. Manila folders were sprawled across the top and stacked in a haphazard fashion in some areas. Some were labeled, some weren't. Price sheets stuck out of several folders, and some price sheets were thumb tacked on a board on the wall to her left. If Madison had any kind of organizational system, it was lost on Raleigh.

What was missing from the chaos was anything of a personal nature. There was that picture, of course, a small air fern in the corner, and a candy dish filled with peppermints teetering dangerously on a stack of wobbly folders. It had been a disappointment to find nothing here, but she supposed it wasn't realistic to believe that she'd open a drawer and there would be a note saying, "I'm here, come and get me".

The front door jangled as it swung open. Raleigh looked up from the desk to watch stripper girl stroll in the door with a short, pleated black skirt and a burgundy blazer. Her hair was slicked back into a bun, and her make-up was minimal enough to pass as normal. Raleigh could imagine what kind of party she'd be throwing. Did Denise even go there? She didn't seem the type.

Raleigh noticed Jenny's confident stroll stiffen as her eyes locked onto hers.

Denise emerged from the back room just as Jenny's lips parted soundlessly.

"Can I help you?"

Jenny redirected herself toward Denise, but her gaze lingered a moment longer. "I'm here to inquire about the job opening."

"I don't have any openings right now." Denise leaned against a white faux column she'd pulled from storage this morning. "You can leave your name and number though. We do need workers for events now and then."

Jenny frowned. "I was told you needed a secretary."

Denise shook her head. "I have a full-time secretary, and I'm not replacing her right now."

Jenny drew up her shoulders. "I was promised first shot at the job. She doesn't even live here."

At this, Jenny thrust her arm in Raleigh's direction. Raleigh straightened up in the chair. How had she become a target so quickly?

Denise's forehead crinkled to those three straight lines. Raleigh had noticed it often in the last few hours, especially when it came to the business side and not her creative side. "My secretary will be returning, hopefully really soon. Raleigh is only a temporary fill in. I'm sorry someone led you to believe there was a job available."

"Oh, whatever! I should've known this would be a lie, too. She's lied about everything else."

With that Jenny turned on the heel of her black pumps and stormed out the door. Raleigh watched her slide into her sporty car and speed off, tires squealing.

Denise looked to her, and Raleigh shrugged. "Isn't she a strange one?"

Denise picked up her stack of messages from the in box. "I don't understand why she thought I'd give her the job. I have someone nearly everyday ask me about a job."

"And I'm sure most of their resumes don't read stripper."

Denise looked up from the stack, frowning. "Do you think Madison told her I'd give her the job?"

Raleigh considered it. Jenny had said she was promised. Had it been Madison who made the promise? Then, why would she give up a job she loved? "Even if she had, Madison didn't quit. She's coming back."

Denise turned to go back into her office, but stopped. "I don't know. A few weeks ago, Madison came into work crying. She said everything was so messed up right now she just wanted to get away. Do you think that's what she's doing?"

Raleigh shook her head. "She would never leave Mason."

Denise smiled. "I just wish she'd be back."

Raleigh looked at the desk again that was covered in folders. Could she come back to help her decipher her system, or at least communicate where she could find this week's event folder? Of course, Madison not communicating with her was a good thing, Raleigh reassured herself. It meant that she wasn't dead or dying. She tried to push down that nagging voice reminding her she could just be blocking her out, but the nagging was chewing around the edges of her concentration.

The day dragged, and dragged, with the most interesting part being the very entertaining Ms. Marsha Crosby. She flipped her long blonde hair no less than fifteen times, and laughed a forced, high-pitched fake laugh no less than ten. By the end of the thirty minute meeting, Raleigh was cringing at each nasally pronounced word.

Finally, four thirty ticked by, and it was time to go home. Raleigh allowed the door to click behind her, and then yanked twice on the handle to make sure it was locked. Denise had left after the Crosby meeting to check on the location for Wednesday's party. It made Raleigh nervous locking up on her first day. It also made her question Denise's judgment.

As she turned toward Paw's truck, she was startled by Max leaning against the driver side door. His hands were stuffed into his jeans' pockets, and his green polo shirt was draped over the front of his tailored jeans in a relaxed way. The overall effect was not the uptight detective look, until she reached his green eyes. Though they weren't boring through her at the moment, they hinted at an inquisitiveness that always burned below the surface.

Raleigh approached, his gaze never wavered and his chiseled jaw and angular face did not flinch. She studied his face for a sign of his reason for being here.

He kicked at the gravel. "I thought maybe we could talk."

Raleigh stopped four feet from him. He was standing between her and the truck door. He didn't seem to be taking any chances that she would refuse. "Every time you talk, I get angry."

His pupils contracted and his lips stiffened. She squirmed under his scrutiny, though she held herself stiff against any physical reaction. "I admit I was a little freaked out the other day by your display. Joey had explained it all, but it was difficult for me to understand that it was even really possible. I'm truly sorry for my reaction."

Raleigh frowned. Apparently, she needed to be more convincing. "What do you want to talk about?"

Max looked around at the parking area. People were leaving the dentist office next door. A freckle face, red-haired boy balanced himself on the concrete divider ledge between the two buildings, as his mother called to him over and over again to get into the car. "Not here. I was hoping you'd follow me."

Raleigh shook her head. "I don't know you well enough."

"You can trust me." Max straightened up. "My son will be there, you'll have your own truck, and a meal is involved. Just give me a try."

She couldn't figure him out, and now throw a son into the formula. What was his story, and why did she keep trying to figure him out? Maybe she needed to start asking him personal questions. "I'll give you twenty minutes, but I'm warning you, it better be twenty minutes of importance."

He opened the truck door and Raleigh climbed inside. Who did that anymore? Chivalry was supposed to be dead. He jumped into his car, and she followed him onto the highway toward the outskirts of Barbeaux. They passed run down shacks to their right, and trawl boats were docked along the bayou to their left. Several boat sheds rose upward, blocking the view momentarily of the water. This was the in between part of Barbeaux and Bois, not that either town was much different than the other. A stranger wouldn't know the difference.

After ten minutes or so, he pulled off the road near the bayou. Three boats were docked in a line along a rotting cypress wharf, and Max pulled off the highway into a parking slot for the boat on the left. She pulled in and shut the engine, but she remained plastered to the vinyl seat. Her heartbeat increased, and her breathing became shallow. He had to be kidding, right?

He approached the truck, and Raleigh swung open the door. She hated for him to see the fear. It was enough that her hands shook and her insides trembled.

"Is this where you live?"

Max looked off toward the boat. "Yes, I inherited the boat from my dad and had to call it home after the divorce. Temporary, of course. Mark is at the neighbor's boat playing one of those video games, but you'll be able to meet him."

He had stepped in the direction of the boat, but Raleigh stood rooted to her spot. "I'm not going on that boat."

Max stopped mid-stride. "I told you, you can trust me. I'll get Mark now if you'd like."

Raleigh shook her head and swallowed against the dryness in her throat. "That's not why, though that's a good reason, too." Why hadn't she thought of that first? Why had she just disagreed with him? "I don't do boats or the bayou. Remember that pesky little phobia."

He studied her, and though her face burned in embarrassment, she didn't flinch. She wished she hadn't come. Why hadn't she suggested a neutral location like Me'Maw's house? But how was she supposed to know he lived on a boat? Even on the bayou, not many people did that.

"Stay right here. I'll be right back."

Raleigh followed his long stride as he jogged toward his boat. He boarded in one clean leap, and she leaned against the truck to wait. The stillness seeped in through her boots. The leaves of the willows, river birches, and the one oak rustled in the breeze, and several leaves tumbled toward her feet. A swaying motion eased her body, rocking her into calmness. She sank into the feeling of a boat rocking her. A car whistled as it sped past on the highway.

Raleigh stiffened and danced around her spot, trying to clear her body of the feeling. Boats and bayous. Nope, no good memories there. How had it crept in so easily?

While she was moving around, probably looking like an idiot, a young boy jumped off the middle boat and skipped in her direction. His face and hair were definitely his father's, but the freckles must have been his mother's contribution. She guessed he was nine? Ten? She wasn't good with children, as she'd told herself on more than one occasion. At some point in her life, she might have to reexamine that and just admit that they terrified her.

He approached with a smile that was missing a tooth. "Are you my dad's date?"

Raleigh laughed. Funny, kid. "Your dad's working on my sister's case, and I'm helping out."

"Oh," he licked his lips as he fidgeted in place. "Sorry 'bout your sister."

Raleigh smiled, wondering what Max told him about his job. She'd imagine most of the details were left out. "Do you live with your dad?"

"I wish." He shook his head. "Mom's on vacation with my step dad, again."

Raleigh noticed the side of his lips twitch down, and his eyes shift away from her. She didn't need to know anything about children to understand that he was feeling some serious sadness about his situation.

Just then Max emerged from the boat's cabin loaded down with an armful of items. Mark saw his father and took off running in his direction. Raleigh couldn't hear their conversation, but she smiled as Mark ran circles around Max, and Max's deep laugh echoed in the quietness. It was the first real laugh she'd heard from him. It was full and hearty, and just enough to make you want to join in. She found it sexy.

Raleigh stilled her pulse. It was better she didn't go there, at least not until she knew what he wanted.

Max reached a nearby tree and set his load down. Mark pulled a blue blanket from the heap and began unfolding it on the ground.

Raleigh looked at the bayou and then skirted toward them, arching away from the water. She could still feel the swaying as if in a drunkenness. She just pushed it further down, her stomach churning under its weight.

Mark was like a squirrel, darting here and there. Max spread out cups and plates on the uneven blanket. The leaves of the nearby cypress and pine trees were flirting dangerously close to the blanket's edge. Though the highway was right there, this section of the bayou side was crowded with trees and grassy plants that muffled some of the car noises. To her right in the parking area only one other pickup truck was parked, and the trawling boats offered only a white wall against the view of the complete bayou.

Max gestured toward his spread. "I'm hoping if I bring my famous culinary expertise to you, you'll agree to enlighten me."

She stopped at the blanket's edge. Noticing that he was watching Mark instead of her, which was strange for him. Usually she felt as though she was naked and under scrutiny from his gaze. "What do I need to enlighten you about?"

"I want to know what happened eleven years ago."

Raleigh stepped back, feeling as though he'd slashed at her. "Why would you need to know that?"

Max stood up. He was close enough that she noticed she had to look up at him, and oh, how he smelled delicious. Why was she thinking of this right now? Her anger was dissipating. She needed to hang onto that anger right now.

"I think there's a connection."

A roaring filled her ears like the sound of a boat engine revving. Dizziness washed over her and then it was gone. He was saying it was her fault. That nagging voice in her mind interjected that he wasn't saying it, just implying it.

He held up his hand. "I don't blame you. I just think it's someone who was involved then. After yesterday, I just have this crazy hunch that some of the missing pieces may lie in the past."

She just stared at him, conscious that Mark was running around the trees in the background and the bayou lay to her left, stagnant and waiting. "I thought you read the report?"

Max sat back down, motioning for her to sit. "It was seriously incomplete."

Raleigh hesitated a moment more, and then sat down on the corner of the blanket. She needed to find her sister. She'd told herself at any cost. Would she go no further than the gossip? She'd already delved into her sister's life, but what if it was her past that had led them here? Could her head literally burst from stress? "It was along time ago…"

"Just tell me who and what you remember."

Raleigh frowned. Could she do this with him? She wondered if one of those containers contained a Twix. Her luck wasn't running in that direction these days. "It was a long time ago, but I can still remember the smells. You know it's what I remember most after each time. I'm sure you know what death smells like with your job."

Max nodded, his eyes scrutinizing her. She tried not to see him. He wasn't exactly the type to go unnoticed though.

"I knew what death smelled like. It's usually the first sense they reach me with, but that day I realized that I'd only really had that weak memory of death."

Max's expression was unchanging, but she drew herself inward and forced herself to go back to that day.

"Mike and I had covered a story a few weeks before and had been threatened with suspension. A football coach had been having sex with a student in his classroom after school. Let's just say the principal was furious when we slipped the article into the paper as a last minute substitution. So, we decided to do a story for the Barbeaux Gazette. We wanted something that would get us onto the college paper as freshmen. Rumor had spread through the senior class that someone on the football team was the one to go to for drugs."

"We tried for weeks to get a lead, but it was no good. Neither one of us were in with that crowd. Katherine, however, was dating Ross Blanch. She agreed to snoop around for us."

"Katherine English? The girl who went missing?"

Raleigh cringed, but nodded as she gulped against the pain in her throat. "She was able to get us some names of football players using the drugs, but not the name of the one supplying them. At the homecoming bonfire, Mike and I noticed three players in lettermen jackets leaving together. We couldn't ID them, but we decided to take a chance and follow them."

Raleigh took a deep breath and stretched out her legs. Max was still concentrating that intense gaze on her. She did her best not to look his way.

"We followed them to the old Boudreaux dock yard, now the Zedeaux dock yard. Mike parked down the road and we crossed through the trees to where we could get a good look at the boat. We figured if we could get the name, we could research the owner and possibly find the source."

"And ya'll were in high school?"

Raleigh frowned. "I know it sounds crazy, but Mike and I were really ambitious. We'd been working at the Barbeaux Gazette to lay out the high school paper, and after hearing them talk about their stories, we just wanted to do what they did. Anyway, we watched a group of men talking on the back deck of the boat. Unfortunately, we weren't close enough to see who or hear what they were saying. We'd decided to leave and go back the next day in the daylight to check it out. Mike had already turned around and was walking back when the men on the back deck turned and looked straight at us. I froze, and when I finally turned to run away, an arm came around my neck and something crashed down onto my head. I was out."

"How many men were on the boat deck?"

Raleigh checked that Mark was still running around the trees. He was now bent over a clump of grass studying something not visible from her position. "Three guys were on the boat deck, but there had to be two more. Mike saw one come at him, and he thinks one went around him. When I awoke later, I was duck taped to the generator in the engine room. It was dark, and I couldn't see anything at first, but eventually my eyes adjusted to the light from the crack in the door. I realized Mike was lying at my feet with his arms tied behind his back. He was bleeding from a large scrape on his forehead, and I kept calling to him, but I couldn't get him to wake up."

Raleigh choked up and looked away. She'd remembered the paralyzing fear that he was dead, and how the blood smell had mixed with the diesel to fill her body. She hadn't wanted to feel if he was dead, and she'd prayed and forced the thoughts away. It was the first of many blocks she'd put up to her talent.

"It was a long time before Mike gained consciousness, and a good deal more time before someone came down the ladder to see us. He wore an orange ski mask, and he forced himself on me, threatening what he could do to me before he killed us. Mike lunged at him, and he broke a beer bottle over Mike's back. He climbed back up cursing. Mike took a large piece of the beer bottle and cut through his duck tape. He was halfway through cutting mine when we heard the footsteps above. Mike stood to the side of the ladder, while I continued to cut through the tape."

Raleigh traced the soft indention in her wrist where the glass had sliced through her thin skin. The movies made it look so much cleaner than it actually was.

"He came down pointing a pistol at me. I screamed, and Mike lunged at him. The gun flew toward me. The guy was twice the size of Mike, and he smashed Mike into the wall. I could hear his head echo against the hull. I finished cutting the tape, and I picked up the gun... I yelled at him to stop, to let us go. He lunged toward me, and... and I pulled the trigger. He was only two feet away."

The echo inside the small, enclosed area had shattered her eardrums, and the ringing had stayed with her for hours after.

His eyes had widened in surprise, and then had glazed over as he crumpled to the floor at her feet. Raleigh had had to push her ability so far from her she thought she would collapse on top of him.

"Mike grabbed me and we climbed the four steps to the top and saw two men running in our direction. Mike yanked me over the side of the boat."

Max was still gazing at her in that way that made her feel as if he could see her thoughts, as if he saw things that she didn't yet know about herself. "The report said you nearly drowned."

Raleigh stared into the sun. Seeing the white spots that blurred her vision wiped out the image that had just risen of what had lain beneath the water. "Under the water, I lost Mike. It was so dark I couldn't tell which way to go, and then I saw her in the net. I released my breath and swallowed the water. Mike said he pulled me out and swam across the bayou. I don't remember any of that."

Max nodded. "By her, do you mean Katherine?"

"Yes." Raleigh sighed. "I know everyone thought I was seeing things because I had drowned, but I know she was there."

Max leaned back against the tree. "The report pretty much picks up when the two of you went into the station, and Officer Jean and a few others went out to the boat to check your story out."

Raleigh frowned. "Yes, when they discovered it was Ross Blanch on the boat, everything changed. His father was a district attorney and his uncle was a lawyer, not to mention his mother was the daughter of the richest man here. That was the worst night of my life times two."

Max nodded. "Officer Nick Shane filled me in on that part. Jude Blanch was furious when there wasn't evidence to charge the two of you. The scene had been tampered with."

Raleigh opened the bowl nearest her to find grapes. She was suddenly ravenous. "Yes, and they had already sent us for emergency care before they hauled us back in, which meant we had evidence to support our story. It didn't stop them from trying to spin it in their direction though."

Max leaned forward and opened a container of chicken salad sandwiches, grabbed one, and bit heartedly into it. "I wish we had an ID on those guys at the boat. Let's say one of them wanted revenge or one of them is working for the family, we'd have motive. I have to be honest with you, I don't have a likely suspect or motive in Claudia's death or Madison's disappearance. I've talked to a couple of creeps, but no one seems to be able to tell me about the several hours leading up to their disappearance."

Raleigh frowned, popping another grape into her mouth. "There's a stripper down at the club that may know a thing or two she isn't sharing. Maybe she knows something about what they were doing."

"Who is she?"

Raleigh rolled her eyes. "Jenny something or other. I'll see if I can get more tomorrow. Then you can have a shot at her."

Max leaned forward. Raleigh couldn't breathe in his nearness. "I'm sorry you had to go through all that, and then have the police put you through even more."

Raleigh couldn't speak. He smelled so damn good, and his nearness was enchanting. She loved the way his eyes crinkled when he smiled, and how right now his gaze was unflinching. There was a throbbing from behind her head trying to send off white flags, but it wasn't making it through the fog.

Just then Mark dove onto the blanket. "I'm hungry!"

They laughed and Raleigh was able to breathe again. The white flags sprang up again. She needed him to find her sister, not resuscitate her nonexistent love life. She certainly wondered what was beneath all the intensity. He'd managed to learn even more about her, and again she'd learned only the smallest bit of information about him. Perhaps it would be fair to ask for an exchange next time.

Chapter Seventeen

Raleigh maneuvered Paw's truck between a blue late model Cadillac and a smooth, black Tahoe. Sheri must be busy this morning. Raleigh chewed on her lip, considering if she really needed to stop now. She had boxes of party supplies in the back of the truck, and she was supposed to be bringing back lunch.

She wondered if Sheri had learned anything else useful though. Raleigh couldn't help but feel that she just needed to be pointed in the right direction, and with the gossip that passed through that glass door she might find that direction. She also felt obligated after yesterday's conversation with Max to ask what part Jenny played in Madison and Claudia's party circuit. Not to mention where to find her that she wouldn't disappear or storm out.

Raleigh jumped down from the truck, knowing full well she was not leaving without checking. Besides, she needed help with her hair again. She'd decided this morning that one of her many skills was not in the hair department. The excuse only released some of the guilt bugging her. She didn't like the idea of only coming to Sheri for information, especially since they weren't the closest of friends anymore.

The bell jangled from above, but Raleigh barely registered it as she swept the room for anyone familiar. She'd prefer no one else from her past with a grudge surprising her.

An older lady sat flipping through a magazine with the dryer covering her head. Her starched white capri pants revealed spider veins all the way to her bare ankle, and Raleigh looked away making a mental note to never wear anything but pants when she was older. Sheri was at the back rinsing the hair of another lady showing off her legs in tulip pink Capri pants. Sheri glanced up as Raleigh walked in.

A smile spread across Sheri's face as she popped her gum. "Business or social?"

The woman sat up, her hair wrapped in a towel and walked to the salon chair. The woman's heavy make-up was smearing at the edges where it was damp from the wash. Sheri spun her around as she towel dried her hair.

Raleigh sat down in the next chair. "A little of both."

Sheri scanned Raleigh's hair. Raleigh stiffened under the scrutiny. "You need something for defrizzing. I have something you can try."

Raleigh laughed, but she patted down her frizzed hair. "I've also come to ask about this girl Jenny that reportedly hung around Madison and Claudia."

"There were a couple of girls." Sheri's forehead wrinkled as she combed the woman's dark brown hair out. "I think you're talking about the one that works at Danny's Po-boys for the lunch shift."

"Was she part of their party or a guest at the parties?"

"Let's just say she was just as much the life of the party as Winter and Summer."

Raleigh shuddered. That was one of those bits of information she could live without even if it was important. Being visual wasn't always a joy. "Any new bit of information for me?"

Sheri looked back at the woman under the dryer who was still flipping though her magazine. Raleigh had to strain to hear Sheri. "Rumor is that Jeffery Zedeaux is asking around about Madison."

Raleigh could feel her heart slow and pound against her eardrum. "Jeffery Zedeaux? Are you sure?"

Sheri increased the speed of the hair dryer. "Raleigh, Madison was involved with Jeffery in high school."

Raleigh jumped as though the chair had shocked her. "You're kidding? Why didn't anyone mention this?"

Sheri shook her head, and Raleigh glanced toward the woman in the chair who was no longer studying her magazine. "No one was supposed to know."

The bell jangled above the door again, and Raleigh watched as Bethany English came through.

She looked as though the door was too heavy for her thin frame to push open. Black circles outlined her sunken dull gray eyes, and her skin looked brittle. She looked worse today than a few days ago.

She stared at Raleigh, her eyes unfocused. Raleigh watched as gradually before her eyes, her presence registered with Ms. English.

"Hello, Raleigh. You're still in town?"

Raleigh nodded, attempting a weak smile. She shivered as if someone had poured water on her when she'd come in from the cold. "I'm staying for awhile, at least until we find Madison."

Ms. English frowned, her eyes losing focus again. "Didn't stay until she found my Katherine."

She snapped back into focus, and her lips trembled.

Raleigh wanted so much to ask Sheri about this relationship with Jeffery, but she couldn't stay here. Ms. English was falling apart, and Raleigh had a painful suspicion that it was her being here that was causing it.

Six pairs of eyes were glued to them. Raleigh reached out and squeezed Ms. Bethany's arm. She could wrap her fingers around the wrist. "We're going to find both of them."

Raleigh pulled away as she backed away toward the door. "Sheri, I'll talk to you soon."

When she reached the truck, she finally inhaled the sweet, dusty air. She trembled all over and had to pull on the truck handle three times before it released its latch.

What had possessed her to tell Ms. English she'd find Katherine? The only true connections she'd been able to make with the dead were through her dreams. Everything else had been sporadic. What was wrong with her? She wasn't even sure if her sister was alive or dead and that was recent. Katherine had been dead for eleven years.

Raleigh shook herself. She was supposed to be working, running party errands. She still needed to go to Dot's screen printing and pick up the tee shirts.

But they had to eat, right? And what was better than a Danny's roast beef?

Of course if Jeffery Zedeaux was involved, she'd never find out anything. Jeffery Zedeaux's family was the closest Barbeaux had to the mob. The family had their hands in everything, even though to a stranger's eyes they appeared to be successful businessmen running a boat business. Jeffery was also only two years older than she was, and in high school she'd turned him down when he'd asked her for a date. He hated her, and Raleigh couldn't deny the feeling wasn't mutual.

Raleigh signaled and turned onto the back road. Within five minutes, Danny's came into view. It was an old, white crumbling diner with a shell parking area larger than the restaurant. Danny's Po-boys was painted in large faded blue paint across the top. A stranger would think it to be a rundown dive, but it was the best fattening food in Barbeaux.

Raleigh pulled into the parking area filled with about ten vehicles. She'd eaten here on Friday nights when she was younger with Me'Maw, Paw, and her family. Danny's wife had played cards with Me'Maw every Thursdays. Raleigh wondered if they still played cards. Most of the old women had played at that time, and Raleigh could remember those parties being loud with French flying around the room. Of course, she'd only picked up the bad words back then.

Inside, Raleigh scanned the noisy restaurant. About twenty-five tables were placed in neat rows with red and white checkered table coverings. The walls on the inside were simple wood planks stained a warm, honey color. There was a curly haired brunette placing drinks on a table in the corner, and a young teenage girl taking an order at a table in the middle. Raleigh continued scanning, and finally Jenny, blonde hair pulled tightly in a bun, emerged from the kitchen carrying a tray of food.

Raleigh placed her order to go at the counter with Danny's wife, whose name she couldn't remember, while watching Jenny serve and then make her way around the tables. When Jenny was filling up the plastic cups with a pitcher of dark liquid at a young couple's table, she glanced in Raleigh's direction and the pitcher tipped dangerously in her grip. The gregarious hairy gentleman didn't look as though he'd appreciate the cool dip.

Raleigh waited, watching her nervously laugh and bring the pitcher back to the drink machines. She fiddled with a few ketchup bottles and folded a few napkins, before she looked back to check if Raleigh was still there.

Raleigh moved to the edge of the counter where Jenny was forced to pass to retrieve her next order from the kitchen.

Jenny frowned and then crossed to her. "Why are you here?"

Raleigh noticed her eyes twitch, and she fidgeted from one foot to the other. "When did you see my sister last?"

"Sunday evening." Jenny looked down at her white canvas shoes. "I went to pick up my money from Claudia, and she was there."

"Where is there?"

"The old house. Madison's house or whoever's house."

Raleigh noticed her eyes shift away from direct contact. "What were they doing? Did they tell you what their plans were that day?"

Jenny shrugged. "They were adding up the money and paying everyone as far as I know. They were working Sunday night, so they usually slept during the day."

"Who else would have gone to the house?"

Jenny's cheeks reddened, and her forehead crinkled. "I wasn't involved in the business. They didn't tell me anything about it."

Raleigh had assumed she was embarrassed, but her words were spit out with an angry force. Raleigh needed to try a different direction. She'd prefer opening her head up and taking a peek without the attitude.

"Why did Madison promise you her job?"

Jenny frowned, averting her eyes again. "She planned to leave town, move. She said she'd put in a good word for me, help me out. She knew I wanted to get out of this diner."

Raleigh frowned. Move? Since when? How come no one else had mentioned it? "Where did she say she was going?"

Jenny shrugged. "It's not like we were close or anything. She just owed me."

How honest was Jenny? Raleigh didn't know her very well to tell. But if eye contact was any sign, Jenny wouldn't be passing any lie detector tests.

"How come no one else knew she planned to move?"

"I don't know. I guess I was just there." Jenny huffed, and her white canvas shoe began to tap on the floor. "I need to get back to my tables. Just... just leave me alone."

Jenny stalked off, and someone set a white bag down on the counter by her. Raleigh turned around and picked up their lunch. She thought she was acting like a teenager lately. It must be going around.

How could she corroborate Jenny's story? What if Madison had moved and not told anyone? It even sounded ridiculous to her own ears.

Madison moving wouldn't cause Claudia to die. Nor explain why Mason was still here because Madison would never leave Mason. At least she now had a clearer timeline of their weekend, but still that left Monday unaccounted for. What had they done on Monday that no one had seen them? On the bayou, there was always someone who knew what you were doing. Sometimes before you knew it.

Raleigh shuddered. She couldn't imagine explaining pleasure parties to Me'Maw or her parents. She would definitely need something else, preferably something more G rated. She'd probably pass out having to say the word sex to Me'Maw, not to mention explaining what else could go on at a pleasure party.

Raleigh pushed open the door and nearly swung it into Kyle Allemande. He frowned, his whole face pushing downward in the motion, and he skirted away. Raleigh watched as he crossed the diner, and Jenny met him between two empty tables and began whispering to his bent over head.

Was that a pleasure party connection or something else? Raleigh didn't like all these questions with no answers. The two of them were definitely looking guilty of something these days though.

Chapter Eighteen

The screen door snapped behind her, and she crossed Me'Maw's kitchen to the drawer where she'd stuffed several Twix bars. She scavenged in the drawer and emerged with a bar. She'd been trying to lay off the chocolate since Me'Maw's food was an indulgence in itself, but her head twanged in that familiar way of having too many thoughts jogging through it. Exhaustion seeped through her. On top of errands, Denise had her jumping around as if the president was coming to this party. But maybe he was, since Raleigh hadn't been able to find a guest list in Madison's mess.

She bit into the Twix and sparks shot through her. It never failed.

Voices drifted in through the living room. Raleigh moved to the doorway, and saw Me'Maw bent over a familiar older woman. Me'Maw's hands rested on the woman's folded hands, and Me'Maw's brow furrowed in concentration.

Raleigh crept into the room, studying them. Since she was a girl, Me'Maw's healing had fascinated her. She recalled the heat that emanated and grew from Me'Maw's hands as she delved deeper into her mumbled prayers of faith. As a young girl, she'd waited for fireworks to explode or music to pulse from those hands. Of course, it wasn't like that, but she'd had an imagination back then. Now she knew that it was all hidden; something to be felt and believed in, but not seen.

Me'Maw asked a blessing and made the sign of the cross at the blue and white Mary statue on a shelf on the wall. She then sagged back into the orange cushions of her rocker. The healing had tired her out.

"Liz that arthritis is fighting us. I think we should start a novena."

Ah, Liz Duet. She lived on the next street, and when Raleigh had been around ten years ago, she'd consulted Me'Maw every week for one aliment or another. She had added several more wrinkles, and her skin held a grayish tinge, not to mention the gray hairs streaking through the black.

Liz rubbed the knuckles of her thick hands. "We're all getting old these days. Why Raleigh used to fit by your knee."

Me'Maw and Liz both looked up at her. "Are you saying I'm old, Ms. Liz?"

Liz chuckled deep from her hearty chest. "Shoo, I wish I was as old as you."

Me'Maw leaned her head against the back of her rocker, her eyelids drooping. "Raleigh, catch Ms. Liz a jar of my cream. I knew you were coming so I made a special batch."

Raleigh walked back towards the kitchen and noticed the canning jar near the edge of the yellow laminate countertop. Me'Maw's secret recipes were always poured into the canning jars that she also used to can peppers, pickles, and tomatoes. Old traditions passed to Me'Maw from her father and labeled in Me'Maw's shaky scribble.

She handed the jar to Ms. Liz's wrinkled hand.

Ms. Liz snuggled the jar to her bosom. "When are you going to teach Raleigh, Me'Maw?"

Me'Maw busied her hands with a quilt square and dropped her eyes away from them. This was going to be awkward. "I've trained Camille. It's to him to train the next one."

Raleigh smiled at Ms. Liz, reassuring her she hadn't misspoken, but they both knew she had. It was just a sore subject.

"Well, thank you Me'Maw. I'll be getting back to the grandkids. Sue Ann is only good with them for short bouts of time."

Raleigh puzzled over the comment. Wasn't Sue Ann her daughter? She wasn't good with her own kids? Raleigh would need to remember to ask later. She could remember not being out of the loop on any of the gossip as a kid. She used to love hearing the stories of the neighbors, even the ones she knew she wasn't supposed to be listening to. She'd imagine writing their stories down and sharing them with the town. She guessed she'd be disliked just as much if she would have grown-up and did that for a living.

Me'Maw's fingers moved rhythmically over the blue toile square, each stitch the same as the preceding stitch. Me'Maw enjoyed making baby quilts, and Raleigh guessed someone was having a boy. She wondered if they knew yet that they were having a boy.

"You understand, right?" Me'Maw sighed, but didn't look up from her square. "Being a traiteur is about tradition, and this is one of our oldest."

Raleigh frowned. What else was she supposed to say? Did it even matter if she disagreed? "I understand Me'Maw."

Me'Maw was referring to the tradition of training a new traiteur. A man trained a woman and a woman trained a man. An old Cajun tradition alive and strong in this family. Me'Maw, trained by her father, had trained Uncle Camille, who had shown the most promise of her sons. It was his duty to train the next one in the family. Raleigh didn't want to tell Me'Maw that the family vocation would probably die with Uncle Camille, which reminded her...

"Me'Maw, has Uncle Camille been sick lately?"

Me'Maw paused in her stitches, but she squinted at them still. "Everyone takes care of their sadness and pain in their own way."

Raleigh shook her head. "I don't mean the drinking."

"He won't go to the doctor." Me'Maw ran her fingers over her stitches. "He's relying on his faith."

Sadness crushed down on her chest; sadness for Claudia, for Madison, for Uncle Camille, and for Me'Maw squeezed tight around her middle. It was one of those moments of awareness she was unable to deny. She would see the death of everyone she loved.

"Sometimes faith is all we have or need." Me'Maw's rocker creaked on the pine floor. "People survive what they are supposed to survive."

Raleigh needed air. Cold, sweet air to inflate her stalled lungs. "I'm going walk next door."

Me'Maw nodded. "Good, your parents will be glad to see you."

Raleigh looked at Me'Maw skeptical, but it only fell on the back of her neck. She crossed to the kitchen door without another word.

The sun lit the sky in shades of burnt orange as it settled over her shoulder. Tuesday was ending. Last Tuesday, she'd connected to Claudia in a dream. Madison had been gone a week with no connection. Where was she?

Raleigh kicked at the grass as she crossed the fifty feet or so to her parent's house. She doubted glad would be the emotion they'd feel, but she wanted to have a look in Madison's room. She couldn't deny that things were strained between her and her parents these days, but it wasn't really much different than the calls she'd receive every few months or so. They weren't exactly close anymore. She wasn't divorcing them or anything that hip, but she wasn't nominating them for parents of the year either.

Raleigh pulled the front door open and stepped into the darkness of the living room.

"Mom, Dad, it's just me."

"I can see you."

Raleigh jumped as the voice came from the darkness of the living room. "You don't want the light?"

Raleigh could hear the strain in her mother's voice. "No, I have a headache."

Raleigh frowned, knowing she couldn't see her. When was the last time her mother had gone outside? She hadn't seen her since the funeral.

"I think maybe you need to get out and get some fresh air."

"Why?" Raleigh heard the deep breath. "I'd rather not see the people talking about us."

"It's not like that," Raleigh stood talking to the shadow of her mother, trying to determine which direction was her face. "People are concerned about Madison."

"Ha," A sharpness had entered her mom's voice. "They just want to see if Madison screwed up like you."

Raleigh drew in a sharp intake of breath. The shock wore off in moments, anger surged in to replace it. "Why do you still hold it against me? It's not like I planned for it to happen or even that it was my fault."

"It would have been nice to hear it from my daughter instead of her grandmother, don't you think? Or your grandfather, or your father, or Doris the woman at the supermarket, or let's see, everyone else in Barbeaux but you."

"Is that what's this about?" Raleigh asked trembling. "You didn't want to hear my story. You told me at the hospital that you didn't want to know."

"I was angry, and then the whole town was talking about it. How this family must have something wrong with it. How do you think that made me feel?"

"I don't know," Raleigh said, staring at her mother's head finally. "I was too busy trying to disappear since no one, including my parents, wanted me here."

Silence. No answer. She could push it, but where would that get them?

"I'm coming take a look at Madison's room."

Raleigh braced herself for the objections, but only silence greeted her again. She waited for what seemed like a year, and then she made her way down the narrow hallway at the end of the living room to the bedrooms. The discussion was over, and now she'd get the silent treatment. Oh, how she hated silence because of her mother.

She reached her old bedroom first, now Mason's, and continued to the next door which was Madison's. Raleigh turned the doorknob and took a deep breath before stepping inside.

On first glance, the room hadn't changed much from Madison's childhood. Dolls and teddy bears lined the shelves above the full size four-poster bed. Her desk stood in the corner overflowing with papers and envelopes, and her closet overflowed onto the beige carpet.

The rumpled navy blue comforter on the bed was a new addition as well as a chair loaded with clothing that sparkled. The air smelled of cinnamon. A candle on the nightstand was responsible. Madison loved the smell and would buy several candles at after Christmas sales to stock up for the year.

Raleigh moved further into the room, an eerie feeling prickling her neck. Only the slate walls stared back at her, but she felt as though eyes were watching her.

With a mental push, she crossed to the desk and scanned the top layer of the mess. Cell phone bills, Mason's school papers, and a few magazines made up the top layer. She pushed some magazines to the side and found unopened letters from Alex. Raleigh returned the cell phone bills on top of them. It seemed to be too personal for her to read. She gathered Mason's coloring sheets into a nice neat stack. She guessed

Madison's organizational system was the same at home as at work. Under the top layer of art, a blue photo envelope from the local drug store rested on top of more magazines.

Raleigh picked this up, justifying that anything that could have been printed at a local store couldn't be too personal. Didn't they have laws about that?

Raleigh sank onto the bed and pulled the stack of pictures out of the envelope. Mason sticking his tongue out greeted her.

Raleigh smiled as she flipped to the next picture of him making a silly, wide-eyed, open-mouthed expression for the camera. She hadn't seen him look that happy since she'd been here.

Raleigh drew in a breath as she flipped to the next picture of Madison, Claudia, and another scantily clad shiny young woman dancing on the coffee table she'd seen the other day at Aunt Clarice's old house. Okay, she'd never look at that table the same again. Raleigh flipped to the next picture, which had Claudia dancing in some eager young man's lap. He was holding a beer in one hand and making a lewd gesture to the crowd with the other. Raleigh thought she'd seen him somewhere before. The next one had a woman dancing with another woman. Was that Davey's wife? The next one was a wide shot of a crowd of people who seemed to be paired off.

Raleigh's stomach lurched forward, and she put the pictures down next to her. An aching grew in her wrists, and she rubbed them. The smell of cinnamon now filled her throat, nauseating her.

She looked around the room and tears burned her eyelids, but she blinked against them falling.

Maybe she needed to leave this job to Max. She didn't want to know these things about her sister. What was she supposed to do with this knowledge? Anyone in these pictures could be guilty. Hell, anyone who had a wife or husband in these pictures deserved to be guilty. Max was right about her being too close.

Raleigh's wrists throbbed again. She studied them, and they appeared normal and unbruised, except for the slight indentation of her scar. They throbbed again, a familiar throbbing.

As when she'd been bound with duck tape.

Raleigh rubbed the soft tissue of her scar from the glass bottle. It wasn't quite the same pressure. The feeling was rougher, more brutal.

Raleigh stood as her body trembled from the sudden chill. She didn't want to do this. She didn't want a connection in her sister's room surrounded by her things. Was it Madison bound at her wrists or was it an echo from Katherine and the past? She couldn't tell anymore.

Her wrists throbbed again.

Raleigh grabbed the package of photos and sprinted from the room.

Exhaustion rolled through her, followed by a wave of frustration. She'd never find Madison this way. Even to her, it didn't seem as though she really wanted to find her.

Raleigh pushed the back door hard with her shoulder as it stuck. It wasn't used often, but she wasn't going back through the front. She inhaled the air, filling her lungs with the smells of vegetables, and she waited for the black spots from her sudden emergence into the sun to evaporate.

She bounded toward Me'Maw's house clutching the pictures in her hand. When she was half way there, she saw Me'Maw standing on the back porch holding the screen door open with one hand.

"What's wrong?"

Me'Maw's voice cracked. "Phil just called that Camille's passed out at the bar, and your Paw's not back from looking on Joey's tractor."

Raleigh gritted her teeth. This day just kept getting better. How many angry family members could she fit into one day? "Old man Phil's bar?"

"The one right up the road." Me'Maw nodded. "He walks there."

Raleigh looked toward Paw's old truck, which she'd left out of the barn, still conscious of yesterday's weird feeling about the mud. "I'll go get him."

Me'Maw squinted. "Are you sure?"

"No, "Raleigh shook her head, "but I'm not going to leave him there."

The truck's air was stifling, but she set the pictures to her side and started the engine. She'd probably put more miles on this truck in the last week than Paw had in the last few years. Something she needed to think about. Of course, she didn't think anyone would sell a jobless person a car. But, who knew?

She pulled onto the street and waved to Ms. Margaret as she passed. The bar was only a few yards down the road on the bayou side. Raleigh eased the truck onto the highway and then signaled right at the bar. Only five trucks were parked out front. Raleigh guessed it was early for patrons, or Phil's business wasn't looking too good.

The apricot building was literally falling to pieces. Raleigh could see sections of its siding broken off at the bottom. The front door dipped some on the left side, and the roof still had the blue tarpaulin from after Hurricane Katrina. It certainly didn't look like a place open for a beer after work.

Raleigh pulled hard on the door, and it finally gave. A wave of ice cold air hit her from inside the darkness. Obviously, the air conditioner still worked.

She squinted into the darkened room and saw old man Phil behind the bar drying glasses. He nodded toward the bar stool, and there was Uncle Camille with his head down on the bar. Raleigh approached slowly.

"I only served him two drinks today." Phil lay his towel down on the bar. "I'm afraid he's drinking more before he comes in these days."

Raleigh frowned. "It's his way of dealing."

Phil nodded. "Poor fellow. I'll help you get him outside."

Phil walked around the bar, and Raleigh put her hand on Uncle Camille's shoulder and he stirred.

Raleigh waited as he picked his head up and tried to open his sagging eyes. "Another drink?"

Raleigh picked up his arm. "No, we're going home right now and get some sleep."

He waved his arm wildly, and Raleigh jerked back to avoid contact. "I don't want to sleep. I want another beer."

"We all have our problems today." Raleigh pulled his arm roughly as Phil eased his right side off the barstool. "You can have another beer at home."

His head lulled to the side, but he didn't fight them as they half carried, half dragged him toward the door. Not surprisingly, he wasn't very heavy, and his arm gave Raleigh a true picture of how thin he'd become. She guessed he hadn't been eating between beers.

Phil maneuvered him to the passenger side of the truck, and they were able to coax him into climbing in. She caught a strong whiff of alcohol as she thanked Phil and closed the door. He nodded without a word as he walked back toward the door.

Raleigh took a deep breath and then climbed back into the driver side. The smell of alcohol and body sweat had swallowed the insides. She scrunched up her nose as she started the truck. This was going to be a long two hundred yard drive. She should have asked if they could stick him in a shower, or maybe they should have thrown him in the bed of the truck to air out.

Uncle Camille had roused himself, and he was looking around the truck's insides. Raleigh eased the truck onto the highway without looking at him.

"My Claudia shouldn't be the one dead."

Raleigh gritted her teeth. Her jaw ached, and she stiffened her body. There wasn't a quota to fill on family arguments. She could be strong.

"I tried to tell her to come home. I went to that raunchy place, but she wouldn't talk to me. Said I was a drunk, and I wasn't a good father. Why would she say that? I took care of her."

Perspiration was beading on her neck and her fingers were burning from her grip on the steering wheel.

He'd taken care of her between drunken spells. Weeks without food in their house, and then he'd show up with a bag of candy. At ten, Claudia had gone weeks without seeing him because he'd been crashed at some druggy's house. Sure, if neglect counted, he'd taken care of her. When Claudia's mother had died in a car accident when she was nine, she'd lost both parents.

Raleigh eased the truck in front of Uncle Camille's house where her father was leaning against a tall pine. He crossed over to them as Raleigh shifted into park. He was still in his blue jeans and khaki work shirt. He must have just driven up.

Uncle Camille looked at her. "Why none of you turned out normal? We raised ya'll good."

Raleigh scowled at him as her father pulled open the passenger door.

"Come on Camille. Let's get you some sleep."

"I don't want any damn sleep." Camille pushed past him and stumbled out the truck. "I'm going get a beer."

Uncle Camille staggered into his yard. For a moment, Raleigh thought he was going to keel over, but he made it to the green chair on his front porch and sank into it.

Her father still held the truck door. "Thanks, Raleigh."

Raleigh released a deep breath. She was probably blue in her lips from holding it for so long. "Just doing my best not to mess things up."

Her father shook his head and then closed the truck door.

Well, one out of three. She could at least tell Paw she'd made progress.

She eased forward and parked it in front of the barn, telling herself she could wash it for Paw. It didn't even sound plausible to herself. She just didn't want to go into the building, and she knew it. Now she was cowering away from the shed. Why was she being such a coward? Wasn't she the one who'd climbed on the roof of that shed and jumped off into a bail of hay, which had really turned out not to be such a soft landing? What had happened to her?

Before long she'd be one of those people who didn't leave their house.

She really needed to get over this.

Chapter Nineteen

Raleigh added ice to the containers holding the salads and scanned the other food stations. Her feet ached, her head throbbed, and the event was only beginning. The guests gathered on the back deck, listening to Father Lucas's blessing. Denise was adjusting the tables and fretting over the set up. Raleigh wasn't sure how many different arrangements could fit in this small area, but Denise seemed intent to find out. Raleigh was in charge of keeping the food station organized and stocked. Even with it set under the small tent, conveniently advertising the LED's new boat named *Alyssa*, the sun was warming things up.

Raleigh sighed as she poured more ice into the pirogue containing canned drinks. She'd thought it would be more practical to keep the drinks in the ice chests, but she'd been told it wouldn't be in keeping with the boat theme. What did she know? She was just stand-in help.

She glanced back toward the boat. Thank God they were on land, or Denise would have had to find that help somewhere else. She'd listened to the lapping water for the two hours of set up, trying to pretend she was no where near the bayou. The massive boats blocking the water front view helped.

The party felt like a respite, keeping her mind busy and off her sister momentarily. The party would be over in a few hours and the next big event, a wedding, was nearly complete after months of planning. After, she could go back to stressing over her sister's disappearance. Oh, goody.

"Excuse me, you're Raleigh Cheramie, right?"

Raleigh turned from the ice chest to face an older woman with brunette helmet hair and deep pink lipstick. Her forehead was plastered stiff against her skull, though the thinness of her skin revealed the aging. Botox, maybe?

"Yes, Ma'am."

"Has there been any word on your sister? I was so sorry to hear about the situation."

Raleigh dug up her fake, sympathetic smile. Lately, it wasn't ever too far from the surface. "We're still searching. Did you know her well?"

The woman nodded and her hair did not shudder with the motion. There must be a thinner layer in the ozone layer above her house. "She helped plan our ladies' socials, so four times a year she and I worked together. Such a sweet girl."

She hobbled off in her deep pink flowing pantsuit. Raleigh would bet today's paycheck that she had money. She could see it in the upright posture of her walk, the tilt of her head, and the shiny rings on her fingers.

Of course, it wasn't a far stretch. The invitation's prerequisite must have been a bank account five hundred times her own. The only normal people here were the ten or so crew members. Raleigh wasn't sure what boat crews were paid these days, but chances were it was more than she was being paid.

The napkins began to flip in the wind again, so Raleigh grabbed a paperweight printed with the LED Marine logo and placed it on top of the napkins.

Questionable attractiveness, but certainly practical.

Voices approached, and Raleigh turned to notice the guests moving toward them from the shiny new supply boat. She hastened behind the food tables to oversee any serving issues that arose. She wasn't even quite sure what that meant. The only serving issues she'd ever experienced were breaking her plastic spoons.

Forty or so people converged on the tent at once, and Raleigh's forehead heated. Why had Denise said they didn't need any servers? Was she supposed to be superwoman today? She would have insisted on a cape.

The first few guests moved down the line smoothly, picking at the fruit trays and sandwich trays.

"I heard he was stealing from the collections."

Raleigh's head snapped up to see a middle age mom with a short bob grabbing a napkin and looking at the similar looking blonde bob woman behind her in line.

"Sister Marissa said that wasn't true."

The woman frowned. "Sister Marissa adores him and wouldn't say anything negative."

The blonde bob lady picked up her cheese, turning to leave the serving line as she shook her head. "The Diocese just wanted to shake things up."

The two's heads remained close together as they headed to the seating area where Denise was shepherding them into seats.

Apparently, even the priest wasn't above scandalous gossip these days. How would that sound in confession?

A few men moved along the line wearing LED Marine logo navy blue polos. Raleigh smiled as each passed, their eyes barely noticing her, and then on the fourth one she froze.

He looked familiar. From his smooth face and bed hair, she believed he was younger than her. She'd seen the guys her age and age hadn't been that kind. His almond eyes crinkled at the corners, and he had this big goofy grin as he stared at her. Where had she seen him before?

Her brain ran through all possible scenarios. A picture, maybe?

Ah, yes, she'd seen him in her sister's pictures. He'd just been showing a little more flesh with his black satin boxers.

Raleigh diverted her gaze away from him and busied herself with checking the food. After he left the line with the others in his group, she watched his group, all wearing similar shirts, walk the four rows of evenly spaced tables all with a sunflower and cattail arrangement centerpiece to a back table.

Maybe she could ask him about the party. Exactly what she wasn't sure, but maybe he could tell her something. She'd just have to stop picturing him in his boxer shorts so that shudder would stop creeping down her spine. If she stayed in Barbeaux, she might have a difficult time dating. She'd want proof that the potential date had never attended a party. Kind of like proof before purchase.

The line progressed and Raleigh tried not to make eye contact, but towards the end of the line she cringed at a familiar voice. How could she remember his voice after so long?

She busied herself with switching on the coffee machine as Jeffery Zedeaux mingled with the big shirts in line. His appearance hadn't changed much since high school. Wouldn't it be great if the outsides matched the insides?

"Is the boat lined up yet?"

A middle age balding man nodded his head. "We had a contract before it was completed."

Jeffery turned to the second suit. "Did you take care of the problems with the crew?"

The suit frowned. "A few have been resolved."

Suit number two's furrowed eyebrows and deep frown did not indicate pleasure with Jeffery's questions. Both suits moved out of the line without anything further, but Jeffery remained.

A young man in a LED Marine logo shirt approached him. As Jeffery looked around, Raleigh bent down and pulled out the tray of coffee cups from under the tablecloth.

"Did you look into it?"

The young guys voice was jumbled, his pronunciation tangled. "Can't find any clear lead."

"Not the answer I was looking for."

"I know sir. I'm still working on it."

"You do that. I want to know if it's one of my own."

"Yes, sir."

Raleigh straightened up and began placing the cups next to the dripping coffee pot. Jeffery turned to grab a sandwich from the now empty line and noticed Raleigh for the first time.

"Is this what you've done with yourself? Explains your absence at the reunion."

Raleigh grimaced at him while still stacking the cups. "Just filling in until Madison returns. I see you haven't changed since high school."

"Don't fool yourself," Jeffery laughed, the sound filling the tent. "You're assuming that Madison hasn't met the same fate as Claudia. The two did have a knack for trouble."

Raleigh glared at him, and for the first time, she noticed the green flecks in his acorn eyes. Eyes she'd seen in a different setting before. She couldn't imagine where though. "I don't see much change, but then again I've been away for awhile. Madison is alive, in case you were interested. You wouldn't happen to know anything about that, would you?"

"Now, how would I know anything?"

"We both know how you've become successful. I'd hate for any of it to really come out. Well, I guess I wouldn't really care."

"Raleigh, you can't threaten when you have no means." Jeffery smiled, but his eyes twitched. "As always it's been interesting."

He strolled away, his cocky gait becoming more pronounced the further he walked away from her.

No one stood up to that jerk. No one ever had. It had caused his head to swell even larger than it was in high school, if that was even possible. She supposed some of her animosity toward him came from his being Ross's cousin; the rest was all his own.

Raleigh moved away from the tent, intermingling with the crowd. She could no longer see boxer short guy with so many people standing around, but she was headed in his general direction.

She brushed against someone and turned to say 'Excuse me' and came face to face with Father Lucas.

"Why hello, Raleigh. Didn't think to see you at an event such as this."

Raleigh smiled, looking ahead through a gap in the crowd. Boxers was still sitting with the others, leaning back in the white fold-out chair. "I'm taking Madison's place until she returns."

Father Lucas frowned, his blue eyes crinkling at the corners. "So I suppose we haven't had any word on her whereabouts then?"

Raleigh shook her head, "We will."

"Faith." Father Lucas's thin lips curved upwards. "The one thing we must never lose."

Raleigh scanned the crowd once again and frowned as she witnessed Jenny talking to Jeffery Zedeaux. What would he be talking to a stripper about? And what would a stripper be doing at a party whose guest's income never dropped below the six figures? A stripper in Barbeaux couldn't possibly make that much money.

Raleigh looked up at Father Lucas, who she realized was still staring down at her. "Excuse me, Father Lucas; I must get back to work now."

"Certainly, it was great to see you."

Raleigh weaved through the crowd, edging toward the odd pair. They whispered fiercely to each other so that they didn't glance in her direction until she was ten feet from their table. Jenny's pale face stared at her a moment, before she turned and darted in the opposite direction, leaving Jeffery Zedeaux staring at Raleigh. She pushed forward and walked past him toward the table with boxer short guy. The only hint revealing her embarrassment was the warmness burning her neck.

From the quiver up her spine, she would swear his eyes followed her all the way to the table.

Boxer short guy gawked as she approached. It wasn't the 'I know who you are' gaze, but the 'is she checking me out' gaze. Raleigh shuddered at the idea. It was like the child on the playground with the cooties.

Raleigh walked around the table, and leaned over close to his shaggy hair. She noticed the lingering scent of heavy, spice cologne, much too strong and overpowering. "Excuse me sir, but would you mind if I speak with you alone for a moment?"

He grinned, standing up. Raleigh stepped back to avoid touching him. "Call me Shane. Do I know you? You look so familiar."

She guessed he hadn't connected her to Madison yet. Raleigh scanned the crowd. No one near enough to hear them. "Actually, no. I'm Raleigh Cheramie, Madison's sister."

Raleigh watched as horror slid into his twinkling leaf eyes. She guessed that he had figured out that she wasn't checking him out.

"I have a few questions about one of Madison and Claudia's parties."

"I never attended one of those parties." Shane glanced back toward his table, now ten feet away. "I heard about them though. Everyone knows about them."

Raleigh moved closer and leaned in. "I have pictures."

Shane studied her, his eyes widening. "Look, I only went that one time. I would've never done anything if I hadn't taken a little acid to loosen up. Man, there are pictures?"

Raleigh nodded. "I want to know what you know about the parties."

Shane shifted in his spot. "All I know is that every weekend, either a Friday or Saturday, they would have a party. You had to pay twenty-five dollars to put your name on the list, and more when you received your invite. There were fees for other things at the party. You could pretty much have anything you wanted if you had the cash."

After Raleigh found Madison, she was going to kill her. If she was already dead, she would bring her back to life and kill her again. She may repeat the process a few times. What was wrong with Madison? Raleigh wasn't going to be the one explaining this to Me'Maw. No way.

"Claudia and Madison ran the parties?"

Shane shrugged. "My cousin put our names on the list and paid the fee. They were running things when I got there."

Raleigh scanned the area again for something to do besides look at him. She'd remember to ask her sister for a list of anyone who attended. That was before she killed her. Kyle Allemande was talking to one of the navy LED Marine shirt men.

Raleigh looked back toward Shane. "Did any of the guests seem to be angry at Claudia or Madison?"

"I know a couple of guys who were angry after." Shane pushed his hair out of his eyes. "They felt as though they'd been scammed. Many of the guys were married. One even had his wife there, but it was the same crowd most of the time my cousin told me. It took us a month on the list before we got in."

Raleigh suddenly had that feeling of hearing too much on a subject and wanting to cover her ears to block any more out. "Thanks, Shane. I'll find you if anything else comes up."

"Please don't show anyone those pictures. Man, the girl I'm dating now would freak out if it got back to her."

Raleigh bit her lip against telling him he should have thought about that before going to the party. She just smiled and turned away.

Kyle glanced in her direction as she approached. He turned and shook hands with the man he was talking to and walked toward the parking area.

Twice today she'd been avoided. People usually had something to hide when they did it so openly. What were Jenny and Kyle hiding, and more importantly did it have something to do with her sister?

It would have to wait. Denise was signaling her from the food tent. She guessed she'd been gone too long. Oh well, at least she wasn't starving anyone. They could survive without the coffee.

After what seemed like many hours later, but was really only two, Raleigh pulled Paw's truck into the yard. She was careful to pull it just shy of the barn entrance. Paw hadn't said anything yesterday, and Raleigh thought he'd actually enjoyed pulling it inside. Raleigh shivered as she got out the truck and quickly walked around the side of the old barn. She'd have to get over this. How could someone develop a phobia of damp dirt? The water phobia was enough for her.

Paw was not walking the rows of his garden nor was he sitting out on the back porch. The air had chilled as the sun began to set. It was the perfect time of year to Raleigh.

The porch board creaked as she sank onto it. Couldn't find a better place to sit and think.

What did she know?

Winter had said Madison's ex-boyfriend had been harassing her. Alex had admitted to that already. He wanted a reason for the breakup. Raleigh still had no clue about that reason. Winter had also said an old man had come to talk to Claudia. If Raleigh had to guess, she would say that man was Uncle Camille. He didn't have the best track record as a father, but Mason could probably beat him up in his present condition. Jeffery Zedeaux on the other hand. What was his involvement, if any? Jenny and Kyle were behaving awfully suspicious as well.

Raleigh kicked at the grass in frustration.

"I guess your day isn't going too well?"

Raleigh looked up to see Max holding the screen door open.

"I didn't know you were here."

Max allowed the screen door to snap gently behind him. "I just got here. I actually came to talk to you."

Raleigh grinned. "Well, at least someone isn't trying to avoid me."

"Huh?"

She shook her head. "Just the kind of day I'm having. Most people don't seem to want to talk to me today."

Max eased himself down next to her, his shirt wrinkling with the position. "Yes, I know what you mean. We brought Jenny in today, and she's not saying anything. Well, she has much to say, but it's not anything of importance."

Raleigh frowned. "She was at a boat christening today that we hosted. She was pretty upset and avoided me. I don't know if she is responsible for Claudia's death, but she's certainly acting like she has something to hide."

Max nodded. "I agree. We're doing some checking."

Raleigh looked at him. The breeze encircled her with his light cologne and his eyes now stared down into hers. It was difficult to look away from those eyes. It struck Raleigh that suspects must have a difficult time lying to him. His gaze was like a magnetic force reeling her into him, assuring her that if she spoke everything would be okay somehow.

His lips were smooth and rounded. Raleigh's body tugged at her to lean in closer.

As soon as she thought "he's going to kiss me" something flew against her leg and stuck. Raleigh hesitated and then looked down. Ross Blanch stared at her in a tuxedo on the arm of Katherine wearing her teal Junior Prom dress.

Raleigh reached down and grabbed the picture and couldn't pull her eyes away, although she really wanted to. It was the formal picture of their junior prom that Raleigh had tucked away in an old album, but this one was blown up on a sheet of computer paper. They looked so young with Katherine's long blonde hair in the hot roller curls they'd spent hours perfecting.

"Nanan! Nanan!"

Raleigh looked up as Mason came running around the side of the house with the same picture clutched in his hands.

Max stood. "Where did you get that, Mason?"

Mason's eyes widened, and his body was jumping up and down in his excitement. "They are all over the front yard. There's hundreds of them, thousands of them!"

Raleigh groaned as she stood up. "Did you see how they got there?"

Mason nodded. "A huge black truck thingy pulled up, rolled down the window, and threw them out."

To that list of what she knew, she'd forgotten to add someone wanting her gone. She felt good about assuming that they wanted her gone because of the past, and this had nothing to do with Madison's disappearance. But if Max was right, then the two were connected. She wasn't doing a good job at eliminating the possibilities.

Raleigh followed the bouncing Mason around the corner of the house. Max was at her side when they turned the corner to see the front lawn littered with white paper.

She caught one as it flew against her. She groaned and then began the job of picking them up.

To think she could have been kissing instead. She looked over toward Max who was also reaching and gathering the photos. At least there will be a nice view she thought as she picked up the trash community service style.

Chapter Twenty

The wind whipped the paper around the tables' legs, and Raleigh clutched her sweater tighter around her chest. The weather in October was crazy. This morning it had been warm without even a breeze, and now the wind blew straight threw her. Mike jotted down a few more notes in his notebook with a smile as he moved on down the row of empty booths.

Raleigh followed along, wondering what could possibly make him happy about a festival story. "I just don't understand her life. There are so many people involved. How do we begin to narrow it down to someone who could even qualify as a suspect?"

Mike shook his head. "What we need is a timeline of who they had contact with and when. We're not going to get anywhere if everything is scattered."

Raleigh looked around at the festival workers preparing the tables, setting up the booths, and carrying in supplies. No one even looked their way. The festival was one of the biggest events of the year, and they were working as if royalty were attending. "Are you done here?"

Mike scanned the area. Only a few remaining fair volunteers were preparing their booths for tomorrow. Most of the booths were wrapped in paper, and some even had ornamental grass decorating them. "Just a few more. He wants a community interest story. You know, the festival is good for our town, and all that hype. I also have to bring in the people element. So I'll be back here tomorrow night while it's in full swing. Lucky me."

Raleigh laughed. Mike loved hardcore investigative journalism. She wondered why he hadn't moved to another paper where he wouldn't be stuck covering a town festival. For reasons Raleigh couldn't understand, he'd been determined to return here after they had graduated college. Barbeaux held its appeal, but career wise, journalism wasn't a competitive market. Heck, he was it. No competition at all. In South Louisiana, men made their money through the oil field. Men weren't lined up to take his job for the measly thirty grand a year.

Mike had dropped in after work for a quick hello, and she'd tagged along on his assignment. It seemed less stressful than listening to Denise ramble about Saturday's big wedding or trying to find Madison from Me'Maw's front porch. Her inactivity was putting a strain on her conscience, yet she didn't know what else to do.

"Hello, Ms. Mabel. How are you doing today?"

Ms. Mabel stopped putting up her ticket sign and turned their way. "Hello, Mike. I haven't seen you in church for awhile."

Mike nodded. "I've been going to the later Mass because of work."

"They keeping you busy, cher. Everyone's too busy these days." Ms. Mabel smiled. "Why, Raleigh Cheramie, I almost didn't recognize you. Any word on your sister?"

Raleigh frowned and her stomach churned. "No, we're still searching."

Ms. Mabel nodded, though Raleigh noticed Ms. Mabel's eyes didn't meet her own. "She'll turn up. Everything works out for its own reasons."

"It was nice seeing you, Ms. Mabel." Mike began walking. "Must be getting back to work now."

"Good to see you, Mike, and Raleigh you too. Good luck."

Raleigh cringed as she followed Mike.

"You know it's all anyone is talking about right now. It will pass when something new happens."

Raleigh grumbled. "Yes, let's hope they don't find out that Barbeaux has progressed to the modern age of sex parties."

Mike chuckled as he turned toward the beefy guy in the suit.

"I think I'll wait this one out right here."

Raleigh leaned against a table already wrapped in white paper.

"I'll only be five minutes. Just need some figures."

Raleigh watched him leave, and then she looked around the tent. As a girl, the festival had been one of her favorite events. It was the only time her parents would turn her loose as long as she checked in every so often. Of course, as a teenager it wasn't such a good idea, but it was the only time during the year she actually saw her parents have fun.

She tensed as a short blonde, plump woman approached. She was familiar as in shared classes in high school, but a name was not coming to her.

"I thought I recognized you over there. How have you been doing?" Then she frowned, dimples forming on her cheeks. "I'm sorry that was an insensitive question. I'm sorry about Claudia. Any word on Madison?"

Raleigh cringed, a name still not forming, but she remembered her being in her algebra class. She had turned around in her seat often to laugh and flip her long hair and make sure everyone was watching her. Now her hair didn't even total six inches, and she definitely would not fit into that cheerleading outfit she'd worn on Friday's game days. Had she reached her peak in high school? "We're still looking."

"Truthfully, I thought you would've come back home with Mike. Where have you been living?"

"I was living in Texas, but I moved to Baton Rouge six months ago."

She knew that would quiet some of the gossip about where she'd been. She didn't remember her name, but she was sure she was like the rest of the bayou in their love of gossip.

"Got it." Mike strolled back in their direction. "Why, hello, Molly. I haven't seen you since the reunion."

Molly Turner. The homecoming queen of the homecoming she'd missed. She'd been tied up, literally.

"Four kids will keep you busy. Are you working with Mike, Raleigh?"

Raleigh shook her head. "We're just collaborating on a story."

"Still working on making it more than one story." Mike smiled. "We need to get going though."

Raleigh began walking toward the tent exit and called over her shoulder. "Nice seeing you again."

She didn't wait to hear Molly's response.

Mike chuckled as they reached the outside of the tent. "I can imagine that conversation. Molly is the leader of this network of moms whose main item of discussion at the weekly play dates is gossip."

Raleigh shuddered as the wind blew through her sweater. A feeling of weakness fluttered in her stomach. "Figured as much. Are we done now?"

"Just need to swing into the center and pick up a schedule of events."

"I'll wait by the Jeep. I'm not feeling so well."

Mike stared down at her. Raleigh squirmed under his evaluation. "A moment ago your face wasn't so pale."

Raleigh shook her head, avoiding his gaze. She felt a little shaky. "I'm sure it's just anxiety."

Mike stared a moment longer. "I'm just going to run in. I'll be right out."

He jogged toward the darkened glass door. Raleigh walked toward the parking lot, an oddness creeping through her flesh. Suddenly her head began to spin and blackness dropped in before her eyes. Raleigh reached out and steadied herself on a post she'd reached.

Something wasn't right. She felt as though she were splitting in two.

Another wave of blackness washed over her causing her body to sway.

Raleigh felt her way to the back bumper of a truck in the parking lot and sank down onto it as another wave hit her.

Her stomach began to churn and swish with the blackness, and she put her head down feeling as though she were going to be sick.

What was wrong with her? It didn't feel like insanity, but would you really know if you were insane.

She could see Mike running toward her, but her eyes wouldn't focus on him, nor could she hear what his mouth was moving to say. She felt far away, outside of her body. She was drifting, leaving behind the white shells of the parking area and the shiny metal of the parked vehicles. It was like before... and then understanding squirmed through her with the next wave of blackness, and she allowed herself to be pulled away.

She was stumbling against a wall. She couldn't feel her legs as she drug them behind her along the wall. The room spun before her. Whiteness, black sofa, and a beat up coffee table spun before her.

She pulled herself into the room. She was almost to the sofa. She was reaching, her fingers multiplied before her. Blackness crashed down on her.

Raleigh gasped as the sunlight beat down onto her, blurring her vision. Mike's arms holding her up. She looked up into his worry filled eyes, yet knowledgeable eyes. Raleigh looked away.

"We need to get to Aunt Clarice's house now. We need an ambulance."

With his arm Mike eased her up from the bumper of the truck and guided her to his jeep. Raleigh would have smiled at his concern if her insides weren't feeling so shaky.

Raleigh's legs felt like wobbly stilts, and anxiousness jolted through her body.

Was it Madison?

Her chest tightened as Mike's tires spun on the gravel of the parking lot.

Raleigh dug around the floor and finally unearthed her cell phone. She punched in Max's number and he picked up on the second ring.

"We need an ambulance at Great Aunt Clarice's old house."

"Raleigh? Who do you need an ambulance for?"

Raleigh paused. She hadn't seen a face; she'd been the face. A tight ball formed in her chest, but at least the shakiness was easing. "I don't know. It's a female. Mike and I'll be there in less than ten minutes."

Silence greeted her. "I'm close by. I'll be there in minutes. I'll get an ambulance."

Warmth dampened some of the electricity tingling her body. "Thanks."

She hung up and closed her eyes as Mike swung around an old brown car on the highway. Her body swayed to the rhythm of his weaving in and out of traffic, but she kept her eyes closed trying to reach back into the darkness.

Was she alive? Was it Madison?

It was no use. She only reached the blackness of her closed eyelids.

She grabbed the armrest as they swung onto Cheramie Lane, and she opened her eyes to see Mike coast the Jeep onto the shoulder of the blacktop road.

Raleigh swung the door open before Mike grinded the gear into park. The windows of the house were black, and no car was parked in the driveway. Raleigh fumbled with the gate latch as another car coasted behind her. She didn't turn to see. Her heart thundered in her ears with each step on the rough plank wood porch as she hurtled in the direction of the door. The door stuck as she pushed on it, but she knew it wasn't locked. They didn't know where the key was.

She threw her body against it and she fell into the entryway. She felt her way in the dark to the living room with the black couch.

The window light projected into the room spotlighting a woman crumpled on the floor, inches from the sofa, a cell phone inches from her fingers.

Raleigh's speed propelled her forward; the blonde hair registering seconds after her eyes took it in.

She skidded to a stop as Jenny's heart-shaped face came into view. Her heart leapt in its thundering and then stopped. Numbness washed over her, and then a warmth broke through.

It wasn't Madison. She wanted to cheer, laugh, cry, and scream all at the same time. Her chest swelled and ached.

Max dashed into the room and didn't stop until he skidded into Jenny. His fingers immediately searching for a pulse. Mike burst in next leading a paramedic.

Help me.

Raleigh's fingers went frigid and her body froze.

I don't want to die. I can feel it.

Raleigh stumbled backward. Jenny was talking to her. The same Jenny that stared up at the room, eyes blank.

Help me.

Raleigh took another step back. The paramedic was still searching for a pulse. Jenny's voice was getting stronger.

Raleigh only connected to the near dead or dead. They were moving too slow.

"Tell me how."

All eyes turned to her. They thought she was crazy. She felt crazy; a heightened sense of alarm stormed through her, her whole body tingled with static electricity. She'd never tried to talk. She'd only listened. Even her ears prickled in alarm.

I just wanted to stop feeling the pain. I wanted to make it go away.

"Pain?" Raleigh's mind raced. What had she done to stop feeling pain? There was blackness and the room multiplying before her. If the dead had to talk to her, couldn't they be more specific? "Do you mean pills?"

Mike moved in closer. Even his understanding eyes had changed to a squinting concern as he studied her, hesitating to touch her.

I found them in the kitchen. They were hers.

Raleigh turned and ran down the hall to the back of the house. Pills were spilled onto the counter and the bottle lay on its side minus the cap. She grabbed the bottle and sprinted back to the paramedic nearly colliding with Mike.

She hurled the bottle at the paramedic not wanting to touch Jenny.

"She took this. We're losing her. She's nearly gone. Do something!"

A panic gripped her. She didn't want to be in the same room if she died. The connection was too strong. It hadn't been this strong since...oh hell, since she was eleven and that girl had been raped and murdered. She'd numbed herself to death after that and severed the first of many of her connections.

Raleigh's body began to tremble as the paramedic began pushing on Jenny's chest, trying to keep her heart pumping. A second paramedic moved in with a stretcher and lightheadedness washed over Raleigh. The room evaporated into black spots.

Raleigh was going to black out.

A strong arm came around her. She inhaled the scent of earth, tobacco, and lingering Stetson cologne.

Raleigh relaxed into the smells, turning to bury her face into Paw's blue Dickie's shirt, the same as she'd done at eleven.

Chapter Twenty-One

Her stomach fluttered as she swung forward, and then it lurched as the motion carried her backwards. The uncomfortableness of the swing kept other conflicting feelings at bay. Had she liked this feeling as a child? She remembered spending hours doing it in her backyard, but Raleigh didn't understand how with how queasy it was making her feel now.

An excited scream pierced the quiet sky. Raleigh looked over in time to see Mike bring down Shawn, Sheri's son. Mason ran behind holding onto Mike's leg, but Shawn still clutched the football tightly.

Raleigh smiled, her cheeks ached with the action. Her chest felt heavy with disappointment, and her insides still felt funny.

Mason yanked on Mike's t-shirt. It came up revealing tightly rippled abs. Raleigh noticed the two women on their jogging break gaping at him with an open admiration. Mike did not turn from the boys. Was this why Mike was still unattached? Maybe he needed someone to point out the obvious. On second thought, not many girlfriends wanted their boyfriends to have girl "friends". It might be better to keep her mouth shut for once.

Raleigh turned to the parking lot as gravel crunched under Max's tires. She admired him as he strolled toward her. The intensity of his eyes, of his expression, and of his walk shot through Raleigh, and she slowed her momentum to watch him approach. Raleigh didn't doubt her attraction to him. Her stomach fluttered in the same uncomfortableness as the swing. The attraction was usually never the problem. The pesky issue of his being in charge of her sister's case wasn't going away as fast as she'd like.

"I hope you don't mind. Your grandfather told me you would be here."

Raleigh smiled again, her jaw aching less this time. Maybe her body was coming out of its coma... especially with a dose of testosterone. "Mike thought we needed a distraction."

Max watched them throw the ball for a moment. "Are the two of you involved? I mean as a couple."

Raleigh gazed at him, and he returned her gaze. She could feel her heartbeat increase. "Mike and I have been friends since preschool. He's like a brother."

Max nodded. "That improves my chances some. Of course, first priority is finding your sister."

Her heart skipped. Had he read her mind?

Raleigh looked away and kicked hard at the ground, and she lifted high into the air. Her stomach lurched and her eyes closed against the feeling.

She wasn't eight-years old anymore. Max still stood at the foot of the swingset reminding her that Madison was still out there. She couldn't escape by swinging through the air. How come she couldn't find her? Was she blocking out whatever had happened to Madison or was Madison alive? Why couldn't she reach out like Me'Maw?

Because she wasn't Me'Maw, and she connected to the dead not the living. This knowledge should give her more relief than what was sitting inside her chest. Her doubts crowded everything else out though. Me'Maw had never been wrong, but Raleigh made a habit of being wrong on a weekly basis.

Raleigh brought her feet down and the sudden stop jarred her body. "How's Jenny?"

"She's unconscious." Max leaned against the metal post. "The doctor said it will be a few hours or so. The baby wasn't affected as far as they could tell. I have an officer waiting for her to wake-up."

Mason screeched and ran under Mike's legs and stole the ball. Raleigh smiled as he giggled. Then Max's words sunk in. "Baby? Jenny is pregnant?"

Max nodded. "Doctor says she's three months along. Wouldn't happen to have heard any rumors about a father?"

"I didn't even hear she was pregnant." How had Barbeaux missed that one? Maybe the gossip system wasn't as good as she was giving it credit. "I know she downed the pills herself. Maybe she's trying to self-destruct?"

"Any ideas?"

Raleigh sighed. "I think something happened at one of their sex parties."

Max leaned in closer. "Did you find out more?"

Raleigh looked back at him. The intensity was now focused on her. The feeling of standing alone on a stage being critiqued by a judge struck her. How could his eyes do that? She could certainly never lie to him guilt free. "Apparently Claudia and Madison were the hosts of the weekly pleasure party, and Jenny was one of the girls provided for entertainment, at an expense of course. I found pictures to prove it."

Max ran his fingers through his disheveled hair. "I need to see those pictures. I'll need to talk to some of the people involved."

"How could Madison let this happen? Did she completely lose her mind?"

Max sat down on the swing next to her. She couldn't help but notice how the swing cradled his derriere nicely. "Maybe she was trying to escape something."

"Jenny told me she was planning on leaving Barbeaux, but no one else seems to know about this. Madison used to say as a little girl she would never leave Barbeaux. Of course, she's not exactly the little girl I knew anymore."

Max brushed her hand gripping the swing. Sparks singed her hand where he touched. "And you're sure she's still alive?"

"I'm sure," then Raleigh frowned. Was she? There was that doubt again. "I didn't connect with Katherine; I just saw her body, maybe I've missed something again."

Max bumped against her with his swing. "I think you would know. What you did today... well, that was important. If we would've arrived five minutes later, it would've been too late."

Raleigh shook her head. "Katherine was like my sister. I spent most of my time with Mike and Katherine. Madison was so much younger than me. We weren't close. If I didn't see Katherine, then maybe I won't see Madison."

"Maybe you just didn't connect with Katherine because you were so close. Raleigh, I believe you'll know."

"So, you've decided to believe in me?"

"It's not that I didn't believe in you." He grinned. "I'd just call myself a true believer after this afternoon. We'll find her, Raleigh."

"I know we will," she said, frowning, "but how? I don't want it to be too late."

"My way isn't working," Max said. "I think you need to give your way a shot."

Her way. Raleigh shuddered. Asking questions and digging into other's lives like he did on a daily basis didn't scare her. His way was like chasing butterflies compared to being chased by the monsters of her connections to the dead.

She knew that she hadn't connected to Katherine because she'd focused so hard on not connecting to the dead when she'd thought Mike was dead. Then Ross Blanch died inches from her. One shock pounding her after another. She'd pushed so deep, she'd pushed it all away. It had never really come back.

Was she blocking Madison out now from fear? Could she have lost the freaky talent and actually be missing it? She certainly hadn't seen that one coming.

Chapter Twenty-two

The incessant beeping from the nurse's station was wearing on Raleigh's brain. She wished she'd put a Twix in her purse. Of course, the whole trip to the hospital was on a whim. There hadn't been time to prepare for a long stake out. Raleigh watched as the officer again walked to the nurse's station to flirt with the petite blonde nurse filling out charts behind a faux wood grain desk. He really needed to just make a move already. This was painful to watch.

When they were both looking away, Raleigh darted across the white hall from the green and wood wainscoting waiting area and slipped into room 308. She held the latch and closed the door without a sound. Her heart thumped against her chest. Every time she'd done something like this, it hadn't ended well.

If they would've let her in, she wouldn't have to be sneaking around. Of course, that didn't make the adrenaline pumping through her body shoot off any guilt-free neurons.

Jenny lay under white printed sheets, staring out the picture window to the dark storm clouds outside. Her room was empty except for a rocker and an empty food tray next to the bed.

Raleigh tiptoed further into the room, approaching the bed.

Jenny turned her head in her direction and frowned when she saw Raleigh. "What do you want?"

Raleigh moved closer. "I wanted to see how you were doing."

"Like you care."

She returned to gazing out the window.

Raleigh stepped toward the foot of the bed. "I've come to check on you. I wanted to see if I could help with whatever is going on with you."

"I don't want to talk to you. I don't even know you."

"You knew Madison."

"Yeah, like that did me any good. She ruined my life."

"How?"

"Ask your sister."

Raleigh clinched her arms. Anger began to well in her chest. Where was the gratefulness for saving her life? If Raleigh knew where Madison was, that list of questions wouldn't still be getting longer. "Do you know where she is so I can ask her?"

"I'm sure it will all work out." Jenny smirked. "Why don't you go look for her and leave me alone?"

A burst of adrenaline spread through Raleigh. "What is wrong with you? Don't you care that Claudia is dead and Madison is missing? Don't you care?"

Raleigh stepped forward and grabbed Jenny's hand to force her to look at her.

On contact with the Jenny's cold palm, the room swayed before Raleigh, rocked her back and forth. Weightlessness floated her. The weightlessness of water.

Raleigh yanked her hand back, Jenny staring at her with an open-eyed fear.

The door swung open, light spilling into the dim room. The blonde nurse in blue scrubs entered.

"What are you doing in here?"

The officer filled the doorway, blocking the light from the hall. "Ms. no one is allowed in here. I'm going to have to ask you to leave."

Raleigh pulled herself upright, shaking the eeriness that had seeped in. "I was checking to see how she's doing. I found her earlier today, and I was concerned. I was just leaving."

The nurse shuffled to the bedside, checking and fiddling with the machines. Raleigh studied Jenny, who had returned her gaze to the window. It was no use. Jenny knew something, but Raleigh couldn't find a way to get it out of her. Raleigh walked out the room, the police officer puzzling over her with a thoughtful expression.

Raleigh crossed to the elevator feeling the officer's eyes staring at her. She wondered what gossip had spread after this afternoon. Raleigh jammed at the button and told herself that she didn't care. She'd saved Jenny's life, no matter how ungrateful the response. Her mind wouldn't dismiss it though, and she paced in the elevator unable to keep still.

Jenny knew something. What though?

Why would she flash to water and Katherine's death when she touched Jenny? Or was it Claudia's death? No, Claudia had been inside the car, which was different than the openness of the water. Was she missing something about Madison? How was she supposed to know anymore? Claiming insanity and being locked away was beginning to look like a good option.

A spike throbbed through her forehead.

Her thoughts were rambling again.

Fifteen minutes later, Raleigh gritted her teeth and pulled Paw's old truck into the barn.

Her headache welcomed the damp, cool air, but as soon as her boot touched the dirt-packed floor, it slithered up her leg. She staggered into the opening. She'd once felt so comfortable there. It wasn't right that death could take it away from her. What else would she give up? If she could make the list of things she could give up, knowing about Madison's life would have been higher on that list.

Raleigh looked to the field as she crossed the back porch, but Paw was not walking among his rows. The screen door creaked under her tug, and the spicy smell of crab boil filled the foggy kitchen. Me'Maw rocked in her rocking chair with her eyes closed and head leaned back against her faded cushion.

Raleigh leaned over the boiling pot on the stove to see the orange shrimp floating in the white foamy water. On that top ten list, this was one of the best reasons for being back on the bayou.

"Your paw went clean up for supper." Me' Maw's rocker creaked on the floor. "He worked the dirt real hard today getting ready to plant his cabbage, lettuce, turnip greens, and whatever else he decides to plant for the winter."

Raleigh smiled. "I'll get the table ready."

The creaking of the rocking chair stopped. "What is it? Best to get it out before your Paw gets out the tub."

Raleigh pulled the trays out of the cabinet and carried them to the table. Me'Maw could always pick up on when she needed to get something out. "When I went to see Jenny earlier, I touched her and I felt the water. All the signals seem crossed. Why didn't I connect to Katherine? I don't understand how she hasn't reached me in all this time."

Me'Maw coughed, her chest heaved with the action. "And you think it was Katherine?"

Raleigh sank down into a chair at the table. "I always dream about the same thing, the water. Nothing more. Why I felt it when I touched Jenny, I don't know."

Me'Maw rocked back. "You said everything has been crossed since Katherine though."

Raleigh frowned. "I guess, but today with Jenny it was so clear, except for her face."

Me'Maw nodded. "My mom used to talk about spiritual blocks. I think that's what's wrong with you. You've blocked it out because you're afraid."

Raleigh ran her finger over the unevenness of the scar. The soft, thin tissue a curvy road across her wrist. She'd figured that one out for herself. "Truthfully, it didn't bother me much until now when I want to find Madison. It was just always so… too much."

"My mom spent days in bed. She also struggled with it sometimes."

"How did she do it?"

Me'Maw smiled. "Everyone who can help people, should help. Understanding the death of loved ones was her way of helping. She accepted this and it gave her strength, and her ability grew."

"What do you mean grew?"

"Oh, she didn't just receive, she could reach out. She could tell someone how long they had to live and diagnose what was wrong. She wouldn't talk about it, but she had communicated with a few ghosts in her time."

Raleigh shivered. "Ghosts?"

She had the diagnosis part if she wanted it; she'd discovered it by accident with Uncle Camille, but the experience with Jenny was enough. She didn't want ghosts popping up, too.

Me'Maw nodded. "She was a medium to the dead, very powerful. She scared many people, but she continued doing it."

"It sounds great and all, but I think I would rather do what you do."

"Oh, I can't do much." Me'Maw smiled, her wrinkles deepening. "I read the living. Trivial things like their worries, their guilt, if they'll have a girl or a boy. I can't sense if I'm not close, except of course with you. No, what you do is special. Sometimes, Raleigh, it's all the living really need."

Raleigh stood and began gathering the paper towels and cups. As she was grabbing a towel from the sink, she looked out the window and into the face of Bethany English. She stood on the back porch looking around, confusion dimming her eyes.

Me'Maw's voice startled her. "We have company."

Raleigh walked to the back screen door and pushed it open. The creaking sound calming some of the worry in her chest. She mentally added a screen door to what her future home must have.

"Mrs. English, did you want to come in?"

She stared at Raleigh a moment. She looked like a life-size doll equipped with cheap, generic eyes. Slowly recognition crept into those creepy dead eyes.

"Yes… I just wanted to have a word."

Raleigh held the screen door open as Ms. Bethany walked in. She studied the kitchen, lingering over the set table before turning to Raleigh.

"I've heard that someone is trying to scare you off, and I wanted to make sure you didn't feel like you had to leave."

Raleigh leaned against the kitchen cabinet. Interesting. Someone on the bayou had once told her that if people weren't gossiping about you, then you weren't doing anything interesting. Raleigh would like to be boring for a time. "Who did you hear it from?"

Ms. English shook her head. "It doesn't matter, but the person who's trying to scare you off doesn't understand. They're not trying to hurt you, so you don't have to be afraid."

Raleigh sighed. Leave it to her to have the one person who could keep a secret come to tell her. "I'm not going anywhere."

She smiled, color rose to her pale cheeks. "Good." She glanced down at Me'Maw, who was staring up at her. "Well, I'll be going now. Just wanted to make sure… I don't want you to leave until… well, anyway, good night."

Raleigh moved toward the screen door and propped it open. Ms. Bethany walked through and then turned to Raleigh, her voice like a child.

"She hasn't left me, you know. Everywhere I look she's there. I need to find her. She needs peace."

Raleigh shivered; the air had cooled outside as the sun dropped into the pink and orange horizon. "I will do my best. Good night."

Raleigh allowed the screen door to snap close before shutting her eyes.

She was going to need that Twix after all.

Maybe two.

Me'Maw coughed and cleared her throat. "She's such a poor, lost soul. She deserves peace."

Raleigh groaned. Didn't she deserve peace, too? She guessed not today.

Me'Maw's rocker scratched the linoleum. "Raleigh Cheramie, no use feeling sorry for yourself. You at least have tomorrow."

Raleigh couldn't help but laugh before busying herself with the table again.

Chapter Twenty-Three

Raleigh scavenged around the floor of the Jeep before she found Mike's notepad under a stack of mail. "You really need to clean your ride."

Mike laughed as he shifted. "I know, but in my defense, I practically live in here these days."

Raleigh flipped through his notebook until she found the address in his neat scrawl. "It's Cypress Lane like you thought."

"So, what exactly do you want to know from Julia?"

"Well, she and Madison were friends in high school," Raleigh shrugged. "I'm just looking at all possibilities."

"I'd call that a long shot."

"I know," Raleigh nodded. "All I have is long shots these days."

"Ree, why aren't you looking at it from your way?"

Raleigh groaned. "What is it with everyone? I had this same conversation with Me'Maw last night."

"What did she have to say?"

"She thinks I have a spiritual block from fear."

Mike nodded. "Sounds reasonable."

Raleigh stared out the window as Mike slowed and turned. She wouldn't say fear could be reasoned with, but how could she get past it to find her sister? She hadn't been able to come up with a reasonable solution lying in bed last night unable to sleep.

Mike stopped at a simple grey brick home with a yellowing hedge near the front screen door. A boy a little taller than Mason whizzed by on a scooter, and then kicked himself back in the direction of the house.

Raleigh let herself out of the Jeep, and then walked up to the door with the yellowing doorbell. Decent described this house twenty years ago.

The spiky haired, black splotchy-eyed woman who came to the door looked older than Raleigh. They must have the wrong house, or this woman's life had been fast and hard.

"Can I help you?"

Her hoarse voice drew Raleigh out of her daze.

"I was looking for Julia."

"I'm Julia." She eyed Raleigh through scrunched eyes.

"I wanted to ask you a few questions about Madison Cheramie."

"Madison?" The woman ran a trembling hand through her hair. "I haven't seen Madison since high school."

"I wanted to ask you about high school," Raleigh paused as the bruises on Julia's arm caught her attention. They surrounded what appeared to be needle marks. This hadn't been one of her better ideas. "I wanted to know who Madison was dating in high school around the time she got pregnant."

Julia chuckled. "The whole football team as far as I'm concerned."

Raleigh drew back, and whistled as she inhaled sharply.

"Look," Julia pointed in the direction of the driveway. "I had my son senior year. I wasn't friends with Madison at that time. As far as I know, the only real friend she had that year was that girl Claudia who's dead now."

Raleigh frowned. "Thanks, I'm sorry for bothering you."

Julia grunted and closed the door.

She followed Mike back to the Jeep. "I'm telling you, Ree, you need to figure this out your way. This way is taking too long."

"So I've heard," Raleigh seethed. It was like she was supposed to be a 911 hotline for the dead. He was right about it taking too long, though she hated to admit it.

"We're still going to Claudia's place?"

Raleigh nodded. "The landlord wants her things moved. Paw wants me to see if we can do it ourselves or if we need to hire someone."

Mike swung onto the road only to travel three streets down and signal again. Claudia's rent house stood alone at the end of the street. It was a small, yellow shotgun house, but it was well tended.

Max's navy caprice blocked the driveway.

Mike pulled off the side of the road. "Did you know he was going to be here?"

Raleigh frowned, feeling the wrinkles on her forehead. She really needed to stop doing that. Cassie would have a lecture prepared to talk her out of Botox. "No, the landlord was supposed to meet us here."

Raleigh stepped out and walked down the shell driveway just as Max stepped around the side of the house.

"What are you doing here?"

Max's quizzical expression rose on his forehead. "The landlord called this morning about having her things moved. I came to have one last look around."

Raleigh nodded, distracted by the white shuttered window under the small carport. It felt like an image in her mind, an old photograph, but she'd never been here before. "Did you find anything?"

Mike reached out and shook Max's hand. Max hesitated, but then grasped Mike's hand way too long. Some kind of territorial dispute as far as Raleigh could tell. She didn't have those kissing yearnings for Mike as she had for Max. She and Mike had tried it in college. The best term to describe it had been icky. Mike was her friend, and she wasn't sure what Max was.

"Claudia kept a very tidy house."

Raleigh walked toward the window. Did it resemble something else she'd seen? It had this empty flower box attached to the bottom and a plastic unicorn hung from an inside corner. What were the chances of seeing that somewhere else? Probably less of a chance than her having a normal hallucination.

"Ree, what is it?"

"The window," Raleigh said stopping in front of it. Another image flashed before her. A stone with a smiling frog being put in there, an empty stone with a spare car key.

Max stepped closer to the window, examining it, rubbing his hand along the casing.

Raleigh reached into the flowerbox above her line of sight and pulled out the stone. As the frog stared at her, she gasped. How else would she know this? The last time she'd spoken to Claudia, she'd been twelve.

She looked up to the flower box, which was level with her head. The white paint was chipped at the corner. If she touched it, what would she see?

She shuddered, and then reached out with her trembling fingers.

It was a flash. Claudia flailed backwards and pain jotted through her spine as her head made contact with the flowerbox.

Raleigh yanked her hand back as if singed, but not before the echo of a scream pierced through her, Madison's scream.

She staggered back and closed her eyes. "They were attacked here."

Mike's hand grasped her arm. "Ree, are you sure?"

"Claudia hit the flowerbox."

Max lifted his phone to his ear and began barking orders to someone to send a crew to the house.

This was the scene of the crime. She'd found it. She'd thought it would lead to Madison, that somehow Madison was supposed to still be here.

Madison had screamed though. It meant she was alive when Claudia began to die. What about after? Nearly ten days had passed. What had happened since?

Chapter Twenty-Four

The boxes were stacked five high, and of course, the last one on the bottom was unmarked. Raleigh studied the pile, and then scanned the storage room, which was filled with similarly packed boxes, several columns, and many oversized props like water fountains. Party planners sure acquired plenty of junk. If she could find the box of silver vases, she could maybe get out with only a few inches of dust covering her clothing.

Raleigh stared back down at that bottom box. There was no getting around it. She heaved the first box from the stack and set it to the side. After a few minutes, she was down to the last unmarked box.

The box cutter sliced through the tape, and she opened the box. The tops of twenty- four silver vases greeted her.

Raleigh smiled in relief. Denise could stop fretting about the last item on the inventory for Saturday's wedding. Raleigh had decided that Denise could stress out the most laid back person. Madison must really love this job to have stayed for two years.

She was closing the box when something white wedged against the side of the box caught her attention. Raleigh reached in and tugged as it stuck in the crease of the box. She turned it over and her mind froze.

She was staring at a picture of a dead Katherine in a muddy silver and green cheerleader uniform. Her blond hair was darkened with the caked mud, and her face was tilted at an awkward angle, but her eyes stared up into the camera, lifeless. Raleigh's fingers went numb, and the picture fluttered back to the vase's box.

Raleigh's blood jolted through her body in a painful leap. She was hallucinating. Not enough sleep? Maybe she was going crazy? Her heart sped to a rapid humming as she looked down at the picture which had landed face up.

Katherine's white, wet body still stared at her with eyes strangely empty. Raleigh closed her own eyes, but it greeted her behind her eyelids. How?

"Did you find them yet? Raleigh?" The door to the storage room swung open. "Are you okay?"

Raleigh sat down on the two boxes she'd just stacked as her shaky legs buckled under her. Her voice trembled. "Who packed the vase box last?"

Denise crossed to her and glanced down at the box, puzzled. "Oh God, is that girl dead?"

Raleigh nodded, not looking down at the box again.

"Madison cleaned up after the Richard's wedding. What is that doing in there?"

Raleigh inhaled a deep, dusty breath. "I need to go. I need to take this to someone."

Denise nodded, unable to look away from the picture. "Oh...Of course."

Raleigh willed herself to touch the picture, repeating to herself it was just paper. She stuffed it into her back jean pocket and shuddered.

"I'll be back later."

Raleigh hurried out the storage room, remembered to grab her handbag from the desk drawer, and emerged into the crisp air. It was an unusually cool day for October. She kept moving and was able to climb into Paw's truck before her legs collapsed under her weight.

How did Madison get this picture and why had she hid it?

Minutes later she was able to start the truck and turn it in the direction of the newspaper. She'd considered Max for a moment, but Mike shared this experience. It was their history, and he deserved to be the one she sought out first. She reached over to the passenger seat and grabbed her cell phone. She scrolled down with a trembling finger, and the phone dialed Mike's number.

"Ree?"

"Meet me outside."

"What?"

"I'm pulling into the parking lot now."

Raleigh parked the truck and hopped out just as Mike was emerging from the side door. She crossed over to him and wordlessly handed him the picture.

His eyelids blinked rapidly. "Oh shit, where did you get this?"

"I found it in a box that Madison packed up for Denise."

Mike shifted uncomfortably and then turned the picture over so as not to see it. "Come on. I need to think this out."

Raleigh followed Mike to the side door where he scanned his card and then pulled the door open. They crossed the dimly lit office to Mike's desk. He set the picture down on the desk, careful to lay it face down. Raleigh scanned the articles tacked to the board around his desk. Yellow sticky notes covered many of the cuttings.

Mike yanked a folder out from the cabinet and spread it out across his desk. "What if Madison or Claudia got this picture from someone we went with to high school. That would be motive, right?"

Raleigh studied his timeline. Large, blank spots jumped out from his all capital letters, neat print. "Someone who was there."

"We know that there were a couple of guys on the boat, but no one would ever confess to it. Madison and Claudia have been having these parties. Many of the old football players have attended at least one party."

Raleigh pulled the chair from the next desk. "So what guys did she have contact with?"

Mike pulled up a file on his computer, and a list of names popped up. "These are the people that I've gathered so far that have attended at least one party. It's not complete or one hundred percent accurate, because, well, it's from gossip, but we can start here."

Raleigh pulled a notebook from a disheveled stack of papers. "But remember, we don't know if the players were seniors or juniors. Both classes were at the bonfire."

Mike began listing names from his master list, and Raleigh wrote them down. All in all there were fourteen football players who had been in high school with them. Raleigh set the notepad down.

"Fourteen is a big number."

Mike leaned back in his desk chair. "If we knew how she got the picture it would be easier. Someone wouldn't just leave that picture lying around for anyone to find."

Raleigh nodded. "Nor would they just bring it to a party."

The two sat in silence for a few minutes. Raleigh stared at her list. She could remember maybe what five guys on the list looked like. Was high school that long ago? Had she blocked that out, too?

Mike tapped on his desk. "You know, Alex was in high school with us."

"He wasn't a football player. Remember he'd been kicked off after that prank at the end of junior year."

Mike's eyes squinted as they did when he was thinking. "No, but they dated. He must still have some of the same friends from high school."

Raleigh stood, gesturing wildly with her hands as her mind began circling in on an idea. "They would have done things together. Madison would have gotten close to his friends in a year. Maybe close enough to come across it."

Mike picked up his phone. "I heard Alex gave up his place when they planned to buy the house."

Raleigh picked up the list. Who had Alex been friends with in high school? Junior year Katherine dated Ross Blanch, and they'd hung out often with them. Alex hadn't liked Ross much. Ross had been an arrogant ass even junior year. Alex had been friends with the blonde basketball player. What was his name? None of the names on the list seemed familiar for him.

Mike set the phone down. "He's been working on his boat lately and staying there."

Raleigh's skin prickled. She guessed that boat wasn't dry docked. "Really?"

Mike nodded. "Josh says he's not really handling Madison's disappearance very well. He didn't leave for his offshore shift Wednesday, and he's painting his boat."

"He seemed pretty upset the night I talked to him. He wants to work things out with her."

Mike shook his head. "Why didn't she tell him or someone else for that matter?"

Raleigh shrugged. "When I find her, I can give her the long list of questions I have for her."

Mike stood. "I'm going to head down to the boat and see what I can get from him. If you want, you can wait here for me."

Raleigh looked around the empty office. A safe place. No fear or uncomfortable murky water. But her sister needed her, and so much time had passed already. "I'm coming with you."

Mike looked into her eyes, a look Raleigh could not look away from or she'd admit her doubt. "Are you sure? He might be in the boat."

Raleigh nodded, feeling her stomach twist. "I know, but I think I can... need to do this."

Mike shrugged. "Okay, but I understand if you want to stay behind."

Raleigh smiled before following him toward the door.

Me'Maw had said she had a spiritual block. It was as good a time as any to face those inner fears, especially with her sister out there somewhere having a proven connection to Katherine. Max's hunch may be correct. Raleigh briefly thought about calling him, but she dismissed it. Not yet. They didn't have anything to go on yet. Maybe after they talked to Alex, she'd have something definite to tell him.

Chapter Twenty-Five

Raleigh quivered as she studied the trawl boats and fishing boats docked neatly in their strips. Five boats faced her as if in salute.

Yeah, as if she deserved to be saluted for the panic balling in her stomach. Her body swayed with the gentleness of the wind on the water. This would definitely require some control and motivation.

Mike swung his Jeep door open, and Raleigh took that as her motivation to do the same. She didn't want to give him any reason to make her stay in the Jeep. It would be hard to argue if she vomited or passed out. Three other vehicles were parked in the shells bordering the bayou, and Mike had pulled in behind Alex's old Nissan truck.

The two had reached the front of the Jeep when Alex came bounding down the cypress deck.

"Did you find her?"

Raleigh frowned, her stomach swishing slightly as she watched the smooth ripple of the water. "No, we just came to ask you about something."

Alex closed in on them before they had cleared the front of the pickup truck. Alex towered over Mike by nearly a head. Raleigh remembered how awkward their junior prom pictures looked and swallowed a nervous laugh. "What is it?

Raleigh looked to Mike. Mike looked up at Alex with a blank face. In college, Raleigh had dubbed the look his interview grimace. It was actually the reason they worked so well together. Raleigh was good at asking questions, and he always knew who'd have the answers. "We think Madison found a picture of Katherine taken after she died from someone you knew."

Alex twitched and his face paled.

Raleigh stepped closer. "We think it's why she's missing. We need your help."

Alex glanced back at his boat, the second to the right. "Are you sure? I mean, I don't think anyone I know would have that."

"I found the picture in a box Madison packed." Raleigh frowned. Shouldn't he be more helpful? "We believe it's the only way Madison could have come across a picture like this."

Alex checked out his boat again, and then kicked at the rocks. "I really only ever see Josh Duplais anymore. Claudia dated a couple of the guys, and well, I heard Madison had a thing with Davey Griffin. He played sophomore year for awhile until he flunked pretty much everything."

The swaying had reached her ears, dulling the sound of the traffic from the road and the chirping of the birds from the surrounding pine trees. Raleigh could feel her energy draining into the shells. Unless her fear had grown, something strange worked on her now.

The gravel flew under spinning tires as a red Miata swerved into the parking lot, nearly nicking Mike's bumper when the driver braked at the last second. Raleigh turned to see who was in the driver's seat, feeling as though she didn't have the energy for the motion. It was as if a director had flipped a slow motion switch. She tried to shake her head against the encroaching sickness. She wasn't even looking at the water. This was something different than her bayou phobia.

Jenny threw the door open and stalked toward them. At first Raleigh thought she was going to fling herself at them, but she stopped just inches from Alex. Though she came only to mid-chest, she raised herself up with her toes and puffed up her chest.

"Where is it? She promised it would be mine. I know you took it."

Alex glanced towards the boat, and then back toward them with a deep sigh. "I don't know what you're talking about."

"Like hell you don't." Jenny flung out her hands and pushed him backwards. "She lied to me. They both did, and she promised that I could have the deed to the house for not exposing them. Where is it?"

Raleigh looked to Mike. Sounded like blackmail to her. So, she was who the act of donation was meant for. What else was she willing to do besides blackmail?

Alex shrugged. "We don't have the deed, never did. We didn't even buy the house, Madison's grandmother bought it."

Raleigh frowned. She'd never gotten around to asking Me'Maw how she could afford to buy the house. Social security didn't send that much money every month.

Jenny growled and yelled a string of profanities.

Raleigh's vision began to blur and four Alex's grew before her. She reached out and touched the old pickup to balance herself. "Mike, I'm going to go sit in the Jeep for a minute. Stay here."

Mike stared at her, concern pouring from his eyes, but he did not move to follow her. They both understood this was important.

Raleigh climbed into the passenger bucket seat and put her head in her lap. The dizziness began to retract, but a strange empty feeling still clinched her stomach. The water swayed her again. Raleigh popped up and looked at the bayou. A gentle breeze caused the water to ripple, to sway.

Jenny was pacing in a circle, yelling at Alex and then Mike. Alex glanced back at the boat again, and Raleigh followed his movement. The boat swayed in the gentle rolling water.

Something about the motion, the feeling cradling her.

Before she could think to reason the hunch away, she quietly opened the Jeep door and crept out the Jeep, stepping lightly on the gravel. She crept along the truck, hoping that the string of insults and Madison bashing that Jenny was doing would cover any sound she made. At the end of the truck, Raleigh watched closely and waited until after Alex glanced back at the boat, before she hurried as fast as she could to a rotting pirogue propped up against a piling. She peeked and could see Mike enlisting Alex to help herd Jenny back to her car. He was offering Raleigh a distraction.

She seized the opportunity and quickly made the leap to the boat and climbed over the ledge.

The feeling of being on and this close to water hit her as her boot hit the deck of the boat. Her stomach lurched and for a moment she thought she'd be sick. She pushed a breath out through her lips repeating to herself that she wasn't in the water. A moment later the feeling eased, though her heart continued to hammer against her chest. Here's to rushing head first into fear, Me'Maw.

Raleigh peered over the side of the boat and Mike and Alex had cornered Jenny at her car door. She would need to hurry. If she'd just gone crazy, there was no way to explain this.

She crept to the door and let herself inside the darkened cabin. It took a moment for her eyes to adjust to the shadows of the small cabin. The steering and controls were to the front and a small kitchen type area was to her right. To her left was a bunk area covered in a heavy blue blanket.

Raleigh peered closer. Under the blanket was an unmoving lump. She hurried to the bunk and threw the blanket back.

Madison's wide eyes stared at her with a handkerchief covering her mouth. Raleigh's numb fingers fumbled with the knot before finally the handkerchief slipped off.

A hoarse croak escaped her dried lips. "You need to get out of here before he comes back."

Raleigh focused on the rope binding her hands together. "I'm not leaving without you."

The knot would not budge. Raleigh scanned the boat for something to use, opening the lone drawer in the kitchen area. Several knives lay mixed in with other utensils.

The knife must have been recently sharpened because it sliced easily through layer after layer of rope.

Madison rubbed her wrists. Raleigh remembered the feeling of the unbinding. It had hurt just as much as the duck tape she'd been bound with.

"How did you find me?"

Raleigh moved toward the door. "Just a hunch."

She threw the door open, but it stopped halfway. Alex glared at her from the doorway.

Raleigh gathered herself up, but she didn't feel too powerful only coming up to his chest. "We're leaving. This is over."

Alex stepped closer. "No, it can't be."

Raleigh looked under his arm, and Mike lay crumpled on the shells. His body faced the road, and from her vantage point, she could not see his face. Was he breathing? Oh, God he was too far away for her to see the rise and fall of his chest.

"What are you doing?" She looked back up at Alex. "This is insane."

He stepped closer, inches from her. "Get in the boat and sit down."

He reached around her to an overhead compartment and pulled out a shiny metal hand gun. Raleigh stepped back, pushing Madison behind her with her arm. Fear and guilt washed over her like a cold shower. How could this be happening again? Wasn't there some kind of guarantee that a person should only be taken hostage once? Even that reasoning sounded wacky to herself right now when she wanted so much to believe that this wasn't happening.

"Alex, what are you doing? This is crazy. You don't want to do this."

Madison sobbed behind her, and Raleigh could feel Madison's body trembling against hers.

Alex ran the hand gripping the gun through his hair. His eyes closed and his forehead crinkled. Raleigh recognized the desperation in the lines on his face.

Damn. They were in trouble.

Alex lowered the gun. "Sit on the bed and don't move."

He pushed the door closed behind him and pushed in the bolt.

"Alex, don't do this. This won't turn out good for you. You know this."

Alex stepped forward, knuckles clinched. "Damn it Raleigh, why do you have to always ruin things? I could have had everything fixed, but you always come and stir things up."

He backed away and looked out the front windows. He was silent for a moment, and Raleigh hoped he was thinking about letting them go, but a moment later he looked at her and from the smoothness of his forehead and the twitch of his lip, she knew he hadn't.

"There's no other way." He ran his hand through his hair again. "Sit down both of you."

Madison scurried backwards and sank onto the mattress. Raleigh moved slowly to her side, studying the interior of the boat.

She'd thrown the knife back into the drawer, and nothing lay around. A wooden life preserver hung on the wall in a resemblance of decoration and a wooden paddle to stir in a boiling pot hung by the bunk wall. Alex's name was scarred into the weathered wood. No weapons and definitely no button that read push for a quick escape.

The boat began to vibrate beneath them, and Raleigh swallowed against a wave of nausea vibrating through her with the engine rumbling.

She pushed the surging fear of the water down into her feet, and her toes grew numb. She glanced over at Madison who was crying silently, her shoulders trembling. Raleigh reached over and squeezed her hand.

Alex glanced back at them, and Raleigh met his eyes, unblinking. She needed to convince him to let them go. This needed to go better than last time.

Alex maneuvered the boat out of the slip, and Raleigh's heart sank as the dock receded and the bayou took its place. "I blame you, you know. None of this would have happened if it wouldn't be for you."

"How do you mean?"

"Junior year you broke up with me, so I did something stupid. We weren't supposed to get caught tearing up the football field. Then I got kicked off the team. I was at the boat that night because I wanted to still be part of the team, and then you two showed up. It was supposed to be another prank."

Raleigh swallowed hard. Her mind racing against the fear and now the anger that it was Alex all along. How could it have been him? She'd actually liked him, thought he was a decent guy. So many others better suited for the bad guy. "It didn't feel like a prank to me."

Alex grunted. "No, it wouldn't. Ross was so damn stupid, but it was supposed to be in the past. Something I could forget had ever happened because we weren't caught."

Raleigh watched him. He was steady and intent. He wasn't going to be reasoned with. Why did she always find the crazies?

"Madison was supposed to be the person I spent the rest of my life with until she found that picture. Damn picture. I'd only kept it to make sure it didn't all come back on me, but she found it."

Raleigh peered around him. They were headed toward the canal, which could then take them anywhere. Where did he think he was going to take them or was that just it? Shove them out into the water to drown. This wasn't good.

"And Claudia?"

Alex shrugged. "An accident. That bitch attacked me. Madison had told her about the picture, and I didn't mean for her to hit her head so hard. I just wanted Madison to listen."

Raleigh glanced at Madison whose tears had subsided.

"Claudia was alive in the car before she drowned. If you wanted to prove yourself to Madison, you should have helped her instead of kill her."

Without another word, Alex steered the boat forward with the gun held loosely on the steering wheel. Raleigh wondered how much time had passed. Was Mike okay, and if he was, had he called for help?

Raleigh sighed. What if he wasn't alright? How was she going to get out of this one? Even if she could get past him somehow, they would have to jump off the boat and swim. It's not as if she knew anything about boats.

Dying didn't bring the fear and trepidation to her chest as much as the idea of having to jump into the water. A nice airplane to jump from sounded better, and her feelings for heights weren't too clear either.

Madison moved closer to her, and Madison's iciness chilled her own body. Madison's body had weakened. If Raleigh had connected to her, Madison was near death.

If she was going to do anything, she needed to do it before they left the bayou.

Each second of silence ticked by in the boat cabin until it felt as though she were back in the interrogation room, Detective Jean staring at her waiting for her to crack. She wasn't sure if this was tying for most uncomfortable; Raleigh wasn't sure how much time had passed as the boat crept steadily down the bayou before Alex began looking out a side door, his brow furrowed.

He mumbled. "It can't be."

Minutes later, he glanced out the door again and mumbled, "He doesn't know I took the boat. He can't know."

Someone following them? That sounded like an option. Options were good. Raleigh studied the paddle. It hung flat on the wall by a small silver hook. If Raleigh leaned across Madison, she could reach the middle section of the paddle.

Alex stuck his whole head out the window again. "Shit, what is Jeffery doing?"

Raleigh's heart sank. Of all the people following them, it had to be the least likely knight in shining armor to the rescue, but she needed to get them out of here somehow.

Alex stuck his head out of the window again, and Raleigh reached over and grasped the handle of the paddle. She wiggled it free of the hook, and pulled her arm back grasping the paddle. She stuffed it between them as he stuck his head back in. Her heart didn't even to do the jig it had started because he didn't look back at them. He was too distracted by the approaching boat.

Raleigh hesitated in her fear. If she did this, there was no going back. She doubted she could knock him out completely. She hadn't hit the gym since Texas and any small muscle tone she'd achieved was long gone. She'd have to get off this boat one way or another, and she hadn't brought a parachute or blow up life raft. Her heart hammered in her ears, and panic gripped her body.

Madison leaned into her, squeezing her hand. It was barely more than a touch. Could Madison even swim to the bank of the bayou? Her luck they would be swallowed by an alligator before they reached the bank.

Raleigh gripped the handle baseball bat style with a clammy hand. A moment later, Alex stuck his head out the window again, and Raleigh lurched forward, gripping the paddle. When his head came back in, Raleigh swung with all her strength. The paddle contacted with the side of his head with a loud thwack. He staggered sideways. Raleigh pulled back again and swung, coming down on the top this time. He fell toward the control panel.

Raleigh reached with her free hand and slid the bolt open. Madison hobbled uncertainly toward her. Raleigh pushed her through the open door and jumped out after her. She dragged and pulled Madison around the ice hold and around the large chests on the back deck.

Standing on the edge of the back deck, Raleigh looked into the muddy brown water and froze. She couldn't do this. A loud thump sounded behind him.

"Get back here!"

Alex's yell drew her attention to him, and he brandished the gun in the air, glaring at them through squinted eyes.

Madison's fingers trembled in her hand.

Raleigh closed her eyes, her chest tightened in the grip of pain that caused a yell to well up inside of her. "Jump!"

The bullet exploded in her ears as the air rushed around her for a moment before she sank into the dark, cold water. Darkness surrounded her, and she fought against the fear throbbing like a broken leg through her.

Madison's fingers gripped her own, but she wasn't moving.

Damn. She didn't have the energy to surface. Raleigh pulled her closer, gripped her waist tightly, and heaved her upwards, some of her air escaping in the process. Raleigh sank further into the water with her efforts, but Madison broke free of the darkness.

Through the muddy water, Katherine flickered before her. Raleigh sputtered and swallowed the water as she pushed backwards from Katherine, who with white face and hair fanning behind her, smiled at her.

Raleigh spit against the dirtiness of the water. Her eyes and lungs burned.

Whiteness surrounded her, and Raleigh's thrashing slowed as she stared in amazement. A spotlight seemed to be shining down on Katherine. Raleigh closed her eyes, and when she reopened them, a movie reel rolled before her.

Raleigh watched Katherine coming onto the boat, glimpsing Mike and Raleigh in the engine room as Ross tried to close the hatch, and then arguing with Ross, threatening to call the police. Katherine turned her back on him, and he reached into the drawer and pulled out the gun. He told her to come back, she kept walking. He screamed at her, he wasn't going to jail for this shit. Alex grabbed for the gun, but Ross pulled the trigger as they wrestled. Katherine collapsed, dead. Alex and Ross argued, but threw her into the trawl net when Jeffery Zedeaux pulled up in his sports car.

The reel slowed, suspending Raleigh in the water. A dark figure in a pirogue, digging into the bayou side and throwing Katherine inside. Raleigh looked up to the cypress tree and the backside of the white shotgun house beyond. Katherine appeared again with a smile twitching at her blue lips. She closed her eyes and blended into the muddy bayou, evaporating with the spotlight.

Calmness prickled through Raleigh. She closed her eyes against the darkness, the mud. She kicked hard as her lungs scorched her chest. She wanted to rip them out to stop the searing pain.

A strong hand grabbed her wrist and yanked her up in one smooth motion. Raleigh gasped as her lungs burned with the oxygen, and then her chest heaved as the muddy water erupted from her lungs.

She opened her eyes to see Max's green eyes burn into her. Her ears were oblivious to any sound, but she stared at the smooth movement of his lips. She couldn't make out anything he was saying, but she'd like kissing those lips one day. It all had such a dreamy quality that Raleigh closed her eyes.

She struggled to open them as she felt herself being lowered, and she could see Madison wrapped in a blanket, cuddled up against the side of the boat.

Raleigh smiled, and then slipped into unconsciousness where the feeling of calm spread through her and warmed her insides.

Chapter Twenty-Six

A jolt stabbed through her shoulder, and she opened one eye to the sun drying her drenched body. She heaved herself upward into a sitting position and immediately felt strong arms steady her. She blinked against the tears from the brightness and stared up into Max's smoldering stare.

His mouth was inches from hers. Such smooth lines curving down into an angular jaw. He was so sexy. Why had he never kissed her? Absolutely no thoughts formed in her brain right now. What bliss.

Raleigh edged herself upward and found his lips with hers. Warmness seeped through her body, and a heat began to grow. God, he felt so good against her.

She gasped for air as he pulled away. "Sorry, I've wanted to do that for awhile."

His fingers caressed her arm. "It just may not be the best place to start."

Raleigh pulled away from him, and soaked in the scene before her. Two ambulances stood before her. She could see Madison, covered in a thick blanket and her dark hair appeared black in its wetness, stretched out on a stretcher with a medic twittering with an IV bag. In the ambulance to the right of her, Mike sat on the back with a second medic swabbing his head with gauze. His face was flushed, and he was staring her way with his out of focus expression.

She scanned the outside of the ambulances and saw Jeffery Zedeaux standing with a police officer near the wharf. She supposed it was his boat that had saved them. Damn. She may actually have to thank him if she didn't choke on the words.

As she was soaking in the other officers and their cars blocking several bystanders from approaching, her mom and dad rushed in their direction. Her mom pounced on the stretcher holding Madison. Raleigh could see her shoulders shaking and tears streaking down her bare face as she leaned in and clutched Madison tightly.

Mason burst through the other side where he'd run around the police car and darted toward Madison.

Tears brushed Raleigh's eyelashes. She guessed she was a sucker for happy endings. She wouldn't have believed it.

She pushed herself up with effort, wondering at her exhaustion. She walked the twenty feet toward the ambulance. Her dad watched as she approached, no sign of his feelings visible in his expression.

Madison was pale, her eyes were drawn, but she was smiling.

Raleigh reached over and squeezed the arm above the blanket and grinned. "Next time, let's find a pool to go swimming."

Madison's chest heaved as she laughed.

The paramedic pulled a disposable oxygen mask out of its package.

"Excuse me. I just wanted to check on Madison before I left to go deal with Alex at the station."

Raleigh stepped back and frowned as Jeffery inserted himself into the group. He stared down at Madison with an expression bordering on kindness. Raleigh had never seen it before, at least not on his face. Mason's head barely reached over the stretcher where he was trying to rest his chin, but he was about an inch too short. Mason looked up at Jeffery, and then back toward Madison.

Mason's green flecks inside an acorn setting had caught the sun. Raleigh glanced back at Jeffery, and his green-flecked brown eyes met her gaze and the kindness was gone.

Raleigh's heart hurtled ahead. Sheri had said that Madison and Jeffery had once been 'involved'. She shook herself before her thoughts traveled any further.

It wasn't possible. She hadn't done anything to deserve that happening. Right?

Madison closed her eyes. "Thank you."

The medic nodded his head at another EMS man in a jacket. "Okay people, we'll be transporting the young lady to the hospital now. Someone riding with her?"

Mom stepped forward and climbed into the back of the ambulance after they lifted the stretcher inside. Raleigh turned away, pushing down the nagging thoughts that her mother or father hadn't even asked how she was. Mike was staring at her from his seat on the back of the ambulance. She crossed over and gave him a smile.

"Are you going to live?"

Mike grinned. "I think my ego is bruised more than my head. I can't believe I didn't see that coming."

Raleigh lowered herself next to him. "How did he figure out I was on the boat?"

Mike reached up and felt the bandage. "When we turned away from Jenny, I guess he saw the Jeep was empty. He knocked me out with this old plank of wood. When I came to and saw the boat gone, I freaked. Luckily, Max was already talking to Jeffery at his boat."

Raleigh studied Max, who was talking with several officers with notepads. Now that she was away from his intoxicating scent, she wondered at her urge to kiss him. It wasn't like her to do something like that. Usually she had a voice in her head talking her out of it. And why had he been talking to Jeffery? It was all too deep for her right now. Exhaustion was weighing down her thoughts, and not in the ignorance is bliss sense.

A haggard Kyle Allemande approached with his hands inside his jean pockets. His chin held a two-day stubble and dark shadows bruised the skin under his eyes. He kicked at the shells as he reached them. "I just wanted to check and see if everyone was all right."

Raleigh squinted at him, noticing a curious look of repentance in his sheepish expression. "We're alive. What are you doing here?"

"Guilt, I guess." Kyle lowered his chin even further. "I should've known it was Alex, but with everything going on, I didn't want to say anything. Then when he didn't say that he saw me Monday with Madison and Claudia, I should've known something was up. I'm really sorry about the whole mess."

Mike cradled his head with his palm, and his eyes squinted in that busy thinking way. Raleigh was confused, but too tired to care that she was confused. "Back up a bit. Explain all of this to us."

Kyle kicked at the shells again. "I knew Jenny was blackmailing Madison and Claudia, but I was still reeling from her being pregnant with my baby. So when everything went down with Madison and Claudia, I thought it might be Jenny. It's why I didn't tell anyone I saw Alex going into the house Monday when I was leaving. I had gone to talk to Madison about Jenny, and I knew it would look bad for her and me. I thought Alex would say something though. I should have suspected him when he didn't."

Mike released a deep breath. "So you thought it was Jenny?"

Kyle nodded. "Yeah, and she had threatened my wife, my marriage. She's a little crazy right now, and I didn't know what she was going to do. It doesn't matter now. My wife kicked me out yesterday when she heard that Jenny was pregnant."

Raleigh leaned in closer to Mike, shivering against the breeze. She could use some dry clothes and a little less smell of the dirty water. "Why was Jenny blackmailing them?"

Kyle stared off into the bayou. "I met Jenny at one of the parties. Jenny blamed them for getting pregnant. It was her first party, and she wasn't prepared for what was going to happen there."

Raleigh remained quiet, feeling the hum of the people moving around them. She could even feel Mike's pulse against her. She snuggled in closer for his warmth. Madison was alive, but she sure had left a wave of destruction behind her.

And Raleigh hadn't delivered the final blow to Alex yet.

Raleigh looked up at Mike. "I know where Katherine is."

She said it simply, but she felt that her words made his pulse skip, and then thunder forward. He stared down at her, his eyes twitching at the corners and his lip pulled thin.

"She showed me when I was under the water. Alex buried her in the bank of the bayou by old Fred Thibodaux's house. Ross shot her because she knew we were at the bottom of the boat and she planned to turn him into the police."

Mike hung his head and gripped the bandage tighter. Raleigh remained quiet, and they sat there allowing the people to move around them. Kyle drifted off to an officer he seemed familiar with, and Raleigh watched Max as he led a photographer around the area. He was comfortable on the scene, alert in a way she hadn't been in awhile. She needed something like that now that Madison would be taking her job back. Thank goodness.

But what was she left with?

She'd lost her job and her rent-a-car. Cassie had brought all her things to Me'Maw's. Take that as a hint that she wasn't welcome back.

She was left with a headache, that's what, and the feeling that she could sleep for a week.

Chapter Twenty-Seven

She gripped the bunch of daylilies from *Julie's Floral and Gifts* and knocked on the trailer's screen door. Raleigh looked around, noticing that the white trailer looked abandoned, unlivable. Its whiteness had turned a dingy gray and grass grew up to the small porch that was nearly four feet from the ground. A metal trim was hanging lose and the screen door was torn in the corner. Not the trailer she'd spent most weekends at as a child.

Bethany English came to the door and pushed the door open. "I was wondering when you were going to come."

Raleigh smiled, though the sadness that had balled in her stomach after they dug up Katherine throbbed. "I brought orange daylilies. They were always Katherine's favorite."

Bethany inhaled deeply and crossed to the other side of the kitchen. As Raleigh stepped inside, she pulled a vase out of a cabinet and began filling it with water. "I'll bring them to her later. Have a seat."

Raleigh hesitated, and then sat down on a bar stool facing the kitchen. "I came to say I'm sorry. You know about everything with Katherine."

Ms. Bethany arranged the flowers in the vase. "It's strange, but I haven't been this happy in over eleven years. It was the not knowing that was driving me crazy. I needed to know what happened to my baby, and I'm grateful you could tell me."

Raleigh studied the pictures of a younger Katherine hanging on the wall. In one she was dressed as a punk rocker for Halloween in t-shirts they had made with neon paint. In another picture, her blonde braids hung down her shoulders as she held a gray kitten they'd called Shadow. "I'm sorry I couldn't give it to you sooner. But after everything, I couldn't breathe here. Everyone talking and telling stories about what they thought had happened. And truthfully, I didn't want to communicate with the dead. It was all too much."

Ms. Bethany nodded, leaning on the bar counter. "I understand, but when you came back I didn't want people like Mimi Blanch to scare you away. I had waited so long already. It may have been selfish, but I was glad Claudia had brought you back here."

So Mimi Blanch was responsible for her car. Raleigh chewed on the side of her lip. She guessed it would be insensitive to send her the bill.

Raleigh looked up. She could count the crinkles on Ms. Bethany's forehead and the imprints around her eyes. She remembered at twelve she'd thought she was beautiful like the women in the magazines. For a fleeting moment, Raleigh could see Me'Maw's advice staring at her through the wrinkles of grief. She could help both the living and the dead. She'd always looked at it as the dead needing the help, but really it was the living, too. "I came because I hoped you'd found the peace you wanted, and to thank you for always believing. Most mothers would've said I was crazy, not wanting to believe."

"I went through my moments." Ms. Bethany sighed. "But I knew Katherine would never run away. I also knew you were right; I could feel it. I hope you never have to feel it."

Raleigh smiled, hoping she would never have to feel it again, but the nagging voice in her head, that sounded way too much like Me'Maw, said "It's your talent." She'd always feel death someway.

Raleigh said her good-byes and walked to Paw's truck parked in the driveway of a thin layer of shells. The wind blew her hair into her eyes, and she threw her head sideways to send it away. The old tree swing hanging from the withering Oak to her right caught her attention.

A blonde girl in pigtails sat, her legs straight out in front of her. The girl watched her, eyes squinting in the sunlight, as Raleigh stared. Though Raleigh knew she wasn't really there, she couldn't help but smile.

Raleigh mouthed the words, as they rang out in the eight-year olds sing-song voice. "Tell me a secret."

Raleigh's eyes burned against the unshed tears. "I can talk to the dead."

"Then I'll have my best friend even if I'm dead."

Katherine smiled and blended into the trees and weeds. The swing blew forward in the wind.

And Raleigh was not sure if it had happened just now or if it was her memory of what had happened then, but it left her with that joyful aching nestled in her chest.

Five minutes later, she pulled into the barn and shut the engine. She wiped at her eyes before jumping down onto the flat dirt floor. Her shoes only felt the surface, and the coolness washed over her in a gentle caress. Everything was as it should be. She walked out into the mid-day sun.

Me'Maw called from the porch. "Help your mama with that tray."

Raleigh looked toward her parent's house and saw her mother balancing a large tray. She crossed over and took one side of the tray.

Raleigh swallowed, feeling uncomfortable. "What's going on?"

"Oh, we're having a crab boil to celebrate."

"Madison feeling better?"

Raleigh knew not to expect an apology or a thank-you. It would never come, but she must move on. Suppression, her specialty.

"She's dressing Mason, again. He took a spill into Paw's watered garden."

Raleigh laughed. It felt good.

Paw and her dad were unfolding a table, and Raleigh could see the butane going under the boiling pot on the side of the barn. The screen door snapped behind Mike as he lugged out a stack of newspapers. She set the tray down on the table, and after Mike placed the papers on the table, he scooped her up into a warm, comfortable hug.

"How was it?"

Raleigh shrugged. "Better than I thought. She seems at peace."

He squeezed her again, and then moved to scoop up a charging Mason. Madison approached slowly. Raleigh had noticed that she hesitated to talk, to come into a room, to be near them. Raleigh wondered if she was worried they knew about her life.

Raleigh moved in, blocking her from edging away from her. "How are you doing?"

Madison looked away. "I'm just a little shaky."

Raleigh reached out and touched her arm. "Madison, all they know is that you are safe now. It's all they need to know."

Madison looked up at her, and finally a smile twitched at her lips. "It seems we have something in common after all. Getting into trouble."

Raleigh laughed. "Speak for yourself, Sis. I've had my fair share. I'd prefer not to do it again."

They laughed as they walked toward the others. Raleigh noticed the change instantly. Madison approached mom and helped her spread the newspapers across the table, and didn't hesitate to look at Me'Maw on the porch. Wasn't this how families were supposed to be? She'd read about it somewhere.

Max walked around the corner of the house swinging a case of Coors. Raleigh smiled as he approached; liking the black t-shirt and jeans look on him. He smiled as he focused on her, the crinkle in his forehead smoothing out.

"I brought the beer."

Madison appeared at her side. "And the cute factor."

Raleigh laughed. "Hey, I saw him first."

"No fair, I was tied up."

Raleigh smiled, feeling Max's eyes on her, warming her body. "That will teach you to have better taste in men."

Madison laughed. "Anyway, I didn't get to thank you for your part in rescuing us. It was very timely."

Max nodded. "It's the part of my job that I enjoy."

Madison bounced away, running toward Mason and Mike, who were tossing a football.

Raleigh shook her head as Mason charged Madison. She hadn't seen his smile this big before as he tackled her to the ground. She looked back at Max who was waiting.

"Alex backed up your story about Katherine, though he claimed to know nothing about burying her. He's still facing several charges, including the murder of Claudia. I don't think he'll be bothering your family again."

Raleigh nodded. She still liked the shape of his lips. "So now that everything is over, I was wondering if you'd like to go on a date, with me not Madison that is."

Raleigh smiled as he stared down at her. She was reminded of his intensity that held a force of its own.

His lips relaxed into a smile that reached his eyes. "Damn, you beat me to it."

"I'll take that as a yes."

"Hey girl, don't keep him away. Bring that beer over here."

Raleigh laughed, a feeling of lightness in her chest, as her Paw called to them from his perch on the porch.

They crossed through the yard and Max handed Paw a beer. Raleigh watched Me'Maw frown, but she didn't comment. Paw would always drink, and Me'Maw would always disapprove. It's how it had always been. Somethings never changed and that was okay.

Her dad called from the boiling pot, "Max, wouldcha' mind giving me a hand?"

Max crossed, set the beer on the table, and walked over to the pot to help her dad dump the crabs onto the table.

Madison ran screeching through the yard, laughing uncontrollably as Mason tried to tickle her. Mike kept blocking her path of escape. Her mom was filling cups from a bowl of ice, and Me'Maw and Paw sat on the back porch.

Life was good, even if it took connecting to the dead to bring it to this point. She may be able to get used to this… as long as it didn't happen too often.

Paw leaned over. "Girl, you reckon you're going to stay 'round this time?"

Raleigh watched as Max walked along side her dad to the table to dump the crabs. It felt good being here, in this place. It wasn't perfect, but it held possibility. She could deal with possibility.

Raleigh looked up and smiled at him. His eyes were actually twinkling with a suppressed laugh as if he knew what she was thinking. He couldn't though. That was Me'Maw's job, and Me'Maw was pretending she wasn't listening as she stared down at the porch boards, rocking in her rocker. "I think I can find a few reasons to stick around for awhile."

"It's 'bout time." Paw laughed, a big throaty laugh, one she hadn't heard in a long time.

Raleigh laughed, inhaling the mix of crab boil, dirt, and the distinct air of her childhood. Max and Mike both looked toward her and smiled.

ABOUT THE AUTHOR

Jessica Tastet is the author of the Muddy Bayou series. Presently, she resides in her hometown with her two children where she surrounds herself with good books and family. To learn more see www.jessicatastet.com.